"What do you mean? What's the real, ultimate plan?"

"We're going to kill the gods."

The words hung in the air. The impossibility of it. The audacity.

The appeal.

"How?"

"Well, it's going to take a lot of magic," Aral said. "We'll need the most powerful mages in the world. I've been getting to know them, corresponding with them, and gathering them for years. You're one of them, Thera. I've had you in mind from the start."

Flattering. Undeniably flattering.

But it didn't keep Thera from realizing that it wasn't actually an answer.

"Do you know how to kill a god?"

"Not yet."

The Arcane War

THE ARCANE WAR

By Tam Chronin

The Arcane War Copyright © 2019 by Mary E Simon. All Rights Reserved.

All rights reserved. No part of this book may be reproduced in any form or by any electronic or mechanical means including information storage and retrieval systems, without permission in writing from the author. The only exception is by a reviewer, who may quote short excerpts in a review.

Cover designed by Joshua Stomberg

This book is a work of fiction. Names, characters, places, and incidents either are products of the author's imagination or are used fictitiously. Any resemblance to actual persons, living or dead, events, or locales is entirely coincidental.

Tam Chronin
Visit my website at www.tamchronin.com

Independently Published

*To the most important men in my life,
Bryce, Adam, Richard, Liam,
And my Grandpa Alan,*

*I would have slayed gods
for any one of you.*

Thank you all for being you.

CONTENTS

The Arcane War	3
Chapter One – Marked for Death	8
Chapter Two – Chaos and Confusion	20
Chapter Three – Searching for Answers	31
Chapter Four – Adrift	48
Chapter Five – Minor Impositions	69
Chapter Six – Acts of Desperation	81
Chapter Seven – Escape	98
Chapter Eight – The Price of Knowledge	106
Chapter Nine – Subterfuge and Sabotage	116
Chapter Ten – Smoldering Embers	132
Chapter Eleven – Fanning the Flames	147
Chapter Twelve – The Fall of Anogrin	158
Chapter Thirteen – Refugees	176
Chapter Fourteen – Gathering of the Armies	194
Chapter Fifteen – The Beating of the Drums	214
Chapter Sixteen – Vengeance	235
Chapter Seventeen – The Arcane War	251
Chapter Eighteen – Ends and Beginnings	264

Acknowledgments	270
About the Author	272
Also By Tam Chronin	273

CHAPTER ONE –

MARKED FOR DEATH

Aral Tennival dipped her quill in the ink, watching it drip back into the well. There was a lecture going on, and she had half a mind on it, but the pitch-black ink held her attention longer than Master Lanrin's monotone.

Dip. Drip. Dip. Drip.

Thera kicked the side of Aral's foot.

Splat.

Damn it. Right on the paper. Aral blotted the drip, thankful it didn't blot out anything important. She'd have glared at Thera, but her friend was only looking out for her. This was supposed to be an important lecture, so Aral had asked Thera to help her keep focused. It wasn't her fault it wasn't working.

There were too many late nights, lately. Too many sleepless nights. Too many nightmares.

Aral scribbled a title on her page. Transportation. So far, it was a history lesson. Horses. Carts. Wagons. Carriages. Boats. Ships. All of it mundane and resoundingly boring.

If only she could be in two places at once. One version here, taking notes, learning the boring fundamentals. The other version running through the streets of Anogrin with her brother Naran, and her best friend, Davri.

Unfortunately, magic didn't work that way.

She should have skipped class to spend time with Davri and Naran. They were going to see the Temple Magica, the grandest structure ever built.

Aral was stuck learning about how wheels had revolutionized the world.

So much excitement.

From his first glimpse of the Temple Magica, Naran was awed.

There were other temples to other gods that they'd passed. They were grander than the temples had been at home. The very first one they'd passed, he'd turned to Davri, his guide for the day, and asked, "Is this it?"

Davri laughed and shook his head. "You'll know it before you see it."

Now, Naran knew what Davri meant.

There was a shimmer in the air above the buildings they walked past.

The shimmer surrounded what looked like an enormous violet jewel in the sky. The jewel drifted in an arc overhead. Two other jewels in crimson and teal followed the same path, circling the apex of a golden spire that could be seen for blocks. Naran didn't know what it was at first; he'd glimpsed this spire when he'd arrived in Anogrin. He'd gone directly to the University Magica, around the curve of the mountain Anogrin had been built into the top of. If not for that mountain, the spire might have been visible from the campus.

"I was told that the architects who built the temple had something more ordinary in mind," Davri said.

Naran looked at the approaching corner with anticipation. As they walked, the floating jewels they'd seen in the distance seemed almost overhead. Over the sounds of the street vendors and traveling peddlers, he could hear a gentle tinkling of bells, like wind chimes, though the air was still. The boulevard ahead was broad, and he could already see crowds milling along it.

Davri leaned close as he continued, so he would be heard over the din. "The priests, however, wouldn't accept anything less than complete awe from those who beheld the goddess's temple. Magic is anything but commonplace."

As they turned the corner Naran froze in place, eyes wide.

He wasn't alone.

The temple was elegant and impossible. It grew seamlessly from the ground in graceful lines and curves that blended solid stone with golden veins and sprinkles of crystals that scintillated and glowed with inner light. Naran was an art student, and he'd asked Davri to bring him here so that he could learn. Instantly, his mind was overwhelmed. His fingers itched to pick up charcoal and his drawing tablet. He could sit there all day, sketching the opulent beauty of it all. The outline would be simple. The details would be impossible, though. The structure breathed and pulsed like a living thing, though it was still as stone. Naran would never be able to translate that feeling onto something as static as pigment and paper. He imagined that even the best of artists would go mad, trying to capture what made it such a spectacle.

Naran was only nine. He shoved his hands in his pockets. For now.

He almost started walking again, but something new caught his eye. Or, rather, he realized his eyes had been deceived. Something that looked like a giant tree was growing from a point within the Temple Magica. The spire that had caught his eye from afar was floating at least a foot above the canopy of that tree. His eyes had filled in supports at first, but there were none. It floated above the tree.

The tree itself should have been incongruent with all of the artifice. The flow of the curves made the tree seem an architectural trick. But, no, it was a real and living thing.

A breeze stirred the leaves of the tree. As they caught the light of the sun, the leaves shifted from green to gold. One of the overhead jewels occluded the light from the sun momentarily, and every leaf became that jewel in miniature.

It was the essence of magic made manifest in this world.

"Travel by magical means," Master Lanrin's voice filled the lecture hall, "has always been the forefront of magical research. The ability to move from one place to another faster than someone else is, of course, a great tactical advantage in battle. The course of history has been carved by mages who understand this."

Aral furrowed her brow. She felt uneasy at the thought that any one of them could have such a vast effect on the world without even using some sort of destructive spell, like calling down a column of fire at someone. Something as simple as being able to move faster than the other side could make that much of a difference?

"Most of you here are more concerned with theory than application. That's to be expected when you're young and idealistic, and it is not a failing. Hard truths are part of your education here, however. Battles and wars sound distant and ominous from our perch up here at the top of Mount Selyst. We've seen peace for longer than any of your lifetimes, but the lowlands are different. One never knows where any one of you might get hired after your time here. Knowing how important it is to be able to transport any amount of people from one point to another might lead to more lucrative wages in your future. Or, your own survival."

A few students tittered, Aral among them, but most were still taking notes without thinking too critically about what was being said.

Master Lanrin cleared his throat and continued. "As far back as the first elves, mortals have tried to use magic to accelerate transportation. Ancient elves, long before the gods created humans, began by enchanting boots to propel the user faster, with as much effort as walking. These boots were clumsy, awkward, and of limited usefulness, but they worked. Centuries later they created a network of enchanted paths that shortened travel by weeks, if not months. Those quickly became corrupted, however, and putting something similar in place has not been attempted again. Less than a handful of elves live today who know the secret of how that massive spell was worked.

"Teleportation and portals are ideas that have been hinted at in literature and tales. Many spellsmiths have wasted years of their careers working on the theory of instant travel across distances with nothing to show for their efforts in the end. I am not saying that this is dead end research, however. Pair up with your study partner and next week we will discuss what ideas you can find about why this elusive magic is still worth pursuing. Go beyond the obvious wish fulfillment. I want facts, examples, and documents. Those who have tried to create a reliable spell for this have not all been ignorant fools. So, explain to me why, despite failure, they keep trying."

Davri put a hand on Naran's shoulder. "It's stunning, especially the first time you see it. I'll never tire of watching the colors dance."

"Is it just as pretty on the inside?"

"Yes, but in a different way. The outside is show and spectacle to draw attention. The inside is subdued, focused on learning and worship, but just as beautiful."

Naran couldn't imagine it. Wasn't subdued just another way of saying boring? How could something boring be just as beautiful? Well, there was only one remedy for that. "Okay, let's

The Arcane War

go."

They walked together, hand in hand so they wouldn't be separated. Naran took strength from that. He was excited. He was also scared.

The last time he'd been to any temple had been at home.

Sacrifice the boy. One child, and the gods will bless your family with long life and prosperity.

His parents were sick. They'd sought intervention from the god of healing.

The gods need proof of your faith, Master and Mistress Tennival. If you are not willing to sacrifice your son, the god of healing cannot cure your disease.

Naran tensed all over. It was as if he was there, listening to the priest talk to his parents, talking over Naran, as if he wasn't even there.

It's your choice, of course. But if you don't give up the boy to the gods, both of you will die.

No. Best not to think of that. Best to not remember at all.

"Have you heard the story of the god of death?"

It was as if Davri had heard Naran's thoughts. It brought him up cold as they reached the steps before the temple.

Naran shook his head. "Mom and Dad didn't talk much about the gods." Damn it. There was a quaver in his voice. He'd been trying to be strong and be brave. Just like Mom had told him to be.

"It's all my parents ever talked about," Davri said with a rueful grin. "You're probably better for not hearing all the myths and stories, to be honest. Some of them could be very dry. I think you'll appreciate this one, though."

"Okay." Naran smiled a little. It might have been more of a grimace. He was trying.

"The goddess of magic was the mother of the god of death. He and his brother would listen to her and defer to her when they were young. They were watching. Listening. Learning.

"The gods were still creating all the races of the world. There were only elves, sprites, mermaids, and imps. The first of those races were all creations of the gods, in union with the goddess of magic. They lived, they had children of their own, and the years didn't touch them with age or an end to their lives.

"The goddess of magic began to wonder if this was a good thing. Eventually they'd overwhelm the land if they had too many children. The other gods and goddesses wouldn't listen to her concerns. The world was vast, and they were still angry at her for setting them against each other when those races had been created.

"The other gods were having godly children with each other or on their own, as gods do. One of those children was the goddess of birth and growth. The goddess of magic knew that there had to be a balance to this new force. She had two children on her own, with the intent of bringing forth that balance.

"The goddess of birth and growth met this baby god of death. The other gods had cautioned her not to go, sure it was a trap since the goddess of magic had intended balance. Instead of being afraid she smiled and kissed his cheek. She said that the god of death would be her favorite."

"What about his brother?"

"The god of secrets? That's a story for another day. Today you're thinking of death."

"And death is bad, isn't it?" Naran asked. He'd been so wrapped up in the story that ascending the steps had been an afterthought. Davri had walked, Naran had followed, and now they paused at the top. "Wouldn't she hate him?"

Davri shook his head. "They created a place together where the souls of the dead could rest and remain, never to be forgotten. A place where they wouldn't suffer hardships that physical bodies endured. So, every death is a birth in another form."

"So, Mother and Father are with the god of death, and they're okay now?"

"Yes," Davri said, smiling as they walked through the enormous arch that brought them into the temple proper. "It's sad that they can't be with you, but they haven't been destroyed. That's why there is a god of death, so that there are ends to go with beginnings, and so—"

Aral turned to Thera and grinned a bit. "This should be fun," she said. "Do you have any ideas where we should start with this?"

"Everyone else is going to go with Dernad's Miracle," Thera said, gathering her papers and putting them in her book bag as she thought. "He never replicated it, but it was obviously teleportation, wasn't it?"

"There's no proof. Just personal testimony from people who may have been swayed by money, or the desire to be a part of something great. My father always said it was a dead end. We're probably safe in skipping that line of research." Aral started grinning from ear to ear. There was something else she had in mind. "Dernad's story is popular, but what about scripture?"

"Scripture? I don't remember any passages about people popping from one place to the next."

"Not people," Aral said, eyes sparkling. "Gods. They appear and disappear all over the place, and it's not just in what's been written. People who have encountered the gods in person, like priests, have said that gods teleport whenever they feel like it."

"Hm…" Thera's brow furrowed. "Counterargument: what if they're not teleporting? They could be using illusion, or they could be creating and destroying little puppet bodies. They're not mortal, so they're not stuck in one body, right?"

"I don't know," Aral said. "That's why it's going to take research. We'll look in the library first, but they probably won't have anything. I'll ask Davri if he can set up an interview with one of his priest friends. I'll bet no one else will think of that. If gods can actually teleport, and use magic to do it, why can't we?"

"I like that," Thera said, smiling. She blinked a moment later. "Davri and Naran are at the temple right now, aren't they? Do you think they'll see a god while they're there? I've heard that it happens once in a while. Wouldn't that be amazing?"

It was possible. Not likely, but possible. "At Temple Magica? The only one who would dare appear there is the goddess of magic herself." As a mage, that was an almost overwhelming thought. "I don't think amazing is a strong enough word. I'd probably faint, or trip over something, or just make a fool of myself."

There was a heavy scent of incense mixed with burning candles. Aral whipped her head around, confused. This was a theory class, books only. Who was casting in class?

"When the world was new, the gods gave it the name 'Kayan'. They saw that it was formless, pulled from the chaos of creation, and desired to make it their home. From the chaos they created mountains and fields, oceans and skies. There were five of them at first, harnessing the five forces of creation, creating Kayan to the vision of their dreams."

Aral couldn't see who was talking, but the lecture hall had disappeared around her. There were crowds of people around, creating noise with their mouths, words that blended together to obfuscate the meaning behind the conversations around it.

The walls were marble and gold, opening to a large space with benches…pews. It was a temple, and a grand one. The vaulted ceiling made every voice carry and mingle in a cacophony. Above the din that one voice continued, the only sound that her mind could parse from the rest.

"Bogradan had dominion over the winds and the skies, giving the breath of life and the gift of air to Kayan. Atherva had dominion over the seas and lakes, marrying Bogradan and bringing to the world the rains. Atherva's sister was Egridaea, goddess of the earth, and with the help of the others sprang all life from her domain. She loved Fotar, god of fire, above all."

It was like scripture from the holy texts, but there were names. In everything Aral had read the names of the gods were omitted. They were referred to only as "god of" or "goddess of".

"And, finally, there was Nalia, who held herself and her gifts apart. Her domain was magic, part of all things, giving the unifying force necessary to all that the other gods created, but separate from all. She granted them her magic freely, as excited as they were over giving life to Kayan, a world that was much like a child to them all."

"Hello?" Aral kept looking around, trying to find who was speaking. "Who are you? Where are you?"

There was a whisper in her ear. "You don't want to be here for this."

She caught a glimpse of Naran and Davri walking into the temple. Aral opened her mouth to shout a warning to them.

If she didn't want to be here for this, they should leave, too.

The strange vision abruptly disappeared.

"Aral?"

She was back where she'd been before, in the lecture hall. Thera was looking at her with obvious concern.

"Sorry," Aral said, patting her friend on the arm. "Just an odd train of thought. It's fine, we should go to the library."

Something was wrong. Something was very wrong. But she knew in her gut that there was nothing she could do about it. Not yet.

"Sir!"

A chill ran down Naran's spine.

There were throngs of people in the temple. The priest rushing in their direction could be addressing any number of people.

Naran's heart was pounding anyway. He knew. He shouldn't have come here. He shouldn't have asked to come, to see the beauty of the place.

The priest tripped over the hem of his own robe in his hurry. It was a momentary stumble that should have looked comical. Something about the long limbs flailing about seemed sinister and spider-like instead.

"The goddess surely blesses you for this." The priest stopped in front of Davri, catching his breath, the picture of disarming benevolence. His brown hair was hanging in front of his eyes like a puppy. "You have done the right thing in bringing this child to us. Do you know...did he wander off from another temple, or did he run away? Ah, it doesn't matter. I'll take him for you from here."

The silence that fell at those words seemed to encompass the world. The priest snatched Naran's hand, pulling him from Davri's limp fingers. Everything slowed down around them, and he watched sorrow and resolve settle on Davri's face without a hint of surprise. It confused Naran at first, then ice seemed to form in his veins. Davri, his sister's closest friend, was letting this happen. He was being stolen away, and Davri was just watching it happen. The back of his throat turned sour, like the moment before vomiting.

So. This is what it meant to be sick with fear.

Naran could see the eyes of the priest from home.

The one who had spoken so pleasantly of killing him.

The one who thought the world would be better if he would lie down and die instead of his parents.

The one he still secretly agreed with every night as he lay in bed, staring into the blackness around him.

He took a deep breath to scream just as Davri clenched his jaw, narrowed his eyes, and yanked Naran away from the priest. The scream came out as an oddly malformed squeak. It heralded the chaos that erupted a moment later.

Sound returned to Naran's world.

Voices rushed in at him from all sides.

One word floated above the cacophony.

"...sacrifice."

The priest was speaking.

He was saying something to Davri as if Naran were an object rather than a child.

That one word swam through his head and drowned out the rest.

People were pressing in around them.

Naran pulled his hand free of the priest and clung to Davri with all his might.

"No!" Davri was shouting. "His parents died! You can't!"

"He's a sacrifice! He's been marked! The gods—"

Davri picked Naran up and ran.

The last thing Naran saw of the temple was the priest falling in a graceless heap to the ground.

Chapter Two –

Chaos and Confusion

They were down two dozen steps in an instant, Davri's heart pounding, drowning out all other sound. He hadn't even had time to think. Just react.

What have I done?

He pulled Naran around the closest corner, panting a little. He kneeled in front of Naran, taking in the wildness and fear in the boy's eyes.

"Don't say a word."

Davri traced a sigil on Naran's forehead, whispering words of magic to seal it. It emitted the faintest blue glow for a mere moment before sinking into the boy's skin and disappearing.

"I have somewhere we can go. Somewhere to hide. I need you to keep quiet until we get there."

Naran nodded.

"We'll walk slowly, like we're simply enjoying the clear weather and wandering around." Davri then took Naran's hand and gave him a gentle squeeze. "We'll get through this."

As soon as they emerged Davri saw familiar faces from the temple, searching faces in the crowds.

Don't run. Don't act suspicious. Just...don't.

It was hard. He would have given his last copper nub to have a cloak with a cowl right now. It would have looked suspicious on such a sunny day, though. Sure enough, one of the temple supplicants confronted a man from out of town. "Chilly up on the mountain," the man was explaining as Davri forced himself to walk past.

There was a haberdasher hawking his wares from a stand in front of his shop. That would do, perhaps. Temporarily. Until they started using magic in their search.

"Good Master," the haberdasher said as they approached, "it's a powerfully sunny day. A hat for you and your brother, to shade your eyes?"

Brother? Well, they were both pale of skin and had blond hair, though Naran's was golden where Davri's was ash.

"I was thinking the very same thing," Davri said, slipping into the accent of his homeland for the first time in a year or more. He'd shed it quickly so that he wouldn't stand out as an outsider while attending University Magica. But, in this case, he was grasping for any disguise he could find.

Of course, branding himself as an outsider increased the merchant's prices. They haggled, and Davri couldn't express his indignation too strenuously without drawing attention. He walked away paying a silver wheel too much for a pair of matching felt and fabric hats of questionable durability. He relaxed once he put his on, though. Any change might be the difference between escape and capture.

The priests and supplicants from the temple weren't looking at anyone haggling over merchandise, yet. It bought him a bit of time, but at the cost of mobility. They were well within the perimeter being searched now. Soon the faithful would start scowering the stalls and shops rather than looking for people fleeing.

So long as those searching were supplicants and the younger, newer priests, they could hide in the open like this. Davri had a few magic advantages over most. The problem would be when the older priests and the high priests joined the search. For that, he'd need help.

He knew where to go. Getting there unnoticed was the problem. Even with magical aid, bringing those looking for you to your hiding place did no good. He wandered through the streets with Naran in tow, sometimes stopping to talk to a person at random to seem less conspicuous or have an innocuous excuse to hide his face. It was tedious and dangerous, leading them in circles to avoid one searcher or another.

Was it worth it?

That was the question he asked himself as his feet began to ache. He'd almost let them take the boy. Almost. A lifetime of obedience to the gods and their priests was hard to set aside in one moment of injustice.

Ultimately, what would the boy's death cost the world? Davri had seen this day coming in dreams and visions. There was a war coming, whether the boy lived or died, and Aral would be at the heart of it.

There was the answer.

Aral.

She'd already lost her parents earlier in the year, in the spring. She'd lost her freedom so that she could take in her brother. She'd lost the joy and the sparkle in her eye that Davri had loved the first time they had met.

What would losing her brother cost her?

This was what he had to do. Saving the boy was the right thing. It might not make a difference in the end, but this was the point of the upcoming war. The worth of an individual life. Davri would be no better than the gods if he ignored that now.

The Temple Magica halls grew unusually silent.

Guests and worshippers were being ushered out, following the incident. The priests and resident supplicants were about to be too busy to watch over the uninitiated.

Krecek Alavraneth extinguished candles, one at a time, with the plain brass snuffer usually reserved for the end of the day. As always, he was reverent and careful, mindful of the prayers

The Arcane War

symbolized by each flame.

His fist clenched around the handle of the snuffer tightly for a moment; he should be outside, tending to the garden this time of day. Not this.

The whole morning had been an irritation to him, interrupting his routine for a small bump on the head. The fact that they were closing down the temple over a minor altercation was beyond belief. Ervain's grandstanding and hysterics knew no limits.

"I saw my life again before me," Ervain was wailing from the bench he was sprawled out upon. "I almost died!"

There'd been a lot of blood. It had been a scalp wound, so of course it bled profusely. The stench of burning hair had been the better excuse to close the doors. It wasn't as if Ervain had bled to death.

Krecek came upon the offending candle. It was now useless due to the singed hair stuck in the cooling wax. He threw it in the bin. Such a waste.

Once the candles were extinguished, the rack itself was simple to clean. It required a minor spell that Krecek could do fast asleep at this point. The bend of a finger, a subvocalized word, and an application of will. Simple. He'd cast the same spell every day for decades.

In other temples, most tasks were traditionally done by hand. The time it took to perform the action was a meditative sort of worship, done with mindfulness, to the glory of the god or goddess in question. It also ensured that the tasks could be done by anyone, with or without magical talents.

The Temple Magica was dedicated to the greater glory of the goddess of magic. Spells were expected, even in the routine.

"We need to gather everyone!" Ervain was still ranting, filling the sanctuary with his cries. "The boy is going to get away if we stand around doing chores!"

Krecek could feel Ervain's eyes boring into the back of his

head.

Yes. The menial chore of cleaning up blood and burnt hair before it had a chance to set in and stain. How dare he?

Also...had Ervain said boy?

Had he been toppled over by a mere child?

The thought amused Krecek for a moment. How pathetic to whine and moan over injury caused by a little boy.

The amusement dried up as quickly as it had surfaced, however. Ervain seemed to be out for blood. He wouldn't put it past the other priest to punish the child for an accident. Ervain's pride knew no limits.

The priests attending Ervain did their best to soothe him. The cries for action eventually calmed. Word was then spread that all were to gather within the sanctuary.

The garden would have to wait.

"What inanity is it this time?" a priestess, Shania, was muttering as she walked past.

It was a common sentiment.

Krecek took a seat, crossing his arms over his chest as others filtered in. He resented being called to meet over what seemed like hysterics. It sounded to him like the incident was probably an accident. This was time he could be spending by maintaining the splendor of this temple. Elevating the awe people felt upon seeing her works and her wonders.

The supplicants and the younger initiates were conspicuously absent. They'd been flitting in and out of the doors, talking to the high priests quietly before slipping outside again. That left the core. Those with actual power. The ones who kept the temple running behind the scenes.

Porrellid, one of the high priests, walked to the front and cleared his throat.

It took but a moment. There were perhaps fifteen or twenty priests and priestesses in the room. It seemed like such a small group.

"We all know Davri Beran," Porrellid began in his nasal voice. "He stops in regularly, full of questions, claiming to be a seeker. Claiming to want to be among our numbers."

"Claiming?"

Krecek wasn't the only one who looked confused. He knew Davri fairly well, in fact. The two had become close, as the young man was one of the few humans who did not grate on his every nerve. In fact, Krecek had been the one to encourage the young man to visit often. He'd introduced Davri to everyone.

What did Davri have to do with this?

"He attacked Ervain in our very halls with no provocation!"

Porrellid's declaration cut through the confused muttering. He looked around at everyone to make sure that the appropriate level of dismay was displayed before speaking again.

"This is not the action of a future priest!"

All nodded, concern morphing into anger.

"Do not blame yourselves, however," Porrellid continued, at once condemning and forgiving en masse, "we were all of us deceived. Even Ervain was fooled, welcoming the instrument of his own undoing."

Davri was charming and his talents were impressive. Everyone Krecek had introduced him to had encouraged him to join them. Talented, quick of wit, with a ready smile.

That ended today.

"He and any of his associates found with him must be brought here for questioning. I still hold out hope that this was a tragic accident or misunderstanding, but it is my duty to correctly ascertain his guilt or innocence. Do not take that burden upon yourself. Just bring him and his friends to me."

There was more confusion.

Associates?

Friends?

Why were they being involved with this, when they all had better things to do?

Why hadn't Davri already been found, since so many already knew him?

Why were they shutting down an entire temple, the most important temple in all of Anogrin, to find one young man?

Were they all expected to leave now to chase him down?

Porrellid didn't answer any questions. He and the five other high priests and priestesses left, ignoring the chaos behind them. Krecek realized that Ervain wasn't in the sanctuary with the rest of them. There was no one left to give answers. It seemed the remaining priests and priestesses were expected to go forth and do as they were told.

How long had it been? Davri's mother had known Arlanz Madri long before he'd chosen to study in Anogrin. She said only that she'd done a job for Arlanz's father, and that the two of them should become friends.

When an oracle tells you to become friends with someone, you do it. Mother or no.

His first year of studies, Davri had come to the café once a week. He and Arlanz had spent hours talking together when business was slow. But, business had picked up. Davri's studies had taken up more time. He felt a twinge of guilt that he'd been away so long, and now he brought trouble nipping at his heels.

The café hadn't changed a bit. The door was a soothing shade of green, and a tiny bell rang out as he opened and closed the door. Two men were talking in front of the window, sharing a stimulating drink and equally stimulating conversation by the sound of it. The chairs were large and inviting. Comfortable. The walls were covered with bright tapestries that suggested faraway lands and very different customs. And the smell...the scent of the herbs, the roasted coffee beans, the sweet creams and caramels, was unlike anywhere else in the city. To the rest of Anogrin it was exotic. To Davri it was a breath of home.

"Davri, my friend!"

The time since his last visit evaporated.

They embraced briefly, clapping each other on the back almost violently. "It's good to see you again, Arlanz," Davri murmured softly. "I must avail myself of your darkest hospitality."

Arlanz was a hulking bear of a man. He towered over most men and had the girth to match. His brow furrowed, and the gap between his wild eyebrows disappeared. He didn't say a word, just gestured to the back as he ambled over to the other guests in his establishment. Davri heard Arlanz ask the men if they needed anything refreshed as they slipped into the hidden room behind the shop's storage.

"We'll be safe in here," he told Naran as soon as the door was closed behind them. "You're safe to talk now, if you need to."

Naran took in a deep breath, expelling it in a sudden rush. It was as if he'd wanted to say something but couldn't fit it all into words. He was pale, sweating, and he looked so small and lost. Probably overwhelmed.

"It's okay," Davri said. "It's a lot to deal with."

"The priest—" Naran started, then stopped. Tried again. "He was—"

"I know. I'm sorry. I shouldn't have taken you there."

"No, it's okay. I wanted to go." Naran's fingers curled into small fists. Nine years old. All he was, was nine years old. "It was as pretty as everyone said it would be." A weak smile. Even now, the boy could find something good about it all.

Davri returned his smile and found an old crate to sit down on. He gestured toward the only chair in the room. "Relax. We'll have to stay here for a bit. Your sister will be in classes for a few more hours. Then we'll find her and tell her what's going on."

After a moment the boy nodded and sat down. "Thank you."

The door opened and Arlanz joined them. "We have a bit of time. What can I do for you?"

"I need to hide for a bit," Davri said. "I hate to impose on you like this, but..." He gestured around the room, at the glyphs decorating the walls. "The boy and I are in some trouble."

"What sort of trouble?" Arlanz asked, fingers closing around the medallion that hung around his neck. He didn't look suspicious or put out at the prospect of trouble. Just...concerned.

"Our young friend has been wrongfully marked for sacrifice."

Arlanz went still, not even any evidence of breath for a long moment. He slowly slid the medallion at his neck back into his shirt, patting it deliberately before he shook his head. "They will say that there is no such thing." He looked skyward for a moment, pained. "They are the priests of the gods. They do not make mistakes. They can commit no wrongs."

It was the way of things, and Arlanz knew that better than most. Still...

"I've been studying to be one of those priests. I've made friends with more than a few. Priests are not gods. They make mistakes. Hell, some of them are blithering idiots who shouldn't be in charge of picking a chicken for supper, let alone a human for sacrifice. I'll talk to some people. I'll get this cleared up."

Arlanz opened his mouth to say something, but he looked over at Naran and visibly stopped himself. Another breath, and Arlanz smiled kindly at the boy. "I'm sure that you will. While you are under my roof, you are family. Under my protection. They will not find you."

At that, the proprietor left them. Naran pulled out a tablet of paper and sticks of charcoal and began sketching things he'd seen that day. "They're going to kill me, aren't they?"

"Not if I can help it, no."

The Arcane War

The scritch-scritch sound of the charcoal on the paper filled the room for a moment before Naran looked up. "Can you really stop them, though?"

"I'm a mage," Davri said with a roguish grin. "There's not a lot I can't do." He could do it. He knew that he could. The cost would be great, but he would save Naran.

Humans.

Krecek shook his head as he walked into his small room. He kept it simple, spare. He had hidden magical components there, impossible for most humans to obtain. By appearing as if nothing of value could be hidden there, he'd managed to hold on to great treasures that the high priests would envy.

His personal items, clothing and such, was kept in the trunk at the foot of his bed. He walked past that, to his bedside table, and pulled out a flat wooden box that was secreted under the surface. It unlocked with a command word in the elvin tongue.

He pulled out a vial of water from the lake Orlathannivra. The lake was said to have formed from the tears Nalia herself. Tears once shed for her child, Baedrogan, the god of death. A potent gift from his aunt Siv before he'd left the elvin lands.

Krecek then lifted a small branch from his father's tree. The branch was so small that it was almost a twig. However, the tree itself had been planted by Egridaea, the goddess of the earth, before humans had been created. Again, it was seeped in ancient magic.

Most important, though most mundane, was a trinket of colored glass that danced in the sunlight. It wasn't much, but for this purpose it would ensure that Krecek could cast a spell no one else in the temple would be able to.

The trinket had been a midsummer gift from Davri.

He felt a pang of guilt. It was one of very few gifts he'd received in his years as a priest. Life had been largely solitary for him. The intent behind the present had been friendship, not this.

In the end, Krecek had a duty to fulfill. The gift from Davri gave him an edge over the other priests.

"Seigreathana, beianla erae," he intoned, touching the water to the branch. He held the bauble in one hand, the branch in the other, and he let the gentle urging from them both guide him.

The pull away from the temple was intense, equal to the urge Davri must have felt to run away. Good. Down the stairs, into an alley —

And nothing. No, just a vague hint.

The spell was working, he hadn't miscast it, but it didn't pull him in any real direction or along any particular path. It was no cause for concern, however. He was content to wander around, stop for tea, enjoy the fresh air. The spell guided him forward and stopped again a few times.

That was good.

Whatever magic Davri was using to hide himself with was not perfect, and not permanent.

Krecek would find Davri. He couldn't hide forever.

Chapter Three

SEARCHING FOR ANSWERS

"I don't understand," Aral whispered.

It wasn't an attempt at secrecy or silence. Her voice just wouldn't come out.

Naran put his hand on Aral's arm, but she could barely feel it. She was staring at Davri, mind racing, trying to find a way to make it so that what he'd told her wasn't what she thought he'd said.

"I don't know what to do," Davri said, voice calm, face almost devoid of expression. "They'll be looking for both of us. Do you have documentation or proof that your parents died? Is there anything in writing to explain that a deal was made between them and the priest?"

"I have a letter," Aral said. She placed her hand over Naran's cold fingers, pressing tight to make sure he was still there. "They explained it. They donated their library to the university, too. The headmaster will have documents."

"Find everything you can," Davri said. "Naran, we need to go as soon as we can. Grab only essentials."

Naran slipped his hand from Aral's, packing as silently as he could.

No.

Aral propped herself against the wall just to stay standing. This couldn't be happening.

"As soon as you get this cleared up, we'll be back," Davri said.

"Gods don't make mistakes," Aral said, and she could hear the creeping hysteria in her own voice. "How do you hide from gods? They're going to find you. Then you'll both—"

She stopped, feeling it a moment before it happened.

It was too late.

The door burst open with a loud crack.

Aral had a defensive spell on the tip of her tongue.

Davri was raising his hands in a gesture familiar from one of their more advanced classes.

Naran was crouched in a corner, hands raised over his head protectively.

They found themselves frozen in place, unblinking, unbreathing, as young man walked in wearing the robes of a priest.

"Davri," he said gently, "what have you done?"

The young priest looked the three of them over. Moments passed, his bright green eyes taking their measure before releasing them with a dismissive gesture.

Aral took a step toward him as soon as she was released.

The spell was cast in an instant.

It should have pushed the priest out of the room like a hard shove.

Nothing.

He was unmoved, unruffled, simply looking at her as if mildly disappointed.

"Don't, Aral." Davri stepped between them, meeting her eyes with a warning that was more intense than his words. He then turned to the priest. "I didn't have a choice, Krecek. It's not right. I had to save him."

"You know this person?" Aral's voice was shrill to her own ears. Some detached part of her realized it was the beginning of hysterics. Well, after everything today, it was hardly a surprise.

Davri nodded, not taking his eyes from Krecek.

"We're friends," Krecek said. "We are." Insistent. Hopeful? "We've been friends for years." Now his voice was firm, determined. "They said you attacked Ervain, unprovoked. The high priests want you, and your associates, for questioning."

"You're making a mistake," Davri said. He stepped aside and gestured to Aral. "This is my friend. Aral Tennival."

Aral took half a step back, still alarmed at the intrusion and the way he'd brushed aside her spell. Was he some sort of child prodigy? Is that why he was a priest so young?

"Tennival?" Krecek eyes lit up and his face grew soft, kind. He made sudden gesture, awkward, like he was suddenly nervous or intimidated. It shifted from that first gesture into him tucking his hair behind his ear. His ear that came to an inhuman point at the end. "I am honored to meet you. I knew your father when he attended this school. He was also a friend."

"You…did?" Aral stammered over the words, realizing as soon as she opened her mouth. He wasn't a young man. He was an…elf? No, half elf. The eyes…the ears…the short stature. She realized he could very well be ancient, and she was judging him as if he was a child. She'd cast a spell not just at a priest, but an elf. No wonder it had done nothing.

She was staring. Rather obviously. A fact she only realized when Krecek's expression changed from warmth to resignation.

"Yes, I am a half elf," Krecek said with what appeared to be well practiced patience. "Northern, which is where I get my stature and the brightness of my eyes. My mother was human." He'd clearly said these words so many times, justifying his existence to two societies that would never accept him.

"Oh," Aral said faintly. What else could she say?

Davri cleared his throat. "Her parents, both of them, died half a year ago. I'm sorry you're learning this way."

"But they were so young," Krecek said. His eyes darted down and to the right, as if calculating their ages, making sure that even by human standards it was a short time.

"Yes. It was a tragedy. One that, if you bring us to the high priests, will be compounded."

"They just want you for questioning. What could be tragic

about..." He stopped himself, looking around the room one more time and looking, actually looking, at Naran for the first time. "Oh no. Again?"

Aral met Davri's eyes, and they seemed to have the same thought. Again? This had happened before?

Krecek brushed past them and stood in front of Naran, looking him in the eyes and placing a hand upon the child's forehead. There was a light pulse of magic that traveled through the room, like a ripple in a still pond. Something glowed briefly above Naran's head, and Krecek's shoulders slumped.

"I can't remove it. A high priest placed this mark. Any priest would see it immediately." He placed a finger over Naran's lips. "No, don't say a word. I can feel the spell on you...Davri's work, and well crafted. Don't break it, not yet." He squared his shoulders and turned to Davri and Aral. "I have my duty, but please, tell me what this is about? Why would someone do this?"

"You'll help?" Aral could barely dare to hope.

"I'll do my best," he said. "I need to know everything."

"My parents were sick," Aral explained, hesitating over the word "sick". It seemed so inadequate. "Sick" was something a healer cured. "They went to the temple at home. It's dedicated to the god of healing, so it should have been so easy to fix. Just go in, pray with a healer and a priest, and come home to rest a while before going on." Aral took a deep breath. It was a tangent, but she couldn't help herself. She hadn't spoken of this for months.

Davri put a hand on her shoulder, and Aral grimaced. It was supposed to be a smile, but this was too hard. She ducked away, sitting down on the edge of her bed, gathering herself to go on.

"They sent me a letter. The priest had given them a choice. They could sacrifice Naran, or they would die. They...they tried so hard to have another baby after me. All sorts of spells to bring Naran into the world, all sorts of-- There was no way they'd let him die." Another deep breath. Just facts. "They sent Naran to live with me while they put their affairs in order. They died while he was on the road. I have papers. Documents. Their letters. There was special dispensation made here at the university so I could watch him. They donated books, their research...they died so that this wouldn't happen to him."

Her voice broke on the last sentence. Stupid, weak, crying in front of a priest as if that will make a difference. As if someone like that could be persuaded by emotion instead of strength. He probably saw a thousand tears from a thousand people a day, wanting exceptions, wanting miracles.

Davri handed her a handkerchief. "I've talked to some of the professors about this. There's no doubt that Master and Mistress Tennival are dead. It was a great blow to the community. I didn't think about telling you. I'm sorry. I didn't know you knew them."

Silence.

Krecek's head was bowed, eyes closed. Was he thinking? Praying? Aral almost asked him if he'd help, if he'd decided, but she was so afraid. Would he get annoyed at having his thoughts interrupted? Would he just walk away and leave them to their fate if she asked too much?

"I'm going to help you," Krecek said at last. "It might not be enough, but I'll try, gods help me." It was clear he wasn't using the expression lightly. He'd clasped his hand over a golden medallion, clearly a holy symbol, that hung on a chain around his neck. Round, with a five-pointed star resting over the flame of creation. Aral recognized it at once. Magic. The goddess of magic.

Of course it was. Who else would he worship, in the Temple Magica?

"The first thing I need to do is gather more evidence. I'll need to see their graves and speak to the healers who attended them. I'll need to talk to the priest who did this, if he's still there. The three of you can travel with me, or find somewhere safe to hide, but I can't grant you sanctuary until I have more evidence." He looked defeated. "I'm not supposed investigate. They told us not to. I'm should bring all of you back with me. But if I do that, the boy will die."

"Why?" Aral clenched her fists, fingernails digging into her palms. "You said this has happened before, but you're not even supposed to check? You're not supposed make sure someone didn't make a mistake? High priests can just kill whoever they like, for any reason, or no reason at all?"

Krecek met her eyes, holding her gaze for several heartbeats. Something inside him looked tired, resigned. He looked away first, shaking his head just once. "We don't have much time. Pack a few necessities and meet me at the northern gates. The sooner we leave the city, the better."

He left without another word.

"Can we trust him?"

Davri shrugged. "I trust him," he said.

"Do you think he'll be able to help?"

He hesitated, looking at her with an odd expression for a moment. "I need to grab a few things," he said. "I'll meet you at the gates." He left before she could ask anything else.

Aral stared at the door, heart racing at the implications of everything that had just happened.

She could lose her brother. That was the immediate problem.

Underlying that, her faith in the gods had been shaken. She wasn't ready to think of corrupt priests and sacrifices that might just be murder.

Davri had aspired to be a priest. What did that say about him?

If Krecek helped them, what would that mean for him?

Naran put a hand on Aral's arm, bringing her out of her thoughts. His face was pale with fear, but he smiled at her anyway, faith in her clearly absolute. She didn't have time to chase the darkness of her doubts through the recesses of her mind. She had things to do.

"We're going home," Aral said. "We'll find all the proof we need there, and with any luck we'll have that mark removed by the idiot who placed it on you. We'll get it straightened out," she ruffled his hair, smiling gently. "I won't let anyone hurt you. Ever."

No one spared them a second glance as they left the city. The guards motioned them through with bored expressions as they reached the gate on horses Krecek had obtained. There'd been some creative misrepresentation of the truth in order to get them, as well as the permission to leave for a few days. Sometimes, he thought, a greater purpose justified smaller infractions. The temple could do without the horses, and him, for a little while. It was important to get this cleared up.

After they passed a sufficient distance Davri pulled alongside Naran and removed the spell upon him. The boy thanked Davri, but other than that no words were exchanged. No one seemed in the mood to talk much as they rode.

It was a few hours after nightfall, with the chill wind chasing them down the mountain, when they finally reached an inn. Krecek was glad to get out of the saddle, stretch his legs, and enter a building with an effective warmth spell worked into the walls. He didn't travel often anymore, and he could feel it in his legs. In no time they had a room together and could wash off the dust of the road.

"Get as much sleep as you can tonight," Krecek said as he washed his face. "We have a lot of ground to cover tomorrow."

"Will we be safe while we travel?" Naran spoke up immediately.

"I'm a priest. Where I walk, the gods walk."

"I thought we were hiding from priests and gods," Naran said.

"All of them want to kill me. So, why should you being a priest make me feel safe?"

"Naran!" Aral rushed out from behind the privacy screen, not entirely covered by her nightgown as she rushed to silence her brother's heresy. She froze when she realized it, cheeks almost scarlet before she turned around to fix her gown.

"He has a point, and he hasn't been given the opportunity to ask until now." Krecek wiped his face with the hand towel as he considered his answer. "I hope we're not running from gods. Rebellion against the gods could bring disaster. As for running from priests, that issue is a little more complicated. If you are with me, any random priest we run into will assume I am doing my duty and bringing you to the appropriate temple or transporting you for an upcoming occasion."

"Brigands and outlaws shouldn't be a problem," Davri finally spoke up. "We're three mages, guarding one child. But, we have a different sort of problem. The last I heard, the Tennivals were in Thalanis. We all know how far away that is. Even traveling light, pushing ourselves—"

"It's fine," Aral said. "I'm in no hurry as long as it means this is put behind us. School can wait. I'll write a letter to the headmaster tonight explaining the situation."

"No," Krecek said, "I don't have that much time. If I spend two months to investigate the reason behind a sacrifice that I was told not to ask questions about, there will be consequences. Possibly for all of us." He looked at Davri curiously. "You know what I was going to suggest, don't you?"

"An enchanted path," Davri nodded. "Even Aral is powerful enough to hold her own on one, and the two of us can protect Naran against anything there."

"No! I just had Master Lanrin's lecture on travel this morning, and he went on at length on how dangerous they are. I'm not putting my brother through that."

The Arcane War

"At this point, anything's dangerous," Davri pointed out. "It might be less dangerous on an enchanted path, actually. Nothing there will be targeting us, specifically. We'll be perfectly safe, as long as we stay on the path. There and back within a day, instead of a month or so."

"Wouldn't it be two or three months?" Naran asked.

"No!" Aral repeated, speaking over her brother forcefully. "Naran isn't a mage. He'd be vulnerable."

"He's vulnerable either way," Davri said. "You won't be dropped from your classes. We'll have everything cleared up sooner. And Krecek won't face whatever dire consequences they think up upon his return."

"We're not exposing his young mind to those horrors." She looked resolute.

Naran's small voice piped up with, "You said we'd be going home."

Aral looked like he'd just slapped her.

"Your sister is right," Krecek said kindly. "Enchanted paths aren't safe, even for mages. I shouldn't have brought it up."

"If you're disavowed for investigating, you won't be doing us any good." Davri looked smug, triumphant. "So, we compromise. Aral and Naran stay here, while Krecek and I take the path. I've been down enchanted paths before, and I've lived to tell about it. It would be safer with three, but in a pinch I could do it alone. And I have."

"Now you're just bragging," Krecek chuckled for a moment. "It's a risk, but if two of us went while two stayed behind.... Naran would be safe here with one of us for a single day."

Aral grabbed a pillow almost violently and got into one of the two beds. "I'd better get as much sleep as I can tonight. Davri, you'd better keep my brother safe. If he dies before Krecek and I return, I will destroy you."

"Wait!" Davri's jaw dropped. "It was my idea. I like enchanted paths. I should get to go." He was pouting like a child denied a Nightwatch gift.

"They're my parents," Aral said. "I want to see their grave and pay respects. Krecek has to come with me so that he can see for himself that they are interred there. You've already proven I can trust you with Naran's life. We might be able to find the high priest responsible for this mistake without exposing the two of you to more danger." She smiled grimly. "If we can take an enchanted path, so can the rest of the former mages from the temple. We need to assume that word will spread ahead of us. If Krecek and I are the only ones seen together to investigate, he'll have a plausible excuse for his actions rather than if he is seen with you. Weren't you paying attention, Davri? They're looking for you, specifically. Not Naran. Not yet."

"All I did was push him and run," Davri said, voice weak. "It's not like I stabbed him, or..." He trailed off, looking at Krecek pleadingly.

"Ervain is claiming that you tried to kill him," Krecek said. He didn't bother disguising his disgust and derision at the accusation. "When he fell, he hit his head on the candle rack. We all know he's just being dramatic, but…there was a lot of blood. It won't be easy to defend you unless…"

"You don't sound terribly concerned," Davri pointed out.

"I don't like Ervain," Krecek shrugged. "He's a swine and a parasite. There's something about him, something I can't put my finger on, but…something's off about him. He seems out of place, and he couldn't magic his way out of an open door. Still, as a priest at the same temple, we have obligations toward him."

"You have to take his side, publicly," Davri sounded bitter, "even if the rest of you can't stand him in private. Otherwise, the rabble might rise."

"Yes."

The bluntness of the answer silenced the others. Krecek

finished readying for bed, ignoring the gentle murmur of conversation between Naran and Aral curled up together in the other bed. He lay with his back turned to Davri and agonized. This whole thing was probably a fool's errand, but he had to try. This was once too many for him to keep his silence again.

The heavy pack and shoulder bag Aral had packed were almost useless now, she realized. In the rosy light of dawn, she was moving things around, putting things in the bag that she might need for defense. She'd gotten dressed already, eschewing her student robes for sturdy pants and a long, loose shirt. It wasn't flattering, but it would be practical for the situation.

"Do you want something to eat, before we leave?" Krecek asked in a whisper.

Aral shook her head. "Not hungry," she whispered back, not wanting to wake Naran or Davri. She straightened, patting herself down to make sure she had just what she would need. "I'm ready to leave if you are."

He grabbed one more thing and then they slipped out the door.

"I've never actually taken an enchanted path," she said a few paces away from the door. "All I know is that they're dangerous, but they weren't at first. What are they like? What should I expect?"

"Don't worry, you'll see for yourself soon enough. My father said that when he and the others created them, they forgot to account for something they call temporal bleed. They'd warped time to their purposes to make travel fast."

"Wait." Aral stopped in her tracks. "Your father's that old? And that powerful?"

"Yes."

It left Aral stunned. She followed him out of the inn, at a loss for further words.

"As I was saying, they warped time. The way he explained it to me was that there's some sort of a backlash, where the future and the past are creeping in on the pathways. I can't explain all the things that lurk there, and I don't know what we'll see as we travel. Just be prepared."

Aral nodded. She took a deep breath, let it out slowly. The anticipation was probably worse than the path itself. Unknowns were always worse than reality, right?

"How do we do it? How do we enter the path?"

"You can enter just about anywhere," he said. Krecek then held up a hand, moved it from left to right, and said, "Hasidah."

Aral recognized it as a word of magic that was often used as part of many incantations to find specific items. Hearing the word alone puzzled her. She opened her mouth to ask him what spell he was doing, how it worked, but then she saw what he had done.

In the spot he had waved his hand, reality seemed to blur and warp. In the span of a breath, she was surrounded by it. There were harsh edges and straight lines, deep shadows and harsh lights. There were shadowy figures here and there that were only visible from the corner of her eye.

"If I say run, you run. If I say hide, you hide. If I say freeze, don't even blink. And if I say fight, don't incapacitate. Fight to kill, or we'll both die."

Krecek shivered, rubbing his arms to bring back warmth. The enchanted path hadn't been particularly cold, but fear had spread what chill was in the air to his heart. It was a relief to be off of it, even if it hadn't been as bad as the first time he'd traveled with his father.

"That was…it was worse than I imagined," Aral stuttered beside him, teeth on the verge of chattering. "Those buildings…and the starkness of the roads. The creatures, when we had to go into the darkness…."

"I know," Krecek said, putting a hand on her arm. "It's never easy."

"How was Davri so eager?" Aral frowned, placing her hand over Krecek's briefly in acknowledgment. "He wanted to bring Naran with us…through that?"

"I don't know," he said. A thought occurred to him and he grinned. "Perhaps he wanted to impress you? They say fear is an aphrodisiac."

Aral laughed, and it was a beautiful sound considering all that had happened. "No, no. We're just friends. I don't know how many times I've had to say that to people."

"Are you sure?"

She seemed to have a flippant answer prepared, but she stopped herself. "We've talked about it," she shrugged. "We're both concentrating on our studies. And…I think he's in love with someone else."

"Ah." Krecek took a deep breath, dismissing thoughts about relationships. He looked around, centering himself on reality, on the here and now. "We should get this over with. We still have a return journey through all of that after we're done here."

Aral clenched her jaw, nodded. "I'll show you where the cemetery is. Their headstone was placed just last month. Next to my grandmother, I think they said."

They walked quickly, solemn silence slipping between them.

Krecek kept replaying the memory of Aral's laugh, hating that her joy had been so short lived. Hating more that he had been the one to stop it. He reminded himself, this wasn't some vacation. It wasn't an excuse to spend time with a pretty girl. This was life or death for someone she cared about.

It was easier to keep his mind on track as they walked the rows of headstones. The air here was warm and heavy, compared to both Anogrin and the enchanted path. It made the walk feel tiring, adding weight to what they were here for.

Aral took a few sudden, hurried steps, and then froze.

This was it, then.

It was a granite headstone, chiseled with skill, precision, and expertly worked magic. The names, Haran and Meli Tennival, were fresh and crisp. Grass had not yet spread entirely over the grave.

He paused a moment to remember Haran. Kind. Studious. Irreverent. Wild. Genius. They'd been friends at times. Rivals at others. They'd had a few advanced classes together. Krecek had already been a priest at the time. He'd taken a few of the advanced courses in his spare time, to learn a broader perspective on magic. Haran had helped him out of his shell a bit. Invited him to as many parties as he did study sessions. They talked about expectations. About talent. About the differences between elves and humans. About being an outcast among your own kind, and how it felt. How it shaped both their paths.

That young man, full of life and promise, had grown up and had a family. He'd moved on to live a full life. He'd become a great mage, married to an equally talented spellsmith of great renown. And now, here they were.

Dead.

Krecek took a charcoal rubbing of the headstone, then rolled up the paper and put it safely in a scroll case. First bit of evidence. It was a start.

He then stepped back and gave Aral time.

It was the least he could do. He vividly recalled the death of his own mother. How his life had been upended by her loss. Now, here stood Aral, having lost both parents at once. Krecek could only imagine how much worse that must feel.

She didn't take as long as Krecek thought she would. She turned abruptly and wiped away tears with an almost violent gesture.

"I'll show you to the temple of healing." Her voice was steady but strained, sounding forced. "It's where they would have gone. There's a high priest there. I've known him for years."

"Are you sure you're ready for this?" He reached for her, but she stepped away.

"No," she said. "If we wait until I'm ready, we might not ever move. I just want this behind me." More tears. The hem of her sleeves had to be soaked, but they continued on in silence.

Thalanis was a beautiful town on a hill. There were cobblestone streets and brick houses, and everything was painted in vibrant colors. Children played and parents gossiped, people waved and said hello to Aral. When they saw that she traveled with a priest, with a half elf, the friendly overtures stalled. Warmth turned to hesitant smiles and quickly turned backs as people found somewhere else to be. The furthest anyone got was to tell Aral that they were sorry about her parents, but she only nodded and maintained her pace.

The temple, when they reached it, seemed quaint to Krecek's jaded eyes. The architecture was grander than anything surrounding it. It was obviously a temple. It just looked drab next to the spectacle and show he was used to.

It seemed too innocuous to be the place that had started all this excitement.

Aral pulled herself together, squaring her shoulders before walking in.

So young to have to be so strong, he thought, looking at her. He'd spare her all of this if he could.

"I'm looking for Vigat."

The humble seeming priestess at the doors nodded. "He's been waiting for you." She gestured Aral to the back, toward open doors to the right of the altar. The priestess then turned to Krecek, looked confused when he strode past, with Aral. "Just Aral. We weren't aware of another priest visiting."

"It's just a formality," Krecek said, smiling kindly. "I'm here to see everything is straightened out."

"Show them both in!" someone called from the room. Vigat, presumably.

"Very well," the priestess said with a heavy, disapproving sigh. "It's irregular, but everything has been lately."

They walked into the room and the priestess shut the door behind them.

Vigat sat behind a desk, elbows on the surface, hands steepled before him. He was a thin, balding man with a hooked nose. He wore the vestments of a high priest, but something felt odd.

Off.

"Aral, it took you long enough to get here." Vigat smirked. He smirked! Of all the crass reactions... "All these months? You always pretended to be a dutiful daughter, but now we have the truth."

"I had classes. After everything they did to make sure I was accepted into the university, I couldn't just leave. It would have dishonored their memory. They wouldn't have wanted that; my mother sent a letter—"

"Spare me," Vigat rolled his eyes. He then stood, the very picture of impatience. "What do you want, Aral? I am a very busy man..."

"You know what I want!" She took a step forward, hands clenched in fists, but Vigat didn't move, didn't flinch. "You gave my parents an impossible choice. Their lives, or their son's life. Remove the mark of sacrifice from him! They're dead. You got what you wanted. Spare him."

"Beg for his life," Vigat said. "Grovel at my feet."

He said it simply. So simply that Krecek was dumbfounded.

"Please," Aral said, chin high and trembling. "Please don't do this."

"At my feet."

How could a priest of the god of healing be so needlessly cruel?

Aral slowly got to her knees. She kept looking at Vigat in disbelief, hesitating as if he'd stop her.

He just waited, watching. Feigning boredom.

Beneath the façade he was growing angry.

Impatient.

Her forehead met his boot, and finally Vigat made a low murmur of approval.

"I beg of you. Spare my brother. He is all that I have left."

Vigat reached down and began to pet her, as if she were a cat. He looked up at Krecek, gave a conspiratorial wink. "She'll do anything I ask of her, with her brother's life on the line. Any requests?"

Chapter Four –

ADRIFT

Krecek stared.

"Why are you doing this?"

"She knows why," Vigat said. He reached down, hooking a finger beneath her chin, forcing her to look up at him. "Don't you, Aral?"

She ducked her head and sank somehow lower to the ground. "Please don't," she whispered.

"What sort of priest of Garatara would do this?" Krecek asked, horrified. He felt a twinge of guilt, mentioning the god's name in the presence of one who was uninitiated. The names were considered holy secrets among humans.

"Me?" Vigat laughed. "Do I look like a healer? I'm no priest of his, I just work at this temple." He stood, tilting his head to the side. "What sort of priest of Nalia stands back and simply complains?"

Vigat was right.

Krecek began with a silent prayer to Nalia, asking for her aid against the pretender before him.

Nothing. There wasn't even a hint of response.

"Nalia, please," he said under his breath.

The response was laconic, disinterested.

Busy.

Bored.

"Garatara?" Surely the god of healing, himself, would be interested in righting the wrong being committed in his name.

"Anyone?"

Nothing.

"Did you think you were special?" Vigat met Krecek's gaze and held it. Power emanated from him from some unknown god. "That they'd listen to you, because you're just so pious?"

Nalia was fickle, which was a fact Krecek knew well. A reply would have been helpful, but it wasn't necessary.

There was a reason Krecek had been a mage, first.

He smiled grimly, blasting a wave of pure energy at Vigat. It was sloppy, but powerful. It should have been enough to be effective.

Instead of being pinned to a wall, Vigat disappeared, laughing.

Aral sat up, looked around. "What happened?"

He couldn't have teleported away, Krecek thought. That was impossible.

Had Vigat been an illusion?

Perhaps.

"He's gone," Krecek said, at a loss.

"This is my fault, isn't it?" Aral's voice was high pitched, strained with emotion. "I turned down his advances. In public. I humiliated him for grabbing my breast. I should have just let him."

"No," Krecek soothed. He kneeled beside her, put an arm around her shoulders. "It's not your fault. Any girl of your status would have done the same. There's something more to this. We'll find it, and we'll save your brother."

Aral held him tight, wrapped her arms around him like a drowning victim.

The tears that soaked through Krecek's shirt were still hot when she pulled abruptly away.

She took deep breaths, wiping her face with her sleeves again, roughly.

"We need to get back to Naran and Davri," she said. "They need to know they're still in danger. There's no time for tears and hopelessness." Her chin quivered and her voice was unsteady, but the determination in her eyes had already set in.

This was the first attempt to save Naran.

Not the last.

Agruet paced along the ledge of the building, watching the road beneath.

Watching the shadows grow.

"Mother should never have allowed the elves to create these accursed pathways," he muttered.

The tall, stark structures unnerved him. Their empty, shadowed doorways and windows were gaping holes in featureless walls that reached for blank sky. Even when it rained the sky was a perfectly blank shade of gray.

The paths were dangerous. Unstable.

Paradox and entropy married and at war in perfectly balanced tears in time and space.

The buildings were relics of a distant future. The shadows were ripped from the chaotic nightmare of creation itself.

And even the gods were incidental smudges across the landscape.

In the distance Agruet heard a loud pop. The sound of something whistling past made him jump.

Was someone shooting at him?

Shooting at a god upon an enchanted path?

Well, if they were ever going to have a chance, this was the only place that it could happen. He didn't wait to see what sort of spells were engraved on the bullet or pellet or whatever sort of ammunition they'd devised in the future. He teleported to the bottom level of the building, startling a dozen mutants in the process.

Mages were going to go from dangerous to terrifying over

time. Since the enchanted paths warped both time and space there was no telling what era a mage on the path came from. Even gods could only control for one variable at a time in this hellscape.

Good job, elves. What an accomplishment for the ages.

Thankfully, whoever had shot at him probably did not know they were dealing with a deity. They just saw an exposed figure up high and fired. Any mage from Agruet's era would stick to the safety of the ground. They weren't seen as a threat if encountered.

They didn't know, yet.

Baedrogan appeared at Agruet's side.

"They'll pass here in just a moment. The girl is furious."

"As expected," Agruet said.

Baedrogan opened his mouth, hesitated, and shook his head. "I'd ask what the point is, but you never answer. All secrets, all the time."

"I have a reputation to live up to, brother. God of secrets, and all."

"Yet here I am, the god of death, and I'm not out slaying everything in my path."

It dragged a reluctant chuckle from Agruet. "I just mean to say, she's going to need her anger if she is going to succeed. It will make her stronger for what lies ahead." A non-answer, but it seemed to satisfy Baedrogan at least. "I hate to admit to being wrong, but you were right about the boy. Sparing his life will probably make her fight harder, and smarter. Much as I wanted to spare him from what's to come."

"I do understand death," Baedrogan said, "and how mortals react to it."

Agruet opened his mouth to answer, but he caught a good look at the mortals as they approached. The girl and the half-elf. What a volatile pair. "Well, they're not broken by what happened.

One never knows, with mortals."

As they watched, the girl laughed.

That was certainly unexpected. To be sure, the spells she threw at approaching threats were backed by fury. Agruet could also sense the guilt and despair that tinged her mood, but something her companion said had set those emotions aside long enough for her to laugh.

"She's got a certain charm," Baedrogan said, analyzing. "It will make it easy for people to rally behind her and take up the cause."

Agruet nodded, silent. Aral hadn't been his first choice. Perhaps she should have been.

The halls of University Magica seemed colder now. Lonelier.

Returning without her brother and her best friend had been a blow to Aral, but what choice did she have?

If she'd gone with them, she wouldn't have a chance to beg for their lives.

If they'd returned with her, they'd have been caught and captured.

She fidgeted with the note in her hands, tried not to crumple or crease it, but it looked a little worn at the edges despite her intentions. Davri had scrawled it hastily, folded it in quarters, and asked her to deliver it as soon as she returned. The return trip had been enough to batter it a bit, sitting in her pack unprotected. Now, well, her nervousness was enough that she was proud the paper was intact.

The door before her opened, and she hastily bowed her head in respect. "Master Arsat?"

"Come in, come in, no need to be formal. You're here for an informal purpose, after all."

"Yes sir," she said. Aral glanced up with the closest thing to a smile she could muster. "Thank you, sir."

Master Arsat was an elf, but he looked almost the opposite of Krecek. He was tall, with straight black hair and caramel skin. His eyes were golden brown, and ears longer and flatter. He was a southern elf, while Krecek's elfish lineage was clearly northern. It's what made Krecek shorter, his skin and hair paler, his eyes emerald green, and his ears more resembling a leaf.

Also, if rumors were correct, Master Arsat was much, much older than the priest.

Aral followed him into his office. "This is for you," she said, thrusting the paper forward before he'd done more than step out of the way. "It's from Davri Beran. He asked me to hand it to you, personally." Her tongue almost tripped over the words in her rush to get them all out at once.

He gestured to a chair, slipping behind his cluttered desk without a word. He unfolded the paper and read silently. At a few points he glanced up at her, frowning, but his eyes darted back to the paper before she could read his expression.

"That's quite the tale," he eventually said. "Did you read it?"

"Of course not!" The lie came out immediately, without thought, and Aral's ears warmed as she said it. Some bits of the note had been of a personal nature. It embarrassed her to be privy to it. Why hadn't Davri sealed it, either with wax or with magic?

Master Arsat arched an eyebrow and looked at her a moment, skepticism obvious by his expression. Instead of chiding her he turned back to the paper. "I am sorry to hear about your brother. Sometimes...the gods simply ask too much of us."

Aral nodded, embarrassment erased with a fresh stab of worry.

"What are you going to do?"

Such a simple question.

"I don't know." Aral hated how high pitched and childish her voice sounded. She tried again. "Petition every high priest in the

The Arcane War

city. Send letters. Beg. Whatever it takes."

Master Arsat looked at her, his large elfin eyes inscrutable as moments passed. He seemed to come to a decision at last, nodding to himself. "I can send a few letters of introduction, to help you get an audience with some of the more helpful high priests."

"No," Aral said immediately. "I appreciate the offer. I do. I just can't...Davri's already on the run because of this. Krecek Alavraneth, the priest who helped us, will probably be reprimanded, and might face worse over it. I can't put anyone else under suspicion by association."

"I understand," he said. "If you need anything, if there's anything I can do to help clear Davri's name and keep your brother alive, please come to me. Don't hesitate. I want to help."

"Thank you, Master Arsat. I will."

He smiled, inclining his head toward her. "My name is Byrek. If we're to be conspirators, allow me that level of friendship. At least in private."

She didn't like the word "conspirator", but she knew she would need friends. She would need people she could rely on. And, well, having someone with some authority would be most helpful.

"Thank you, Byrek. It's an honor to be your friend."

The air was thick and the clouds a heavy gray that hid the entire city of Anogrin from the base of the mountain. Once in a while the glow of a fire or some spell of light could be seen through a brief thinning of the clouds, but those were brief, distant. It gave the illusion of safety to Naran and Davri from their vantage. The long road that was carved into the mountain led to nothing.

"Might as well settle in." Davri pulled out a thin sheet and enchanted it to feel like a feather bed. "We've got nowhere to go, and all year to get there."

They'd left the road and had settled into a cave that was fairly hidden but comfortable. There was evidence that it had been used before, but not recently.

Naran just nodded. He picked up a small rock and tossed it out the cave mouth. Picked up another. And another. No point to it. There'd been no sketching. No writing. No wondering. Just one miserable, sullen silence.

"You okay?"

"No."

Two days.

They'd been doing this for two days and had only made it this far. They hid from priests on the road or tried to find safe paths away from the well-traveled road. Krecek had taken the horses back with him, of course. So, they were on foot, and that didn't lend itself well to getting away quickly.

Anyone could turn them in. It took just one person to recognize them. Unlikely, of course, but posters and fliers had been posted with their images drawn upon them. Terrible likenesses, but good enough to a sufficiently suspicious, or greedy, passerby.

There were reasons the road was so well used, of course. It was easy and relatively smooth. It meandered down the mountain with gently sloping curves to make even the heaviest cart easy to navigate.

Everything else was too inconvenient for the average traveler, and this slowed the two of them a great deal. Steep slopes and other frustrating terrain were the least of things that kept Davri thinking of creative use of spells to aid them here and there. As they moved further from civilization he'd have to use a whole new set of spells to keep them safe from wild animals or fellow outcasts of society. What would brigands do with the two of them

The Arcane War

if he was caught off guard? There was no telling.

"Just keep an ear out. Something's bound to hear those rocks you're chucking. It would help if you warn me before whatever it is comes to investigate."

In response, Naran picked up a bigger rock, glared at Davri, and threw it directly at a bush for maximum noise.

Davri closed his eyes. "Everything's terrible for both of us, Naran. I'd like to be right there with you, scaring off birds, tossing things around, maybe blowing up trees just for the sheer joy of destroying something. But we're not going to be able to get away with that sort of thing."

"You don't understand."

Ah, the cry of children everywhere when they were the ones who didn't understand.

No. That thought was unkind. Davri shook his head, chiding himself internally. Naran hadn't asked for this. Hadn't been able to decide, one way or another, if he should be out here, running for his life. He was a scared little boy, and Davri needed to act like the adult here. Nineteen didn't feel old enough to Davri to be suddenly responsible for another human's life, but it was better than nine.

"Okay, tell me what I wouldn't understand." Davri sat, patting a spot on the blanket, inviting Naran to sit down.

Naran, for his part, looked skeptical, wary. He stood where he was, not approaching, but not throwing any more rocks.

"I've never seen you angry before." Since the boy had arrived at University Magica, he'd been quiet and reserved. He'd hidden in Aral's shadow, for the most part. Davri was sure anger had been part of his grieving process, but Davri hadn't been around to see it. "I don't blame you for it, but it caught me by surprise. I thought you'd stay afraid a while longer."

Naran rolled his eyes and sat down. He chose a spot a touch further away from where Davri had indicated.

The Arcane War

"It's all just not fair," Naran said. "I know. You get that. It's not fair to you, either. But my feet are sore. I have blisters. My blisters have blisters. And if we don't move, we die. If we don't hide, we die. It's all my fault that you're going to miss all your school, and all your friends. I didn't even do anything. You didn't do anything. And... now there won't be a party. Aral was going to give me a present. Everyone was going to be there for my birthday. Aral promised."

Naran looked like he wanted to go on, but his voice broke on the last word and it stopped him.

"Birthday?"

Naran nodded.

"When?"

Naran held up three fingers. "Three weeks," he choked out.

Davri picked up a rock that sat nearby and threw it. He hit the cave wall so hard the rock shattered in two.

It was only sandstone, but watching it explode against the wall was satisfying.

None of this was fair, not to either of them.

Naran was right.

It was all so stupid and petty. He'd been thinking that, ever since Aral and Krecek had returned with the news that there'd be no reprieve. It wasn't a surprise, not with the visions Davri had had, but the reason behind it all was maddening.

Instead of looking startled, or scared, Naran just nodded.

"What if Aral doesn't fix it?" The echo of the rock's destruction had long faded before Naran asked the question. "What if she can't? If the priests just don't care. I don't want to die."

"Nobody wants you to die," Davri said.

"The priests do," Naran said. "The gods do."

"If the gods wanted you dead, you'd be dead," Davri pointed out. "Neither of us are powerful enough to stop that. I think they're just too busy to care who dies, and that's a shame. The world's better with you in it. They just don't know that yet."

"You're just being nice."

"No. I like you. Not only because I like your sister, either. You've put up with a lot in the last few months, and you've kept your temper and made things easy for everyone. So far, you've turned terrible things into something good. Every time you draw something, you've turned your pain into something beautiful. It's a rare gift in this world. If you keep doing this, I'll never stop fighting to keep you alive. Even from the grave, if I have to."

Naran huffed, dodging when Davri reached to ruffle his hair. But the anger had gone out of him, and they both seemed more relaxed for having gotten some of their frustrations out.

"This is the strangest cave," Naran finally said with a bit of a frown. "It's very…square."

"You've never seen a square cave before?" Davri grinned a bit.

"Never even heard of one. It's more like a room, don't you think?"

Davri nodded. "It's ancient magic… I can feel it, and I've read about these before. There are a few in the world. No chisel marks or anything like that, just perfectly formed angles, where someone pushed all of the rock out of their way."

"Dwarves?"

"No. I'm pretty sure they'd find this sort of magic vulgar and invasive. I've only met a couple of dwarves, of course. From what I understand they have too much reverence for the natural order of things to, well, squish everything out like this. This sort of thing took more magic than a dwarf has, or any of the races of the world. The technique used here was reshaping reality on a base level. It would take the power of a god."

"A god did this?"

"No. A god would have no desire to." Davri stood, walking over to one of the walls, running his fingers along it. "Someone given the powers of a god. It happened a long time ago, and they ruled the world until they angered the gods and were stricken down. The priests have ruled ever since, speaking for the gods."

"So, they were...human? But really strong?"

"Some of them." There was still so much power left in the rock, and Davri drank it in like water. "They were a mix of mortal and god...children of gods. Mostly elves, from what I've learned. You won't be taught about them in any school and finding a book that talks about them is rare. They existed a long, long time ago."

"We'll be safe here, then?" Naran was looking around, wide eyed. "Since it was made with magic?"

"For a little while. Mages could find it, and we're still fairly close to Anogrin. But... I think we could stay a few days."

Naran nodded, and out came the sketch book. Davri smiled to himself and finally relaxed. If the boy had it in him to draw, everything would work out. One way or another.

The sea was dark gray with frothing, white-tipped waves beyond the shelter of the bay. The wind that whipped it all up was the sort to steal the warmth from any man.

Raev Madri stared out at the foreboding sea, wrapping his winter cloak tighter around his ample frame. He'd been out upon those waters just hours ago. It had intimidated him and made him ill, but his cousin had begged him to come to Anogrin. Obligation to the dictates of their culture and family bonds had prompted him to come. The son of his father's brother faced hardship. Raev had no choice.

The letter Arlanz sent had been short.

> *"They took my Aaria away from me five years ago, despite our lack of children. Now they demand taxes no one can pay. I know you hate travel, Raev, but you have no family to uproot. Please come.*

These priests in this accursed land look upon my skin and lack of magic as an excuse to push me around, and because I am but one man I must comply or lose my livelihood.

"Come quickly, Raev. Bring all of the money the family can spare."

Money was not a problem for the Madri family. They were known for their spices, coffee, and tea, which was why Arlanz had opened his café. There'd been demand ten short years ago. He'd been successful until now.

It was of great concern to the entire family that one of their own would be in financial trouble in one of the most prosperous cities of the world.

There were traces of dark magic upon the letter that made Raev's skin crawl. He was no mage, but he was sensitive enough to magic around him to know.

Arlanz wasn't telling the whole story.

There was something gravely wrong in Anogrin.

Raev's goods were being unloaded and inspected while he waited on a balcony of the hotel. It was a smaller port he'd never heard of before. They would have traveled on to Merwythan, but the threatening storm had forced them to land, and Raev was sick of the sea. There was a good, solid road between here and Anogrin. He'd take that.

The port officials were upstanding and conscientious citizens, enough to stay bribed if the payout was substantial enough. It was also out of the way enough that no one would think to ask awkward questions. He didn't have any contraband, but that was hardly the point. He was paying extra for speed and silence about some of the magical components and books he had decided to bring with him. Some of them could have brought a little more attention than he would have liked, as a foreigner, though it was not exactly forbidden knowledge.

The Arcane War

Sometimes questionable was more dangerous than forbidden.

"Your wagon is being loaded, Master Madri," a young lady walked up to him. She bowed just a bit as she addressed him. "Will you be leaving this afternoon, or staying the night?"

"I will stay the night," Raev said. "The road is long, and I do not look forward to the journey."

The girl bowed deeper and backed away. Raev leaned against the rail of the balcony, watching the sea again. His thoughts turned apprehensive of what he would find at the end of his journey.

"Don't go to Anogrin." The man was short and thin, his hair was dark and hung half in his face. He stood next to Raev and grinned like he was enjoying some private joke.

"Excuse me?"

"Send the money along. Send the merchandise along. I have a counter-proposal for you."

"I am sorry, sir." Raev scowled at the audacity of this stranger, accent thick as he spoke from his heart and without deliberation beforehand. "My cousin needs me, and family comes before all."

"You'll be able to help your cousin better if you listen to me right now, Raev Madri. Arlanz is in over his head, and he has no idea how far." The man leaned in closer and lowered his voice. "I want his business to succeed as much as you do, but don't go to Anogrin. It's better for everyone if you're not seen working together."

"How do you know so much about who I am and what my business is? Who are you to tell me what to do with my business and my family?"

"My name's Agruet." As soon as the name was uttered the magic in the vicinity did something odd, gathering and vibrating on the air, then dispersing in a rush. Raev had never felt anything like it before. "The god of secrets."

It was impossible. The gods didn't just appear on the street and talk to ordinary humans. They didn't tell just anyone their names out of the blue.

Did they?

"Build a shop here. Send your cousin what he needs. I will return. Trust me." Agruet extended a hand and took Raev's as if in a handshake. Raev didn't have time to pull away, or to react at all. Power flowed through Raev as soon as their hands touched. Enough power, enough energy, that it nearly brought him to his knees.

"But...my obligations..." The protest was weak, but it sprang to his lips as if of their own accord. His brain, though overwhelmed, could not allow him to simply turn his back on his cousin.

"Raev, my newest friend, I'm a god," Agruet released Raev with a sly smile. "I take care of my own."

It took a few moments, but Raev nodded, accepting the onus of this god.

"I'll be in touch," Agruet said, and he vanished.

The wind picked up again and Raev stood on shaky legs. He needed a drink. "Arlanz, what have you done to get us both into this?"

His mind was reeling with the implications.

A god. A real, honest, all-powerful god. Had just appeared. And given Raev his name.

The energy that had flowed through him from the moment of contact with Agruet began to shift, integrating into his own. It started to make him jittery and euphoric, and he could feel that his magical abilities had been enhanced. It was as if his eyes were wide open for the first time.

He knew that listening to Agruet was the right thing to do. Something huge was on the horizon. Huge, like the storm that was about to hit the harbor before him.

There was no choice. He would put down roots here.

Arlanz's café was fairly empty in the middle of the week. Krecek had suggested it to Aral as a place they could meet and talk about their progress for just that reason.

They met for lunch most days, spending time getting to know each other.

At first, they'd agreed to meet so they could update each other on any progress. That fell by the wayside over time from a lack of anything new to share. Every night had become routine. Aral would set up a meeting with a high priest of one temple or another, and each time the answer was the same. They would not rescind a pronouncement given by a high priest without good reason.

"Someday I'll find someone who will actually listen," Aral said. "If I have to meet with every high priest, personally, until they're all sick of me, that's what I'll do."

Krecek nodded, gazing out the window.

"What's wrong?"

Her fingers were cool upon his hand, like a splash of water to bring his thoughts back to the present.

"I'm sorry," he said. "I should have been listening."

"You didn't miss anything. I was cheering myself on and hoping I don't give up over time." She squeezed his hand. "Did something happen?"

Why did she have to be so insightful?

Krecek nodded, pulling his hand away and looking out the window again. "We had a new priest initiated last night. To replace Ervain."

"Ervain? The one that Davri almost killed?" Her tone was lighthearted, amused.

Krecek snorted with derision. "Yes, him. He played it up so

much.... They removed him to another temple, somewhere in a small town. I think it was to save his reputation, because no one believed him here. He just insisted more and more that he nearly died." He tapped his fingers on the table. "His replacement seems more even tempered, if naive. I suppose that's how we all start."

The sound of Arlanz clearing a table settled between them while Krecek thought of how to say what had come next.

"At every initiation, the god or goddess they dedicate their service to appears. Not a vague feeling or sensation of having their attention, no. Flesh and bone, so real you can touch them if they let you. You've never seen a god made flesh, I'm sure...it can be anything from ordinary, like the two of us talking now, to utterly overwhelming." He leaned in, lowering his voice. "Nalia was there last night. She decided to be overwhelming. I could feel her omnipotence and awareness filling the room and I was certain she would call me out for disobedience, for loss of faith, but she looked at me as she always has. She smiled at me, and that was all. The evening was perfectly normal."

"That was all?" Her brow furrowed. "Nothing's changed?"

"Nothing at all." Krecek slumped back into his chair. "I don't understand it. She has to know, doesn't she? Does that mean that the gods simply don't care? It's hard, day in and day out, doing everything I did in faith and out of love for the goddess who brought us magic and all things wonderful, and now I wonder why I bother. Every day. What am I doing, Aral?"

Aral finished her drink and set the cup down, playing with it on the table for a bit. "It doesn't make sense, unless she doesn't care, like you said." She pushed the cup aside then. "Last night I had a problem as well."

"I'm sorry," Krecek said. He reached for her hand this time, and she smiled in return. "You were going to tell me, and I wasn't listening."

"No, I understand." She was leaving her hand within his,

surprisingly. "The thing I wanted to talk to you about is...the priest I saw last night at the temple of the god of fire..."

"Fotar," Krecek said. "His name is Fotar." He'd been teaching her the names of all of the gods as they came up in conversation, both to help her and because he felt a rebellious thrill by doing so.

She smiled, nodding her thanks. "I was setting up an appointment, and the priest I was talking to demanded that I tell him where I was hiding Naran."

"It's a good thing that you don't know," Krecek shrugged and grimaced in sympathy. "Fotar's followers generally tend to be rash and impulsive, and more than a bit temperamental. It might be better to not pursue a pardon from them."

"I'm too afraid to miss an appointment with anyone. What if they're the one who would have helped? Or, worse still, what if they spread word against me?" Now she pulled away from him, twining her fingers in her own hair and tugging to emphasize her frustration. "So far, the questions they've asked have been ones I can honestly deny, but I'm scared. One of these days I'm going to have to lie."

"Use magic," Krecek said, shrugging. "You're a better mage than nearly any priest. Your parents taught you more than you seem to realize. When you cast your spell, invoke Agruet and use his power over deception and secrets to aid you. Don't ask, just take."

"You keep doing that." Aral laughed nervously. "You keep telling me the names of the gods, teaching me as if it's nothing. I thought that wasn't allowed?"

"Strictly speaking, as a priest, it's not," he conceded. "As an elf, however...the names of the gods are what makes elven magic so powerful and lasting. I'm not teaching you as a priest to an outsider. I'm teaching you as an elf, to a fellow mage.

"That's not forbidden?"

"No, but it is...rare." He took a deep breath. "It's a matter of power. Knowing a god's name gives anyone a certain amount of power. To keep people from using that power, it's kept from outsiders, either by decree or by sheer arrogance. The gods themselves don't care. Apparently, they care less than I realized before."

They paused while Arlanz cleared the table and left them with a bowl of fruit and some water. A simple and sweet end to a light meal. They probably would have become regular customers of this café even if Davri hadn't suggested it to them, or had mentioned that they'd do well to befriend Arlanz.

"The first time we met," Krecek said when Arlanz left, "do you remember when you tried to cast a spell to stop me, and it had no effect? Your spell was rendered harmless and my spell ignored your defenses."

Aral nodded, picking out an apple from the bowl.

"Set up a shield around your apple." He waited until she set it down and there was a slight shimmer in the air around the apple. "Now, if I only use my own magic, we're about equal in power." He silently cast an attack, and the shield around the apple glowed momentarily red. The apple itself was untouched. "Hm. A touch more powerful than I thought. So, not equal."

Aral smiled. "Stop flattering me. That wasn't your full power."

"Guilty as accused," he said, echoing her smile. "Now, if I use supplication in my spell, it changes the nature of the spell." He took a deep breath, then spread his hands wide. "Oh, Nalia, goddess of magic, please grant me a portion of your power that I may touch this apple, so adeptly protected." He raised his eyebrows and cast the spell again. The apple rolled a bit, hitting the dome-shaped shield, but the shield itself hadn't so much as rippled.

"Oh, I see! Your spell completely ignored the shield!"

Krecek shook his head a bit. "Not quite. Some of the energy of the attack was still absorbed by your shield. It just did so invisibly. You didn't feel it at all, because most of the energy was used up in keeping you from feedback. However, if I just take the magic without supplication or care for consequence—"

Aral jumped and let out a yelp of pain. Her hands flew up to shield her face.

The shield was gone, and there were pieces of apple everywhere. A moment later Krecek had reformed the apple with magic and picked it up casually. Aral stared at him, jaw slack, as he began to eat it.

"No sense in wasting good food," he said simply, shrugging.

"You hurt me!"

Krecek set the apple down. "Only enough to demonstrate the power, and the risks, of what I'm teaching you. If you'd been showing off touch more and had your shield too strong, I could have killed you. I turned your power back on itself, so technically you hurt yourself."

"The intent was yours, not mine," Aral pointed out. "Therefore, you hurt me. You also stole my apple."

"Payment for making you more powerful." He took another bite. "I'll get you a list of all of the gods tomorrow. For now, remember Agruet, Nalia, and Garatara."

Aral paused.

Krecek could tell the exact second that she remembered where she'd heard the final name before. Her back went straight and her eyes narrowed

Damn it. He wanted to apologize for the reminder of their setback in her home town.

"Aral," was all he could get out before she stood up abruptly and turned away.

Elves, even half elves, were quick and nimble compared to humans. He jumped up and placed his hand on her shoulder before she could run away.

"He wasn't. No true priest of Garatara would have done what he did. When you need healing, Garatara's power will help you. He's gentle. I swear it."

"Then how do his high priests, the ones I've seen here, justify turning me away and continuing this nightmare? How do they allow this travesty to continue in his name?"

There was no answer he could give to that.

Aral left.

"Be patient," Arlanz said from across the room. "She is hurting. She will come around."

It startled Krecek a bit, reminding him that they had not quite been alone. How much had the proprietor overheard? Enough, apparently.

Chapter Five

Minor Impositions

Krecek looked over at Arlanz, wary and unsure how to proceed. He hadn't said anything to implicate either of them in harboring Naran or Davri, but he'd shared dangerous names. Sharing the names of gods with Aral was one thing.

Being overheard by another party, however...

"My apologies," Arlanz bowed. "It is hard to run a business such as mine in a city of such wonders without overhearing many things. Your secrets are safe with me, priest, but I have a room where the two of you can be alone and undisturbed in the future."

"A room?" Krecek blinked a few times in confusion.

"It is where our friend Davri was hidden, before he left. It is a place where one may speak freely." He hesitated, and his voice was rough when he added, "Even blasphemies."

"Why are you telling me?"

Arlanz didn't reply with words. Instead, he pulled out a piece of paper from his pocket. It was carefully folded, and it took only a moment for Krecek to realize he recognized the writing upon it.

It was from Davri.

"They're still safe," Krecek breathed in relief. He skimmed the letter quickly before handing it back. "Thank you."

"I received it days ago, but there was always someone else here when you were." He looked sorrowfully toward the door. "I wanted to hand this to the both of you, but...is she the boy's sister? He used no names, in case it was intercepted."

"Yes, Aral is Naran's sister. Thank you. I'll let her know the next time we meet."

Arlanz looked like he wasn't sure he had done the right thing, still.

To that, Krecek couldn't blame him. If someone found the letter, even without names, it could bring suspicion to the café. Especially if they also found some secret room.

Finally, Arlanz nodded as if coming to a decision or conclusion. "I have trusted Davri for some time. If he asks me to extend that to you, I can trust that he knows something that I do not."

Krecek thought a moment. "That's a lot to ask of you. Blind trust, based on the word of a mutual friend?"

"I have had more asked of me, with less potential for reward," Arlanz bowed his head, touching his forehead with two fingers of his right hand.

A memory. Such a gesture wasn't as common in a big city like this, but Krecek still recognized it. He was honoring the memory of someone he had loved.

The gesture would usually be followed by hands brought together to honor the gods, but Arlanz did not follow through.

Krecek understood too well.

Another murder given the name of sacrifice, ignored by the gods.

"I will not betray your trust," Krecek said. "I swear on my father's tree." He couldn't swear by the gods. Not now. Not after that realization. "We should talk and know each other better, so that our mutual trust does not feel so forced."

"Yes." Arlanz looked up and smiled. "I would like that."

Behind a locked door, over many cups of coffee, the two spent the rest of the day getting to know each other very well. From then on, when Aral and Krecek came together to talk, Arlanz joined them, commiserating, offering suggestions, and passing along letters smuggled in from Davri and Naran.

Naran had gotten used to traveling.

Any given morning could be an adventure.

When they traveled closer to any town, they ran the risk of some random priest just happening upon them. In their travels, it happened once. A priestess had come upon them and asked Davri if he knew that Naran had been marked. Davri had bluffed their way out of it like a master.

When they traveled too far into the wilderness, they ran the risk of being stalked by wild animals or criminals. They'd fought their way through those sorts of threats several times. With Davri's magic, such encounters seemed trivial.

Of the two, Naran would take the wilderness. It seemed to be a more honest threat, where they knew to be on their guard at all times.

It seemed that Davri agreed, and they hid in the wilderness far more often than civilization. It would have been more dangerous if Naran had been alone, or if he traveled with someone who had no magic. Most outlaws they ran into weren't mages. The few who were had been more likely to talk to Davri a while than to try to rob them. It seemed even immoral and desperate mages craved knowledge above all else.

On most days, Naran collected firewood when the sun got low on the horizon. Davri set up camp and lured a small animal in with a spell to be their supper. Naran didn't like being there for the killing and the butchering of the animals. It reminded him of the fate he had dangling over him, if they were caught. He felt like a giant baby, hiding in the woods while their food was caught.

Davri didn't seem to mind, though. They never talked about it. After a year, it simply became the way of things.

It was the reason why, even when he'd had an uneasy feeling

all day, Naran took his time to gather more than enough wood. He jumped at every sound. Every shift in the breeze had him on edge as he picked his way across the terrain.

The woods felt darker than they should, but he ignored the dread. He had to bide his time until he'd given Davri enough time to finish.

When he couldn't stand to be alone with his fears another moment, he returned with his arms full.

"I hope this is enough," Naran said. There was a patch of sky visible through the tree branches above them. It was so dark, much darker than he'd expected. Had he been gone so long?

"It's fine," Davri said. He was sitting on a large root beneath the tree they'd decided to call their home for the night. "No meat tonight. I don't know what's scared the animals off. Be on your guard. We'll want the fire for light, not for cooking."

That meant digging into their precious jerky and cereal cakes. They didn't have to do it often, thankfully. Still, it was disheartening.

"It feels like something's wrong." Naran sat down and opened his pack. "All day, I've been worried. Like, something's wrong with Aral."

Davri looked at him, looked down. "I've felt it, too. Next chance we get, we'll send a letter."

"Thank you," Naran said. "I mean, it's not exactly comforting that we both feel it. But if there's something wrong, I'd rather know. I'd rather you tell me, than make me think I'm just getting paranoid."

Davri nodded. He grabbed a medium sized stick from the bunch Naran had gathered. He pulled out his knife and impressed the usual markings on it.

It had grown dark so fast…

The magical fire ignited in a sudden burst.

Naran froze.

The light exposed dozens of faces, glittering eyes gazing at them from the gathering darkness.

"Davri?"

"It's okay," the mage said. "I've been expecting them."

Raev prospered, just as Agruet had said he would.

He sold spices from his homeland that became a popular "secret" ingredient in the flavorful fish dishes that were so popular in Hodarian's Bay. The strange god had even given Raev a few ideas about how to grow the spice plants in a room of windows, as well as a room underneath that would work well for preserving seeds and dried herbs. The design of these rooms gained him further popularity and prosperity, and within a year he was one of the most successful business owners in the small port city.

Arlanz was less than forgiving, at first.

The money had arrived intact, as did the tea and a few other spices, but he wrote back saying that he needed more than gold and riches.

He needed protection.

He needed his family.

He needed someone to mind the café when he was ill or tired.

He needed more than he dared ask for overtly in his letters, but the implications were clear in the subtext. Arlanz accused Raev of failing his family duties for personal opportunity.

It chafed, but Raev could not explain himself.

After a time, the tone of the letters shifted. Accusations gave way to grudging admission of a turn of fortune and eventually of success.

Arlanz hired a local girl out of desperation, and the girl turned out to have a natural talent for both business and dealing with customers. Her name was Bretav, and tales of her slowly began taking up more and more of Arlanz's letters.

She was trustworthy.

She was hardworking.

She was witty and told entrancing tales.

She was quick on her feet, never complaining.

And, Arlanz admitted once, adorable.

She had apparently decided that the café was her favorite place in Anogrin. She spent all of her time there, talking to Arlanz, even when she wasn't working.

One day she proposed marriage to him.

He refused at first, explaining the circumstances of how he lost his first wife, but she persisted. As the letters continued, Raev knew that Arlanz would give in.

"I was right."

Agruet had appeared at Raev's shoulder, peering at the latest letter from Arlanz.

"You are a god. I thought that was a foregone conclusion." Raev set the letter down on his desk and shook his head. He was growing used to these sudden intrusions.

"Let's just say I enjoy hearing it." Agruet laughed, seeming endlessly delighted with himself. "You're both better off, and you're both exactly where I need you."

"I had a feeling that this was coming," Raev muttered darkly. "What is it that I owe you?"

"Hospitality, for just a few friends. They aren't here yet, but you'll know them when you see them. Your cousin will send them here."

"What would happen if I refuse?"

"Why would you do that?"

"To see what would happen. What the consequences would be."

Agruet smiled. It wasn't an unpleasant smile, but the skin on the back of Raev's neck crawled. It made him shiver.

"Mortals were given free will. Do what you like, of course." The smile vanished. "This would be a poor time to test consequences, however. More than one innocent would die."

Raev clenched his jaw. Threats. He would have to obey, or the god would kill. Of course. That was the nature of their kind.

"I'm not threatening you, Raev." Agruet looked weary, sad. "Your actions are your choice. I only thought you'd prefer to have an informed opinion before those consequences befell."

"By taking in these guests, I would save innocent lives?"

It was hard to believe. Gods demanded. Gods took what they wanted. Gods made things happen at their whims.

However, for a year now Agruet had been helpful. He'd been playful and manipulative, but he'd also been kind. The god was annoying and spoke in riddles, spoke in prophesy, but so far it had all been to Raev's advantage. Had it been the bait of a trap? Or did Agruet have some greater outcome to strive toward?

"I will consider it," Raev said.

Agruet nodded, then vanished as he always did once a conversation was resolved.

Even with free will, Raev wondered if he had any choice but to follow what the trickster god desired.

Trying to look impressive in front of Naran had almost backfired for Davri.

He had been expecting the dwarves. It was no feat of magic or precognition, though. He'd realized, too late, that they'd set up camp right outside one of the hidden entrances to their underground kingdom.

The problem came in saying he'd expected them. Dwarves were secretive and didn't trust outsiders. His words had almost

The Arcane War

gotten them both executed for espionage on the spot.

The expression of awe on Naran's face was a bit of a bright spot, at least.

"I'm an idiot," he'd finally admitted when brought before Deeg, master of spies. "It's amazing how smart you can be and still be a complete idiot."

"That's quite a contradiction there, human," Deeg had said, voice a deep and disapproving rumble. "I'll feel better keeping an eye on you and your contradictions for a while."

"The boy did nothing wrong," Davri said quickly. "Please. Don't imprison him for my stupidity."

"Are you saying we should send this child out on his own, to fend for himself?"

Was there a good way to answer that question? Davri gave it an uncertain stab.

"No?"

Deeg chuckled. "Don't think of it as imprisonment. Think of yourselves as involuntary guests until we can take a measure of your character. You'll not be locked up in a dungeon."

"They're all skin and bones," another dwarf said.

That prompted a great deal of talk of feasting and celebration for the brave deed of "capturing" two wild humans. They were jovial, if vigilant. The dwarves joked and sang, but there was no chance of the humans escaping at any point.

To be fair, it was a more pleasant captivity than Davri had expected. They shared a room with Deeg and his family, but the beds were more comfortable than any they'd slept on in a year. They ate their fill at every meal, and any expression of hunger was met with food being shoved at them enthusiastically.

"You don't see many humans here, do you?"

"We deal with a few merchants," Deeg's sister, Vera, said over lunch. "And we keep an eye on the local outlaw bands, to discourage them from our woods."

Davri nodded, not surprised. "I just wanted to point out, you don't have to feed us quite so much. We're not malnourished, just young men. We're naturally somewhere between an elf and a dwarf in girth."

"But...the merchants..." Vera stuttered, eyes wide for a moment. "They're all so big!"

"They indulge a lot to get to that size," Davri said. "Naran and I have been on the road a while. It limits what we can eat. Even still, we haven't starved. To get as large as the merchants are, we'd have to eat this well for many years, I think. You can spread that around, so others don't worry so much."

Vera stroked her beard in thought. "There's a lot we don't know about humans. The merchants won't join us underground, too afraid of the roof caving in I suppose. We see humans so seldom that a few among us thought humans might turn to stone in the dark, the way we will in sunlight, curse Deyson for her petty spite."

"You know the names of the gods?" Interesting to know.

"Just hers. When she cursed our kind, we took her name with us in revenge, passing it to our children to utter as an epithet. My grandpa used to tell us to say her name loud and often, and eventually there'll be so many of us she'll be distracted, and we'll be able to walk in sunlight again."

So many stories of how petty the gods were through the ages. They'd been such common stories that Davri hadn't thought about it until he'd found himself pitted against them and their priests.

"What do the dwarves think of the other gods?"

"Except for the lady of the earth, we try not to think of them," Vera shrugged, setting aside her beer. "There's no love lost, here. None of them have gone out of their way to talk to Deyson about what she's done to us. Most dwarves would just as soon be quit of the lot of them."

Interesting. They may have stumbled over unexpected allies. Davri made a mental note to talk about this at length with Deeg.

"Your presence is requested."

Four words Krecek had been dreading for a year.

The early autumn weather was bright and clear. There'd been a light wind all day, whistling through the branches of the tree hovering above him. He was tending the gardens when the initiate appeared and uttered those words.

"Who requests it?"

Krecek stood, wiping his hands off and willing his face into placid curiosity. Mustn't look guilty or afraid. If anyone was sure of his complicity, he'd be apprehended, not called in for an audience.

"Porrellid."

"Thank you."

He could hear his heart pounding, feel his pulse rock his chest. Krecek managed to walk at a normal pace through an inhuman feat of will. When he reached Porrellid's office door, he only knocked a bit louder than he meant to. Only four or five people looked over, startled.

It could have been worse.

Porrellid opened the door silently, standing aside for Krecek to enter, then closing the door behind them. He was of average height, for a human, but towered over Krecek as most did. The hair that had once graced his forehead had started a strategic retreat, perhaps to hide from the ever-present sneer on his lips. The high priest might have been handsome in his youth. Now his belly was protruding in a mockery of budding motherhood.

Despite the physical flaws, Porrellid wore his power like a suit of armor. It was obvious both physically and magically. The sneer of contempt on his face matched his posture, his squared shoulders, and the aura he needlessly enhanced with glittering gems and jewelry. No one could mistake Porrellid for anything but what he was. A high priest of the most powerful goddess in the world.

"How can I serve?" Krecek asked, bowing his head humbly as he stood in the center of the room.

"I have heard rumors," Porrellid began. He sat upon a cushioned velvet chair and reached for a glass of wine on the table beside him.

There was only one glass. Krecek was not offered a thing.

"What sort of rumors, sir?"

"You've made friends with that girl from the university. The one who's been going around, looking for clemency for her brother."

"Yes sir."

"That's two friends in the same decade, isn't it? Aren't you afraid of getting a reputation?" Porrellid laughed at his own joke, filling the room with it. "They were friends of each other, weren't they? This Aral, and your other friend, Davri."

"I believe so," Krecek said. His stomach roiled and tightened in fear. So this was it, then. The end.

"I've heard she's beautiful." The permanent sneer morphed into a smirk. "Tell me about her. What has she been trying to offer for her brother's life this past year?"

"Well, she is beautiful as you've heard," Krecek said. His brow furrowed as he tried to figure out what this question had to do with anything. "She's determined, and I know she's offered her magical services quite a few times, if she thinks it will help. Aral is quite talented, so it's no small matter. Mostly she's been seeking mercy, though. A favor given out of kindness for a young lady who has been put through so much."

"Ah, one of those," Porrellid said. "She must think we're fools who have never heard someone weep before. A sacrifice is offered for equal blessings. If we offered the gods only our rubbish, what could we expect in return?"

Krecek nodded, one hand clenched in a fist, but he managed to still his tongue.

"I think I'll see what she's willing to exchange. She's asked for an audience. I was going to ignore it. In honor of your friendship with her, I think I'll give her a chance."

"Thank you, sir."

"You may return to your duties."

Krecek bowed and left, walking swiftly to the gardens.

He should have felt relieved. The summons hadn't been out of suspicion. There had been no accusations. He had not been called to account for his lies and subterfuge in aiding the boy's escape.

He was still free. Still in his position.

Relax, he chided himself silently. Aral might get her chance. This might end well for all of them. If anyone could release Naran from the mark of sacrifice, it was Porrellid.

It wasn't until the dead of night that he realized why he was still afraid. Porrellid could remove the mark, true enough. With the magic he had at his command, however, there were many other things he could do.

They were both in very grave danger.

Chapter Six –

ACTS OF DESPERATION

"You've been doing this for a year."

Had it been that long? Hadn't it been longer? Aral had lost track of time, doing this for so long that it had stopped registering. Classes, studying, begging for an audience, begging for her brother's life. If it hadn't been a full year, it was close.

Porrellid wasn't the last of the high priests she could turn to, but there were few in Anogrin she had not yet seen. He, and a few others, had refused her requests for some time. She'd been surprised to meet with any representative of this temple. This is where the trouble had begun, after all. Wouldn't they automatically protect their own?

"Give up, child," he said. "The gods don't ask us to sacrifice more than we can afford to lose."

Aral shook her head. "They've taken everything from me, and now they ask more."

"They're testing your faith, because they know you will be greater for it."

She knew he was wrong, though. The gods hadn't demanded it. One petty man had.

Saying that to him would be a mistake, though. Pointing that out to other high priests had always been met with cold indifference, if not accusations.

"Perhaps...they have put me in this situation to test your mercy?" Chin up. Defiant, but playful. Don't let him take offense.

Porrellid smiled. He reached forward, brushing a lock of hair from her face with soft fingers. "Shouldn't you leave it for men in my position to speak for the gods?" He chuckled, fingers lingering on her skin a moment too long. "You are quite remarkable. I am impressed by the lengths you are willing to go to just for one child. The world is full of so very many children. You could just replace him with a child of your own."

"He cannot be replaced," Aral said, abandoning her defiance for defeat. "Please." Eyes downcast, and do not pull away from his fingers in disgust. "I will do anything you ask if you will remove the mark of sacrifice from my brother. Anything at all." She closed her eyes, held her breath.

A year was a long time to nurture such desperation.

Aral knew that she really would do anything.

She just hoped he would not ask it of her.

He took her hand and placed a gold coin upon her palm. When she opened her eyes, his gaze met hers with clear intent as he closed her fingers around the coin. "Clothe yourself in something other than a mage's robes and come to my chambers tonight. By dawn we shall see how merciful I feel."

Aral nodded, mouth too dry to force out a word. She walked away nervously, glancing around to see if anyone had noticed the unusual exchange. Her eyes were drawn to the brilliant green elfin eyes...Krecek was standing to the side, eyes wide, shaking his head. It was too late, she had taken the coin. If it would bring her brother back, nothing would stop her. Even this. Even him.

She ducked her head, virtually sprinting to get out of the temple. To get away from the alarm and concern in her friend's eyes.

This was the first chance she'd had. The first time she hadn't been mocked. The first time she hadn't been dismissed or accused.

She tried to erase the expression on Krecek's face from her mind, ignoring the guilt it made her feel. She had to do this. She had to.

Aral threw the gold coin on her dresser, adding it to what was left of what she'd inherited from her parents. She had plenty of dresses that would suit her for the evening. Aral preferred the status and prestige that came with wearing a mage's robes. That they were practical and comfortable were secondary. She understood, probably much better than the priest had, what clothing said about a person.

Tonight, instead of having her power and status discarded for a mere dress, Aral would wear her favorite gown. She fingered the maroon velvet with a hint of a smirk. This dress would make her look regal. As the daughter of one of the most renowned mages, and one of the most talented spellsmiths, in the world, it was just as much her right to dress that part. She would remind the priest that she was not some simple girl to discard once used.

Night came too soon.

Aral slipped into the temple as quietly as possible, using a side entrance in hopes of avoiding Krecek, with no luck.

He'd shown her this entrance.

He was waiting for her.

"You can't do this," he whispered urgently. He grabbed her arm to pull her back out the door.

"I don't have a choice," Aral said. She dug her heels in, refusing to budge. "It's the closest I've had to a chance this whole time. Can't you just let me do this, without having to think about it, without having to justify it?"

"No, you don't understand. He—"

"The girl has an appointment with me, I believe," Porrellid's voice rang out through the antechamber.

Aral pulled away from Krecek. "Don't stop me." It was taking everything she had to go through with this. She couldn't listen to him. Naran depended on her to do whatever she could to save him.

Porrellid held his hand out to her. She hurried forward, and the moment her fingers brushed his skin he grabbed her and pulled her in, possessive.

"Perhaps, when I am done with her," he said to Krecek, "she will be more receptive to your own advances. You've been trying for a year, haven't you? You just need to know what a girl wants, so you can get what you want."

Aral felt sick to be used to hurt her friend like that. Krecek turned his back on them, and she started to take a step toward him, to apologize, or to explain. Porrellid's grip was strong and his fingers dug into her shoulder as he guided her away.

"You'll have to try harder than that to persuade me," the high priest murmured in her ear when she still hesitated. "Forget him for a night. Krecek is no one."

She'd apologize in the morning, once her brother was free.

Byrek woke up with a feeling of dread. Someone was knocking on his door ever-so politely. Ever-so patiently. Ever-so persistently.

Something was dreadfully, horribly, terribly wrong.

"Just a moment," he called out, throwing on a robe. He pulled his hair out of his face, tying it back without bothering to brush it as he strode across the room.

Aral stood on the other side of the door, naked. She didn't even have the self-awareness to try to cover herself. Her eyes were as empty as a doll's, and her skin was as pale as milk.

"I'm sorry to bother you," she said, still staring at the door. Her lips barely moved as she spoke. "May I come in?"

"Of course."

He grabbed a spare blanket from the top of the wardrobe.

Aral had taken one step in, but the door was wide open behind her. There were cuts and scrapes on her hands and knees. Bruises in other spots. Her lip was red and swelling up in one spot, and her cheek looked like it might bruise.

Byrek closed the door and wrapped the blanket around her. He put an arm around her to guide her to a chair, but she flinched away with a convulsive shudder.

"Sorry," he murmured, letting her go immediately. "Please, sit down."

Byrek lit a fire and started some tea while Aral sat in silence. She wasn't ready to talk. This wasn't the first time a student had come to him disheveled, beaten, and withdrawn. Power does funny things to some young men and women. He tried not to jump to any conclusions, but whatever had happened…it was bad.

When Aral had her hands wrapped around the tea cup, she let out a long sigh. "Davri mentioned you in his last letter to me. Reminded me I could come to you. I would wager he knew this day would come. He probably didn't need magic to guess something would go wrong. He probably knew I'd have no one else I would want to turn to. Other girls would be spiteful and petty. They'd say that I brought it upon myself and should have known better. I've seen them do it, heard them, and never thought they might be wrong. Other men would fear for themselves, thinking I would cry rape only to sully their names rather than admit what I've been through. I've seen that and looked away in disgust at both parties." She leaned forward and took a deep breath of the steam coming off of the tea. "Krecek warned me, even to the last minute, and I don't know that I'll be able to look him in the eye again." She shifted her tea from one hand to the other, rubbing her battered palm on the blanket. "Master Arsat—Byrek, I've made a terrible mistake." She finally looked him in the eye, but her gaze was still empty.

"Were you raped?" Byrek asked gently.

Aral shook her head. "I let him touch me. He said he would save Naran. He lied to me. He insulted me and violated me and forced my secrets from me, but he didn't rape me. The intercourse itself wasn't horribly unpleasant, though he mocked me and said I lied when I told him it was my first time." She looked down at her hands, at her lap. "Then he learned the truth. That I was. He found my secrets. All of them. He was in my mind and he found everything. Naran. Davri. Krecek. You."

"Wait. He said he'd save Naran? Do you mean to say a priest did this to you?"

"A high priest of Nalia," she said, her voice a monotone, unflinching at saying the name of a god. "Maybe if it had been a high priest of Vaedran or Thebram, they would have had more talent for bringing pleasure." Aral looked into Davri's eyes again, this time her eyebrows drew closer together. "They didn't offer. Isn't it strange? A priest from the goddess of magic would think to blackmail me for sex. But the priesthood for the god of sex, or the goddess of fertility, didn't even bother. I'll bet the priesthood from Egridaea would be adept in such matters, as well. I was thinking of her, in all her earthy and seductive glory, rather than Agruet. I didn't know that intercourse would reveal my secrets."

Byrek winced, realizing what must have happened. "The priests of Vaedran and Thebram wouldn't use sex as a weapon. It's sacred." That, of course, wasn't the point. But it did offer some explanation. "Whoever did this to you didn't do it for sex or out of desire. He wanted information, and the rest was just for fun. So…now he knows." He placed a comforting hand on her arm. "I am so sorry —"

"He knows, but he can't say it. He can't even reveal my heresy to his goddess. I won, Master Arsat. I was a better mage than him. I bound my secrets. They'll rip apart his soul when he dies." She showed her first glimmer of emotion; grim satisfaction and bitter triumph. "He's tarnished my name, thrown me to the streets at first light and called me a whore. He sentenced me to death. But I won. I've destroyed him."

Byrek choked on his tea and coughed for a moment before he could speak again. "To death?"

Aral nodded calmly, lips upturned in something between a grin and a sneer.

It was too much to process at once, so he didn't try. In letting the repercussions go, one question rose to the surface.

"How did you get away?"

"I'm not sure," she said, staring across the room at nothing. "I must have teleported."

"Teleportation is a myth, a mental exercise," he said, brow furrowed. "It's supposed to be impossible."

"I don't know how it happened." She straightened, and the blanket fell from her shoulders to drape around her waist, halted only by the chair she sat upon. She paid it no mind. "My knees were skinned, my feet were bleeding, I was humiliated and afraid, and suddenly it all fell away. I knew what I had to do to get away. And then I was here. Davri said I'd be safe with you. So, it can't be impossible, because I did it. It's...it's exhausting." She closed her eyes and slid forward onto the floor, fast asleep.

The remains of her tea spilled into the rug, and Byrek sighed. The cup was trapped between her thigh and her breast, protected from the fall by her hand. It wasn't quite scalding, but her skin had turned pink where the tea had spilled. It couldn't have been the worst of her discomfort, though. He looked more intently at her knees and her feet, and even parts of her hands where she'd obviously caught herself in a fall. She was all bruises and scrapes growing uglier before his eyes. The bastard must have literally thrown her into the streets in his demonstration.

Byrek lifted her carefully, gently. He set her onto the bed next to the one he had shared it with the night before. "It looks like you were right. If she's caught, they'll kill her."

Agruet sat up and the sheets pooled into his lap. "We'll have to make sure she isn't caught. With all I've done to put her in this spot, it would be a shame to have her executed by my own priests."

"Can't you do anything to stop them?" Byrek frowned, but then he turned away and sighed in frustration. "I know we've had this argument before, but can't you intervene and save just this one child?"

"I could," Agruet said slowly, grinning in his maddeningly devious and smug fashion. "I'm not going to, though. There is a café not far from here." He reached over and touched Byrek on the forehead and the knowledge of where it was and how to get there was suddenly implanted in his brain. "The proprietor owes me a favor, and she's a friend of his. He'll hide her until she's recovered enough to travel. Go with her. When it's safe to travel, get out of Anogrin. You'll find that staying here will be most undesirable, soon."

"What about her friend, Krecek?"

Agruet slipped out of bed and put his arms around Byrek, kissing him gently before answering. "The half-elf is not one of mine. I'll use him, but I can't interfere with him directly without Nalia intervening. It's much too soon for that." He patted Byrek on the cheek and took a step back. "Besides, the little priest boy is about to get everything he ever wanted, now that he doesn't want it anymore. Isn't that worth letting him stick around for?"

Byrek sighed and started cleaning Aral's wounds, knowing that he wouldn't get answers from the god of deception by asking for them. "Tell me what to do, once Aral has recovered."

Agruet grinned. "The answer will come to you when you need it. Before she does, steal as many books as you can get away with and ship them to your homeland. If it were me, I'd empty the whole library."

The library? "Why?"

"You'll see." Agruet's grin took on a deeply sinister look as he disappeared.

Byrek began a string of profanity in his native tongue before he got properly dressed and proceeded to do what the god had suggested.

Krecek had watched in horror as Aral was publicly shamed and sentenced to death. He could do nothing unless he wished to join her.

It was tempting. Horribly tempting.

She'd been dragged through the streets by her hair. Aral clutched a bedsheet in one hand, but she had given up using it to cover herself by the time he worked his way through the crowds.

She didn't see him, but Porrellid did.

When she vanished, no one could believe it at first. People pressed in, feeling around for an invisible girl. No one could find her, even with supplication to the gods, and there was a greater outcry of disbelief.

It only made her character assassination easier. The end of the Tennival family became the primary goal of many of the priests and a substantial portion of the city.

He couldn't say a word.

Krecek's attempts to find Aral had come up with nothing.

Despite their friendship. Despite the secret magics he'd learned from his father. Despite everything, there was no trace of her in the city.

Days passed. Porrellid's story was the only one he heard. The two of them had had their torrid affair, Porrellid had denounced her publicly, and she had vanished. No one had anything further to offer.

Krecek's worry grew every day. Porrellid had to know now just how complicit Krecek had been in Naran and Davri's escape. With Aral being accused of seduction, with her state of undress when she'd been paraded through town, he knew that Porrellid and Aral had shared intimate relations. He knew the spell Porrellid must have used.

All Krecek could do was wait until the high priest decided to set aside his search for Aral and come after her accomplices.

How long would it take?

What would he do?

As time passed, he became obsessed with wondering when the time would come.

He tried to plan what defense he could muster.

What lies he could tell.

How he could save himself.

The confrontation, when it came, caught them both unaware.

They'd pass each other casually every day. Others were always around. Krecek would find an excuse to leave, to be too busy. One time he had simply turned around and walked the other way.

Why didn't Porrellid press the matter, though?

It was the middle of the night, and Krecek's mind was too restless to allow sleep. He'd heard from Arlanz that Aral was safe. The great mage Byrek Arsat had gone underground with her. They were fine, but he should not know where they were.

Just as he and Aral had not known where Davri and Naran were.

It was a relief, but it was hard. It left him completely alone. The sleepless nights became a regular occurrence. Worry ate at his guts and chased sleep away.

He decided to walk through the gardens to clear his mind.

Porrellid was doing the same.

Porrellid's presence soured what had already been a bad evening.

No one else was around.

Krecek squared his shoulders. Better to get this done now. Get it over with. The potential conversations had been running relentlessly through his head. Time to put that to use.

He took a deep breath to speak.

"Your friend has only delayed the inevitable," Porrellid said without turning, cutting him off.

"I'll tell her you said that when you are dead, and she is not," Krecek said. Yes. All those hypothetical conversations, and this was the best he could do. Damn it.

Porrellid turned with a snarl on his face. "I don't know how she got away, and I don't know how she is hiding, but the gods will not be denied."

"The gods didn't sentence her to death. You did. You're just a human. A mere mortal. You attained your position through scheming, lies, bribery, and posturing. I had more faith, more magic, in my toenail clippings a decade ago than you have ever possessed. You and your ilk disgust me, and I'll never know how you became a high priest before I did."

That was better. Words he'd wanted to say for weeks. They'd almost come out the way he'd wanted, too.

"You just said it yourself," Porrellid said. "Scheming. Lies. Bribery. Faith is for the masses. Faith is for the sheep who can't handle a little initiative and determination. Faith is for those who need a pat on the head at the end of the day for following others. Power is for those who take it."

"I've had power all along," Krecek said. "I've also had the wisdom not to abuse it."

Right? Hadn't that been wisdom? He'd thought so, until now.

Porrellid's mocking laughter said otherwise.

"You've made a mistake, Porrellid. What's the point of power if you don't use it to protect those who need it? To take what you know you deserve?"

Krecek took a step forward, buoyed by sudden realization. He was stronger than anyone in this temple. Perhaps the whole city.

The only thing between him and revenge was a rapidly fading fear of some nebulous consequence.

Porrellid took a step back. When he realized he had done so he gave a shaky laugh and planted his feet solidly on the ground. "You think you deserve my position? Is that it? You're just as underhanded as I am. Just as corrupt. I tossed that girl aside because the entire time she was with me, she thought of you. She wanted you, just as much as you want her. It was disgusting, seeing your vapid, hopeless eyes etched in her mind. I almost lost my erection."

It stopped Krecek for a moment. She'd thought of him?

"I'm the one who had her, though." The sneering look of triumph on Porrellid's face snapped Krecek back into focus. "I took what I wanted, while you're still pining for things that could have been. Even if you take my place as high priest, you'll know it was too late to save her. You could have, if you'd only realized. She'd be yours, the boy would be safe, and you would have everything you've ever wanted. Instead, you waited. You had your precious faith. While I had what you don't have the balls to take."

"I'll take it now," Krecek's eyes were narrowed.

"I don't think you have it in y—"

Porrellid's words choked off and his eyes bulged. He gasped for breath that wouldn't come.

He hadn't even seen the dagger Krecek had thrown. He was too busy taunting Krecek. Too confident. Too proud. Too prepared for a magic attack to expect something so banal as a knife in his throat.

"You hurt someone I love," Krecek said, walking over and grasping the dagger and giving it a twist while the high priest bled. While he suffocated on his own blood. "May the gods have mercy on your—"

Krecek stopped, eyes wide. Something was wrong. The man

he was killing—

Porrellid's soul was dying along with his body.

There were no second chances.

No chance for atonement.

No reward for any good he had done.

No justice for the evil.

This was his end, and Krecek had brought it about.

"Gods!" he gasped, lifting his hand to his mouth in horror.

His hand reeked of tainted blood. That, and the thought of what he'd just done, made his stomach roil.

No. He didn't have time to think about it. He had to shove emotions aside. He would be caught, surely. There was no hiding what he had done, only why he had done it.

Scheming. Lies. Bribery. Krecek decided to add one more to the list of what would bring his rise to power.

Intimidation.

It took some work, and he cheated with a bit of magic. Before anyone stumbled upon him and cried out in alarm he had hacked through bone and sinew to remove Porrellid's head. Krecek's hands grew slippery with blood and his robes were hopelessly stained with it.

The night air cooled the blood and the body quickly. Soon it felt tacky on his skin and his robes stuck to his body, but he managed the task at last.

It was tempting to sit back. To take a break. The effort had been exhausting.

No. He had to be the one to surprise them. Not the other way around.

Krecek gripped the hair tight in his hand. His fingers were sore already, his hand wanting to cramp, but will over weakness.

He stalked down the hall that led to the grandiose bedchambers where the high priests and high priestesses slept. The head dripped blood, leaving a trail from the garden to the round antechamber that connected the six rooms. Three for the high priests, three for the high priestesses.

With a blast of magic, he threw open their doors. The five of them walked out in various states of undress. They looked at Krecek, looked at Porrellid's severed head.

They were all silent. Waiting.

"I am taking Porrellid's place, and only Nalia herself can remove me from the position."

He then stalked into the room no one had come out of.

His new room.

Krecek closed the door and wept.

The news of Krecek attaining the position of high priest spread quickly throughout Anogrin. Details of how he did it were never revealed or even rumored. Porrellid was merely said to have met with a sudden and unfortunate end.

His body was never displayed.

If Krecek seemed cold and distant through all of the services, the public chalked it up to nerves. They adored him and his elfin grace, though Anogrin was primarily a human city. He was just human enough to set them at ease, but elfin enough to be exotic, mysterious, and the subject of many idle fantasies.

He would have laughed if he had known of even half of them, but he kept himself aloof as he adjusted to this new paradigm. He couldn't believe he had gotten away with so much. No one protested. No one even cared that Porrellid had been killed. When the mourning period had ended, he was elevated officially to his new rank within the temple. Like all ceremonies at the temple, the goddess appeared.

Nalia gave him an appraising look and a knowing grin, but everything else was exactly as ceremony dictated. His chambers were larger, his robes more ornate, and his duties and responsibilities were fewer but more important. His days were longer, but that didn't matter to him. He had no one left to spend time with. Most of his free time was spent in study and magical practice.

Aral had disappeared. Naran, Davri, and even Byrek were gone. Occasionally he talked to Arlanz. The only news shared was that their mutual friends were safe and alive.

He was afraid to ask for more than that.

One of the first things he had thought to do was reverse the death sentence on Aral and find out how to reverse the mark on Naran. It was something he had killed a man to be able to do, after all. Aral's sentence of death could possibly have been overturned in time. Once public outcry had died down. If he did it quietly enough.

Unfortunately, people loved a spectacle. After her disappearance, a fear of magic and the abuses of magic had reached a zenith. If he pursued the matter, he was putting every mage, and most priests, at risk.

When Krecek asked what those risks were, one of the high priestesses smirked and used Porrellid's fate as an example.

Mob justice could be more brutal and effective than a priest's whim. What Krecek had accomplished, an angry and fearful crowd could trump in the beat of a heart.

Another of the high priests gently suggested that he set aside the idea entirely and simply let events unfold.

It was an idea that did not sit well with Krecek, but he seemed to have little choice. Aral and Naran were safe for now. That was the most important thing. He would sometimes close his eyes and wish for their continued safety, but he didn't dare to pray for them.

It was one thing to tell Porrellid that the gods hadn't sentenced Aral to death. It was another to ask the gods to keep her safe.

"You look sad."

Krecek's eyes flew open and his heart felt frozen in his chest. "My goddess," he breathed, falling to his knees before her.

She was...beautiful. Stunning. Ethereal. Her hair was the night sky, dotted with glimmering stars. Her skin was flawless, glowing with health and life. Soft, curvy, sensual perfection.

"You're not enjoying yourself the way I thought you would. Especially not after such a spectacular rise to power," Nalia said, leaning over him. "Do you feel well? Are you ill?"

"I miss my friends," Krecek slowly looked up. He met her eyes and fell into them. They were haunting, revealing power barely restrained.

"You have me, now." The goddess smiled, and Krecek's heart lightened instantly. It was the most euphoric feeling he'd ever experienced, seeing her like this. "Put them from your mind."

He slowly stood, drawn to her. Nalia's pure power was intoxicating, and the magic within his blood hummed in resonance to her presence. "I thought you would be angry with me. For...Porrellid. For what I did."

Her laughter was light and carefree. "I am the mother of Death! If I didn't appreciate that sometimes people need to die, I would never have given birth to such a monster. You did what you wanted, to get closer to me. You do want to be closer to me, don't you?"

"With all my heart," he vowed. While in her presence it wasn't even a lie.

"Come closer and know me, then."

That was all it took to lose himself completely. His only thought was to please her, in any way he could. The touch of her skin, even as light as letting his fingertips caress her cheek, erased every other thought from his mind. When Krecek kissed her, he was drowning in a sea of her, the sensation of magic all around him. In him. Through him.

Time lost all meaning. There was only her. Him. Them. Together.

He would do anything for her. All that he had. All that he was.

Nalia rewarded his devotion with power. Demanded nothing but his adoration.

With all of his heart, he gave it.

Chapter Seven –

Escape

"How long has it been?" Aral sat up, groggy.

"Lay back down," Byrek said, immediately at her side. "It's been a day and a half, but you're in no shape to move yet."

He wasn't lying. Aral was so sore her hair hurt. She almost asked what happened, but as soon as she had the coherence to think the question, she remembered the answer. The room looked familiar, though it had never had a bed before. It was the storeroom in the back of Arlanz's café. She'd spent many hours in here, with Krecek.

The wards looked updated. Probably Byrek's work. "I can't stay here," she said, though she curled up further under the soft blanket surrounding her. "I'll be trapped in the city. Being here will put Arlanz and Bretav at risk."

"We have some time. Concentrate on recovering, first. You're safe here."

It felt good to have someone else be in charge and looking out for her well-being. She was too tired, too heartsick, to muster the strength not to trust him. "Thank you," she said quietly. "For bringing me here. How did you know?"

"Hush. No more questions." He placed a hand on her forehead. "You're still running a fever. Too much magic will do that. I'll ask Bretav to help you with bodily necessities. Then, sleep."

Her first thought was food, but that was as appealing as a mouth full of road mud. She did need to pee, however. As soon as she thought it, it became urgent. "Please hurry," she said, even as he left.

Bretav was a strong girl, and nimble as well. No nonsense, just helped Aral with her business, then carried her back to the makeshift bed. It was over and done before Aral thought of how fatigued she was.

"I've got some broth, and I've got some tea. Which one do you want?"

Aral's stomach roiled. "Neither," she moaned, curling up around herself.

"Try the tea, then," Bretav said, reaching for one of the cups she'd brought in with her. "There are herbs to settle your stomach, and help you sleep. Here you go..." Bretav arranged herself on the bed behind Aral, propping her up on Bretav's ample breasts.

It wasn't entirely uncomfortable, Aral realized. "I'm too tired to drink," she said, relaxing against Bretav and closing her eyes.

"Come on, we'll get this over with. A dehydrated body doesn't heal. Even with magic."

They worked in concert to bring the cup to Aral's lips. Some part of her lurking behind the exhaustion was mortified that she couldn't hold a cup of tea without help, but Bretav didn't make anything of it. As soon as the cup was empty, that was that. No small talk. No irritation. Bretav sang something soothing, and Aral fell back to sleep.

Many days passed in a similar vein, with Aral gaining a bit more strength each time.

Usually Byrek was the one watching over her when she woke up. He could still move about town freely, but he said he was keeping that to a minimum. The elf wasn't suspected of anything, but he was planning on accompanying Aral once she left.

"You don't have to do that," Aral protested. "I'll find Davri and Naran, and we'll hide together. I'll be fine."

"I've already resigned from the university," Byrek said. "It was time for me to put it behind me. You've handed me the perfect reason to go. I want to help."

"Help me what? Help me hide for the rest of my life? I appreciate the help, but why waste your time on me?"

Byrek gazed at her without a word.

"I'm serious—" she started, upset by his silence.

He cut her off with a shake of his head.

"You are more important than you think." Byrek sat next to her and patted her on the arm. "You proved teleportation is possible for mortals, not just for gods. Ill-advised, but possible. On top of that, you've become a legend overnight. Your defiance is inspiring stories beyond the gates of Anogrin. It's been a mere week, and bards are singing of you in the forests of Shalysalaianleth and the deserts of Sadarenti. That's just among my people. I imagine you're more popular among humans."

"My defiance had me humiliated and sentenced to death," she said, choking on the words. "If not for you, I'd be a shining example of why defiance needs to be quashed, teleportation or no."

"Now you'll be a shining example of the fallibility of the priesthood. They're mortal mouthpieces, not the gods themselves. If they overreach, they must be stopped. If the gods won't do so, it falls on us."

It was too much for Aral to think about. "I have to escape Anogrin, first. That means getting strong enough to walk again. All things to worry about another day."

"True enough," Byrek said with a gentle smile. "One problem at a time. First, regain your strength. Next, we find a way out. Everything else can wait."

The gates were being closely watched still, but they were looking through boxes and crates, searching wagons for anything being brought in or out illicitly. There were mages at every gate to

The Arcane War

dispel all illusions, and half of them would have recognized Aral. Perhaps half of them would have tried to help Aral escape, but that could have turned bad for them considering all the potential witnesses.

Despite these obstacles, escape was simple. Disgusting, but simple. Aral dressed as an old beggar, using mud combined with urine and fecal matter to enhance it. No guard or mage bothered to check her close enough to recognize her. They ushered her out of town.

She traveled alone, on foot, until she reached a pre-arranged meeting spot. Byrek tersely handed her a basket with clean clothing and soap, then pointed her at a nearby mountain stream.

The rags she'd escaped in were smoldering ash on the bank within moments of reaching it.

The water was frigid, but blessedly clean. That's all that mattered. Getting clean was more important than comfort. It was only after her fingers grew too numb to hold the soap that she thought to cast a warming spell on herself.

"Of all the options, of all the disguises, of all the methods of escape, that's the one she chose."

Two men watched from the opposite bank.

Aral was sure the surrounding area had been vacant a moment before. It hadn't been a cursory glance. She wasn't a mage for nothing, after all.

"Who are you? How did you appear here?" Aral didn't shy away from their attention. Misdirection. Distraction. She stood proudly, taking just an extra moment as she stood to prepare the first spell that came to mind. "It's dangerous to startle a mage while she's bathing!"

Flames seemed to appear, roaring toward the two through the air. It was an illusion, and it should have scared them off. The pair didn't even have the decency to flinch.

The taller of the two men turned to the other. "I told you she

The Arcane War

would react poorly. Mortals like their semblance of privacy."

"Nonsense," said the other one with a playful grin. "We needed privacy for this conversation, and she needed privacy to clean herself."

She looked back and forth between them. There was something odd about them, and oddly familiar about the shorter, playful one. They hadn't been cowed by her illusion, and they showed no concern that Aral might use other magic to defend herself.

"Give me a moment to finish washing," she said. "I'll be more open to conversation when I don't reek of shit."

"Do you want some help with that?"

The larger, more serious of the two punched the other in the shoulder for his question.

Aral didn't bother to reply. She glared, arms crossed over her chest, and waited for them to walk away, or at least turn their backs.

They seemed oblivious.

Byrek was nearby. If she screamed, he was sure to come to her aid.

The oddest thing to her was that they weren't staring. They weren't looking at her in any sort of predatory manner. They watched her, but with no intent in their eyes.

A moment of recklessness took Aral. Why not? What could they do to her that was worse than what she'd already endured?

"If you want to help, grab the soap I left on that rock, and help me wash my hair. Just promise not to rape me. I'm in no mood." Gallows humor. As if asking a promise would prevent a thing.

"Rape?" The two of them exchanged an odd look, and the smaller one laughed. "Rape and coercion are games played by the weak and the fearful when they're convinced they must settle for scraps."

He appeared behind her, soap in hand, and reached for her

hair.

Oh no. He was a god.

They were both gods, come to end her.

"Relax," he said gently, stroking her hair, soothing her. "We're not here to hurt you. What Nalia's priests decree are no concern of ours. We're not their hunting dogs."

The other appeared on a nearby rock, settling in to get comfortable. "We have a favor to ask of you, Aral Tennival. Many favors, in fact."

"And none of them are sex," the god behind her said, already washing her hair, separating filth-matted strands with care and patience. "If they ever are, I assure you that you'll be well and thoroughly seduced, not forced. I prefer enthusiastic cooperation."

"Brother..."

He cleared his throat, shook his head. "Yes, I digress. You know my name, but don't yet know who I am. Agruet, master of secrets, would-be savior of the planet. This is my brother, Baedrogan. Keeper of the dead and master of death."

The god seated on the rock nodded as if saying hello and agreeing with everything said.

A shiver ran down Aral's spine. "What could you want from me?"

"Recover, first." Agruet guided her chin so that he could run water through the entire length of her hair. "You've been through an ordeal, and you've used more magic than a mortal should. You're no good to us broken. We need a strong figurehead for the upcoming war."

"I won't be your puppet." Aral straightened, pulled away from Agruet, and got a face full of water for her effort. She sputtered and wiped her face, but it didn't diminish her anger at the thought.

"You're already his puppet," Baedrogan said. "He's made

puppets of us all. Count yourself honored to be aware of it." He laughed, sardonic, with a wry twist to his lips.

Agruet shook his head. "I have all the puppets I need. What I need from you, Aral, is to be strong. Be yourself. Be angry, be righteous, be moral and just. Be everything we gods are not."

"You're going to make her like us." Baedrogan snorted in derision. "Telling her it's okay to do exactly what she wants."

"I'm getting there," Agruet said. "It's only okay to do exactly what you want to do so far as it serves our designs. Otherwise, you are to serve us unquestioningly, in mind, body, and soul." He rolled his eyes. "Is that better, brother?"

Aral couldn't help it. A giggle escaped at their banter, which she quickly covered with a hand. They couldn't be serious.

Then again, they were gods. Perhaps they were.

Baedrogan shook his head. "You don't know a thing about humans. Pitiful, really."

"I know more than you realize."

"You're making a mockery of a serious matter."

"Which is why I am making a mockery of it."

"Thousands are going to die."

"If we can't laugh at death, the very presence of life is an inconsolable tragedy."

A sobering thought, and Aral agreed. Life would be unbearably overwhelming without the ability to laugh in the face of an inescapable doom.

"That's a crass thing to say to my face," the god of death grumbled. He didn't seem to take true offense, however. "Very well. Aral, there's going to be a war. We've worked hard to ensure that it happens. Your death sentence is a tipping point. Of course, our plans rely upon your survival."

"If you don't, we've got a lot more work to do, and I'm tired of doing it," Agruet said.

"You could make me immortal," Aral offered, thinking it an

amusing solution.

"No," they replied in unison.

Well. That was an emphatic reaction to something said in jest.

Agruet laughed after a moment. "Not to stray from the topic at hand, but that's quite a bit to ask from us. You don't have nearly enough to offer in return."

"It was a joke," Aral said.

"That's what you say," Baedrogan said. "Everyone wants to escape death."

"Even me." Agruet's voice was strained. "It's what this is about." He winced, shook his head. "You're sufficiently clean. Dry off and get dressed."

Aral hesitated. Curiosity was gnawing at her. "Even you? But, you're a god..."

"Go. This water is freezing. Get comfortable so that we can talk." His shoulders slumped just slightly. "I'll explain when you're finished."

Chapter Eight –

THE PRICE OF KNOWLEDGE

"My friend is waiting for me," Aral said as she tied her boots. They were stiff and required some handling to lace up tight enough. She hadn't worn them in a while. Hadn't needed to. They were sturdy, for travel or hard work. She'd worn more stylish footwear in town.

"Byrek won't mind the delay," Baedrogan said with an odd look in Agruet's direction.

The other god gave a shrug. "He knows this much of the plan already. We could invite him to join us, but I think I'll spare him the tedium. I'm sure he's enjoying his book."

"He knows?" Had they met him along the road? Why were they talking to Aral, then, when Byrek was smarter, older, wiser? More respected.

Agruet nodded. "You'd do well to listen to him as events progress. He's told me time and again that he wants no part in leading, and I don't blame him."

"What if I don't want to lead, either?"

"If you don't, you and your brother will die."

Baedrogan shook his head at his brother. "You're terrible at this whole motivation thing." He sat down next to Aral. "Death would be your easy way out of this. Your absolution from responsibility. I'm not saying this just because of who I am and what I represent. It's truth. I would take you and your brother into my arms and cherish your souls forever. I hate asking anyone to give up the certainty of that end, but I am asking it of you, and a few others."

He was so much kinder than Aral had expected. Baedrogan radiated warmth and compassion, opposite of what came to mind at the idea of death. She thought of her parents, and for the first time was comforted at the reminder of their fate. This god, this compassionate man beside her, had taken them. Even now, their souls were his. It could have been a much worse fate.

"Our creations go to your care when they die," Agruet said, eyes intense, voice low and full of emotion. "Even I don't know what will happen to us." His hands were in fists. "Aral, we need your help, and you may be the only one who can do this."

"To save your lives?" she guessed.

"No," he said. "To end them."

"Why?" Aral blinked. "How?"

"The how is the easy part," Agruet said. He batted that answer away with a flick of his hand. "The why, though... That is trickier to answer. There's a broad answer to that, but it wouldn't motivate you, only horrify you and paralyze you with fear. Unfortunately, I think you're intelligent enough to understand it if I did explain. I'm doing you a kindness by keeping it to myself. Instead, I'll share with you what your motivation will be."

"How would you know that?"

"I am the god of secrets. I know many things. You won't start a war over your life, or your brother's. It's a good catalyst, but that thought won't help you see things through. This wouldn't work if you were that sort of person, so, well done." He patted her on the head, and she ducked away. "There is a sickness of soul among the gods. All of us suffer this malady. It must be ended."

"What sort of malady?"

"I like her," Agruet turned to Baedrogan. "Don't you? So full of questions. It's like having a child. All that wonder and ignorance. Refreshing."

Baedrogan rolled his eyes. "Stop stalling. If you don't tell her, I will."

"That's no fun." Agruet frowned. "It's a malady of heart, and of mind. We're terminally bored. We've given our creations morals, and the free will to follow them or not as they decide, but we have none of that. At this rate, we'll destroy everything. This planet, each other, and perhaps all of reality."

"I doubt that," Baedrogan said.

"I said 'perhaps'. Of course, if you ask me, that's the best outcome if we maintain the status quo. We're touching on the bigger picture, however. Aral, mortals will suffer and die under our care. We are spoiled children, breaking our toys. Your brother's fate is merely a symptom of this disease. Gods don't care about the lives of their creations. We're amused by the suffering you have wrought. Our high priests and priestesses are usually among the vilest, most corrupt, and most power-hungry representatives of their species that could crawl their way through the filth to serve us, and it makes us laugh."

"I don't laugh," Baedrogan said with a pained expression. He stood, and turned his back on them.

"This will be easier if she can hate us all."

"Right. Sorry." Baedrogan turned his eyes on Aral once again. "If you found out that we, the lot of us, really do not care one way or the other if your brother died, how would that make you feel?" His expression was earnest, sincere, and as serious as the grave.

"Would it make you want revenge?" Agruet added.

"Of course!"

"Then seek it," Agruet said, voice intense. "It is the truth that we do not care."

Aral straightened, looked at them in confusion. The laces of her boots were as tight as they were going to get at this point. She was finished with getting dressed, but far from finished with this conversation.

"Why are you telling me this if you don't care? Why should I do what you want of me?"

Baedrogan shifted his balance from one foot to another and

looked away. "I am more used to honesty than subterfuge. I'll explain. Aral, some gods are what you would consider decent. We don't hurt others for the simple pleasure of seeing them suffer. In fact, I hate suffering. It is why I took on the mantle of death. Somewhere along the line, there must be an end." He paused and took a deep breath, then turned to look her directly in the eyes. "Others of us see no point in adhering to a morality we instilled in our creations. There is no one to hold us accountable, when we created morality simply to keep our creations in line. Well, some of us had other motivations. Watching them squirm as they were put in impossible situations trying to live up to our rules and codes. It amazes me that some of our creatures still try."

"We cannot be redeemed," Agruet said softly. "If there are no consequences for our own actions, why should we care? Why should we stop? It makes me wonder why we bothered creating this world to begin with. Don't think that I'm coming to you from a righteous standpoint to condemn my entire family for doing whatever we wish. I'll let Baedrogan have his illusion of justice and doing what's right. I just know that you'll agree with him, and you'll do what I tell you because of it."

Aral had heard enough. "What sort of army will I need?"

"Mages are the most important," Baedrogan said. "You can't just concentrate on them, however. Your force will need to be big, because whatever you gather the other gods will at least double. Gaining numbers shouldn't be a problem, since your brother is the least of the victims of our brutality. Find some number of mages who are strong. Mages you can trust with not just your life, but with the fate of the world. The strongest mages will eventually need to know that you plan on killing the gods. You'll need them, because you can't do it on your own. As for the unwashed masses, well, they just need to be willing to die for the idea of a better world."

The Arcane War

Aral nodded.

"We'll tell you what you need to know as you need to know it," Agruet said. "For now, you need to hurry to Hodarian's Bay. Raev Madri is waiting for you and Byrek."

Agruet leaned in uncomfortably close. "You want to do this. I can hear it, whispering in your ear. It's the only way you'll save your brother. It's the only way you'll save yourself. And, bonus, you get to do some real good for the world. Doesn't that feel good?"

"I'd feel better if none of this were necessary," Aral said.

"So would we all," he said calmly, placing a hand on her shoulder, looking momentarily as if he had great respect for her and was looking at her as an equal. "The future awaits, such as it is."

The two gods disappeared and left Aral behind to mull over what they said and all the repercussions.

"Here. A letter."

Davri looked up from his book, startled to find the creased sheets of paper thrust inches from his face.

No envelope. No seal.

He looked at Deeg. Scowled.

"You've read it," he accused the dwarf.

"I've also let you know I've read it. Handing it to you loose isn't exactly subtle."

Davri had no reply to that. He grabbed the letter and skimmed over the opening. He didn't need to read it in depth. The underground darkness brought more visions than he was used to. He might as well call himself an oracle now instead of a mage.

Like his mother.

The letter recounted Aral's efforts, her mistake, her flight. The teleportation was remarkable to have confirmed, since Davri had doubted the truth of the vision he'd had about it. Conventional wisdom said mortals couldn't teleport. Her unconscious and weakened state indicated that it wasn't a viable method of travel, but it was possible. Dernad's miracle recreated in modern times.

What happened wasn't important to Davri.

It was a letter from Byrek. He lived for these interludes. For the final paragraphs...

"It feels empty and weak to say these words in a letter when I was never able to say them to your face. I live to see you once again. You became my light, my hope, my reason for being. No human has ever touched me this way before. Be safe. Be careful.

"Arlanz directed us to his cousin, Raev, in Hodaraian's Bay. Your grandfather agrees that this is a good plan. Your family and the Madri family must have been close indeed.

"I will write more when we arrive. I count the days until you are again by my side.

"Yours Evermore,

"Byrek Arsat"

Davri's heart ached. For one moment he wanted to rush to meet them. It was foolish, he knew. The dwarves wouldn't let them leave so casually. Not yet.

Once they did leave, there would be more work to do. Allies to gather. Contacts to make. Stories to spread.

Davri snapped his book shut. "You read the personal parts, too. Not just the recounting of events."

"No other eyes fell upon it." Deeg's voice was calm, even. "We're still assessing your threat to our community, and our secrets."

Good reasons, but it still didn't sit well with Davri. Damn it, those things were meant for his eyes only. Shouldn't words of love be intimate, and not privy to prying eyes?

Deeg pulled a chair up to the table Davri sat at. He settled in and leaned close. "It's my job to know things, and to figure out how they serve our people. To me, it's irrelevant noise, and I'd have forgotten it quickly as something more important came along. It stands out to me now because you're an unknown, and because the name of Byrek Arsat is not unknown. He's a legend, even below the earth."

"Is that why you made a point to let me know that you'd seen it?"

"Yes." Deeg's eyes were intense, wide, and steady as he continued. "It means something that an elf like him, a mage like him, would be in love with you. Someone like him wouldn't say such things to a common brigand. You're a person of note, in your own right, or he wouldn't have given you a second look."

All true, or at least flattering enough that Davri accepted it. "He was my teacher, and mentor. I've been trying to seduce him for years, but he was too circumspect to risk abusing his position, or to seem to. Apparently absence has made his heart fonder of me."

"It happens sometimes." Deeg leaned back, thinking. "You do know that love between a human and an elf is always a tragic tale?"

"I know," Davri said, head bowed. "I love who I love. It can't be helped."

Silence passed between them for many moments.

Deeg cleared his throat and stood. "You have many things in your favor, human. I'm beginning to think our run in on the surface was an actual misunderstanding. However, before we turn you loose, I have some favors to ask. If you do them, you'd be a hero among our kind."

Just like the vision he'd had the night before. They would be easy tasks, but they would occupy him and Naran over the winter, at the very least.

It had to be done. He felt like a puppet on Agruet's strings, but he knew what had to be done.

"I wanted to show you," Raev said in a hushed tone. "We had this plant brought with the last caravan, and the leaves are spectacular."

Master Gethralo leaned in to take a closer look. "What a beautiful specimen. I've never seen such a perfect example of the golden shimmer in the leaves. How did they transport it without damage?"

Raev grinned. "My father discovered a new spell that held it in perfect state for the entire trip. I was worried about shock from a change in elevation and humidity, but they'd prepared for that before the spell was cast. It is already acclimated to this region. It was costly, but in a few months it will—"

Raev broke off as the door flew open and the bell rang. He glanced up to give a greeting, but the words froze in his mouth as he realized that these were the two he had been waiting for.

"Excuse me, sir. I must close the store for the afternoon. Something has just come up."

Master Gethralo looked at the newcomers in mild curiosity for a moment. "I'll return in the morning. Zynth glows even brighter in early daylight." He was a good and loyal customer. One who knew when not to ask questions.

"Arlanz sent us," the human girl said softly, revealing a bit of confusion in her voice as he ushered them into the back room.

"I know," Raev said as he closed and locked even that door behind them. "That bastard of a god, Agruet, told me to expect you. He said I would know you when I saw you, and I certainly did."

The elf frowned, cocking his head to the side. "You've met him, then? That makes things a bit easier."

"I am Raev Madri. This is my shop, as you must know." He looked around, half expecting Agruet to appear and start making demands again, but it seemed this meeting was beneath the god. "You are welcome to stay here, as a favor to Agruet."

"I am Aral Tennival, and this is Master Byrek Arsat of the University Magica. Despite what you owe to our benefactor, I must warn you before you decide to take me in. I've been sentenced to death by a high priest." She raised her chin defiantly, daring Raev to pass judgment upon her.

That was, indeed, a wrinkle. Still, Anogrin was days away even by horseback. Raev considered the risk minimal. "You will find no love of those meddlers under this roof. It may be dangerous, but…I am curious to see how this great plan will unfold."

"Thank you," Aral said. She stepped forward, grasping his hands to emphasize her gratitude. "My life is in your hands."

"And I will do my best to keep you safe."

"Thank you," she repeated.

Their eyes met and held. Raev marveled at how clear her blue eyes were. They were like the sky at mid-day….

Byrek cleared his throat and the two of them stepped apart almost guiltily.

"I have rooms for you," Raev said. "They are underground, for privacy. I was expecting more people than just two, so you will have plenty of space."

Aral grinned. "That's perfect. I'd like my brother and a friend of mine to join us as soon as possible."

Byrek finally spoke up. "Agruet has his reasons for every instruction he gives. Don't worry, the rooms will be filled in time."

"This is cause to not worry?"

"No," Byrek said. "But it's less cause to worry than the rest of what's to come."

"I'll show you to your rooms," Raev said, shoulders slouching a touch. He was afraid that the elf was right.

At least the girl was pretty, and she seemed to smile easily enough. He would not complain.

Raev showed them to the hidden passage behind and below his storage rooms. This additional area was formed and hidden by magic. It was as safe as he could make it.

Of course, with two such accomplished mages now under his roof, his meager precautions would probably be put to shame. Indeed, the two of them were already talking wards and illusions as he showed them around.

Chapter Nine

Subterfuge and Sabotage

Davri climbed carefully, slowly, to the top of the hill. It wasn't steep or treacherous, though there were occasional rocky outcroppings. In fact, it was rather round and gently sloping, covered in spongy grass except for the occasional barren patches of rock. That was part of the problem, really. Gentle slopes and spongy grasses didn't give a person much of a place to hide.

Naran crawled beside him. They were both well practiced at climbing this terrain silently, and the bed of spring grass made it much easier than any amount of snow had.

"That's a good vantage," Davri pointed, keeping his voice to a hushed whisper.

Naran nodded, skittering over to the partial shelter of rocks. His sketch book was in a satchel that rested on is back, along with other drawing supplies. He sat, waiting. Davri was watching him, unmoving, laying in the grass and changing his cloak to blend in with the color of the grass around him. Only another mage would spot him, now.

Eventually they heard the clop of horse hooves upon the nearby road. The grinding creak and rumble of wheels joined the sound. A small procession of people traveled with them, skirting the hill. Children played, running up the slope until parents called them back.

Davri watched as Naran sprang into action, sketching furiously and glancing up and down several times to make sure he was right. They were not yet out of sight when he stopped and gave Davri a quick nod. He was done. They were free to descend, as soon as the caravan was gone. Davri slumped and closed his eyes, in weariness. They'd been doing this every day for months.

Naran slowly crept back to Davri's side. "Greater Stonegore, this time, or I'm a drunk dwarf."

Davri chuckled slightly and shook his head. "Don't let our hosts hear you say that."

"Why not?" Naran tucked his sketchbook away and prepared for the slow climb back down the hill. "They say it all the time."

"It's different when outsiders say it," Davri tried to explain. "Drunk is the greatest insult you can give a dwarf, you know. It's saying they can't handle their drink, and that's an insult to their integrity and strength. So, when a dwarf says it, all they hear is the drunk part because it's obvious that they're dwarves. When you say it, you're obviously not a dwarf, and things start to get touchy. Which part is the insult, since humans don't see being drunk as all that insulting or unusual? Do you see what I mean?"

"Well, that's not fair," Naran said, frowning. "There's nothing wrong or insulting about being a dwarf, either. Just being a drunk dwarf. It goes against na—"

Davri clapped his hand over Naran's mouth and pulled them both quickly back down to the ground. He covered them both with his cloak and they held perfectly still and silent for several minutes. Finally, Davri lifted his head slowly and looked around.

He'd heard something, like a rustle of leaves followed by the snap of a dry twig. He saw nothing, but he whispered a few words of magic to check the area.

A deer. It had just been a deer. The poor thing had probably been more spooked by the twig than he had been.

Davri released a slow breath in relief and they began their trek back to the tree where their dwarven friends would let them in. "The point is, while we're their guests it's not polite to use that phrase. It's a little too insulting to people who are being so generous and helping us hide."

"Okay," Naran said, and the subject was dropped. They

reached the tree line and the giant oak that protected and hid the entrance to the dwarven kingdom. The same one they'd set up camp beneath, months ago.

The roots of the giant tree shifted to reveal the small cave. They had to crawl to squeeze in, but as soon as the roots had returned to their place the back of the cave opened up and allowed them to enter.

"Thank you, Deeg," Davri grinned and stood up straight for the first time in hours. "We barely got there in time, with all the crawling around we have to do. The hill's a good vantage, but it's extremely exposed."

Deeg grunted and tugged thoughtfully on one of his beard braids. "You got there in time, though. That's all that matters. Where were they from?"

"Greater Stonegore, Yargran like the ones last week, and Plath, as always. I'm not sure about this crest, though." He pulled out his sketch book and pointed to a crest of a star to the right of a tree. "Isn't that Lanrinburgh? That's very close to Anogrin."

"What color background?" Davri looked closer, frowning.

"Scarlet," Naran answered right away.

"No, that's Uregom. It's along this route to Plath. Lanrinburgh is deep green, and the star would have been bigger and to the left."

Deeg nodded and tucked the page away in a scroll case to mark it up with notes and trace over it in ink later. "It's a great service you do for us, since it is difficult to make out colors in the night. Still, in all this time, you haven't told us much we did not know or suspect already. Well, boy, go see Merlynd for your supper. She's still convinced you're not eating enough since you're not growing healthy and round."

"Yes, sir," Naran beamed and ran off to join Deeg's wife and children.

"Come on, human," Deeg sighed heavily and began the

familiar walk down to the ale house. "We have a lot to talk about this night."

His earlier admonishment to Naran sprang to mind. Had he warned the boy too late? "What happened? Did one of us offend?"

"Now, now, it's nothing like that!" Deeg drew himself up to his entire four feet height and looked slightly offended. "Nobody's saying you did anything wrong. Even when you're drunk you don't act drunk, and your beard is nearly glorious! For a human, you've done remarkably well, and no one would think to complain about how dutiful a guest you've been."

"What can I do to fix this?" Their statuses as guests had long gone from involuntary to honored, with all the work they'd done, and all their effort to adjust. He did not want to lose the dwarves as allies, and he had grown comfortable accepting asylum from his new friends.

Deeg pulled open the door to the ale house and ordered four ales before he would finally admit what was wrong. "It's the boy. Naran. And people hate even to bring it up, because he's also been a good guest for a lad who doesn't drink."

"There's only so much I can do about that. He's young…"

"That's not the point, Davri." Deeg shook his head. "He drinks fairly well, though you were right about human children having no tolerance. At least you never insulted us by asking us to water it down. You finish his cup yourself, which counts a great deal in your favor. It makes what's at issue here all the more awkward." Deeg took a long drink of ale, slamming the cup down to show the hostess his appreciation by how much he'd had at once. "Now, listen. I hate to say this. It's embarrassing as hell, all things considered. So, I'll come right out and just tell you what's wrong. The lad has no beard."

"Well, no. He's just a child." Davri wasn't sure if he should be exasperated or amused. "Humans don't grow facial hair until adolescence. I explained that."

"The other boys and girls his age are starting to ask some embarrassing questions," Deeg was turning red and he wasn't maintaining any sort of eye contact. "The other day Naran said his mother had no beard, and a girl went home crying. She has a bit of a crush on the boy, you see. And the thought that, if they got married, their daughters wouldn't have glorious facial hair was too much for her. You know the girl, Heda. The one who was so proud when she could finally put a braid and a bow in her little scruff, bless her heart."

"I remember," Davri nodded. "Adorable girl, and very bright. I'm so very sorry she was traumatized by the thought."

"Heda's a tough girl," Deeg said gruffly. "She'll get over it. It's just…one of the boys said something about shaving the other day. It's getting a little out of hand. Shaving's a decision for adults, not for children. They shouldn't have to think about things more than how many braids or what they want to tie their braids off with, or maybe, if the parent is liberal enough, if they should trim for the further glory of their beard. Not shaving off patches, or Deyson be damned, shaving it off entire because they're too young to know better."

Davri winced. "I see your point," he said softly.

"When this all started out, we'd planned on using you and turning you out once we didn't need you." Deeg sank down into his chair. "I was curious about humans, and the pair of you didn't seem much of a threat. As a mage, I figured you'd use your head more than your spells, and it paid off. You're an arrogant piece of work, but it gave me an excuse to keep you around longer." He took another long drink and then shoved the two full glasses over to his friend. "Drink up. You've been a boon I couldn't have asked for, and a friend on top of it all. I'm not kicking you out immediately. I just think it's time to think about moving on before things get any worse around here."

"It's fine," Davri said, and he took a long drink of his own. "It felt good to be doing something to help others instead of just running and hiding. I can't tell you how much I've appreciated having a chance to know your culture and live here this long."

"You and the boy were half dead from starving," Deeg said gruffly. "I couldn't exactly turn you away. Even if I was wrong about the starving bit. I forget how emaciated humans can look. And don't get me started on elves, the walking twigs."

Keedi, the barmaid, walked over with five more mugs and sat down. She was a short woman of ample bosom, and she dressed to emphasize it, keeping her beard in twin braids that rested on either side of her cleavage. "Bah. Elves, now? They wouldn't be caught dead down here in the caverns. Even when our ancestors gave them plenty of head room if they cared to visit. You ever hear about that?"

Davri shook his head.

Keedi took a quick drink to wet her whistle and leaned forward. "Long ago, elves helped us hollow out the caverns, and they taught us the shaping of the earth with magic. They didn't care much for enclosed spaces, however. We'd build smaller rooms and they'd accept them, but they were too polite to say a word. They kept leaving and going out into the world and living among the trees where there were just too many places you could fall down, and we wanted to keep them in the goddess's womb where it was safe. When our ancestors finally found out that the elves didn't like to be closed in we created great halls and huge spaces, but we could never give them the sky, curse Deyson's name."

Davri nodded. "So, there's no bad blood or anything there?"

"Bad blood? With elves?" Deeg laughed. "I told you I respected that boyfriend of yours, didn't I? I'm not the only one down here who does. It's just, they just don't have an appreciation for the finer things in life. They like their sips of delicate wines and nectars. We like a big swallow of a heady stout. They like their delicate flowers. We like solid gems the size of your fist. They like stories of adventure and peril and higher morals. I'd rather listen to the sound of my neighbors having a good row or making a new kid to fill the halls. Or, you know, practicing the act. Now that's entertainment!"

Keedi laughed as loud as Deeg did. "That is such the truth of it, there! I'd much rather hear sex than a song. Something heartwarming about the sound."

"I've heard some of the epic, five-day ballads elves are so fond of," Davri said, though he was blushing as he continued. "I might agree with you, but I think I'd rather give my neighbors their privacy."

The dwarves laughed and clapped him on the back good-naturedly. They drank up, gathering more friends as the night wore on, until it was time to return to their homes and their families. They said fond farewells when they heard he was leaving, and they all drank just a little bit more than usual in his honor. Keedi gave him a kiss goodnight, even though she complained good-naturedly about kissing a man with no meat on his bones.

In the morning Davri packed his belongings and broke the news to Naran. Deeg and Merlynd saw them off and offered provisions for their journey, including a couple of skins of Deeg's best ale. They'd made friends during their stay, even if it could not last. It hadn't been a waste of a stop in the least to cultivate a friendship with the best covert information network in the world.

"Where next?" Naran asked as they looked up at blue skies.

"Plath." He wanted to say Hodarian's Bay, but it wasn't time yet. "Seeing their crest so many times has me curious, and they never struck me as overly religious."

Naran nodded, adjusting the pack on his back for the long road. "I've been wondering what it's like there, too. Grasslands as far as the eye can see. They've also got a lot of renowned artists and galleries, from what Heda and her parents kept saying. I can't wait to see for myself."

"Shall we find ourselves one of those caravans?" Davri grinned and gestured to the road. Just one more step on their great adventure.

The winter had been a harsh one in Anogrin. Snow and ice blocked all trade routes for a month solid, and sickness had driven families into isolation even when the streets were clear.

For Arlanz and Bretav, it had been particularly harsh. She had found herself with child, but could not carry it long enough. Finding a priest or a healer had been impossible until too late.

The loss hit them hard. There were gaps in their network of friends, and those empty spaces were felt hard. There were nights Arlanz would go to bed and wonder how they had made it through.

Still, life went on. Those days passed and were put behind them.

Spring brought new life and new hope.

Arlanz swept the steps and sidewalk in front of the café, clearing dirt, pollen, and withered flowers. The air smelled sweet and fresh. The sun was clear, and it seemed brighter than it had in an eternity. The streets were busy, bustling, but this early these were people with a purpose. Shop help, or merchants making deals. The tourists and the leisurely folks were still waking, or sitting down to breakfast.

As if to disprove that thought, a young lady stood across the way. She looked around, her blond hair glinted in the sun, and she looked Arlanz in the eye for just a moment. He nodded her way and a cluster of pedestrians walked between them.

He did a double take.

"Aral?"

No. It couldn't be. She was safe, with Raev. He had her most recent letter tucked into his pocket even now, with no mention of smuggling herself back into the city.

There were plenty of women with golden hair and brilliant blue eyes in this city. The recognition he felt must have been a trick of lonesome eyes.

She wasn't there when the street cleared.

Arlanz looked down at the steps and decided they were clear enough. There was more work to be done to prepare for opening the café. He closed the door behind him and smiled. Even the thought of seeing his old friends was enough to buoy his spirits.

Aral stood in the center of the room. There was no mistaking her, this time.

Arlanz stared. "You shouldn't be here. How did you get here?"

Aral smiled and came close. She reached out to give him a hug.

He felt nothing. No warmth, no stirring of breath, no touch. He could see her breathing, see her arms around him, but felt nothing from her at all.

"Are you dead?"

"Of course not," Aral said, laughing lightly. "It's a spell I've been working on. Projection. The last letter I sent you is in your pocket. I etched an invisible sigil upon the paper. I'm so glad it works!"

"It's amazing," Arlanz said, passing a hand through her image. Nothing at all. Just air. "So life-like, I can't believe you're not here."

"I've been working on the spell all winter," she said. "I'd wanted to test it with Naran and Davri first, but it's been almost impossible to get a message through to them. The one time they arrived here was the time Byrek and I were traveling. It's been terrible luck."

"Will I need to send them this letter?" Arlanz asked, pulling it from his pocket.

Aral quickly shook her head. "I have a separate one for them. This one is attuned to you. If it's not in your hands, and only yours, it won't work."

"Thank the gods," Arlanz slumped in relief. "This could have been a dangerous thing."

"I wouldn't dream of putting you in danger," Aral said softly. "You've done so much for us. It would be a poor way to thank you and repay you if I put you at risk."

He waved it off. "I have been putting myself at more risk than you could do. A favor for a mutual friend." When Aral look nonplussed, he gestured. "The sigils in the back room." Arlanz sighed and shook his head. Gods were more trouble than they were worth, honestly. "Do you need anything else of me? To get a letter to your brother and Davri?"

She shook her head. Paused.

"I will be sending you a letter with a sigil to one other person, I think." Aral's words were slow, hesitant. She looked downward, brow furrowed. "I should talk to Krecek, but I don't know if—"

"If you can trust him?" Arlanz finished for her, feeling no need to skirt around the issue.

"Yes." She met his eyes with strength and determination. "He was my friend, before we left. He tried to warn me, and I didn't listen. I need to know, but I don't want to put you at risk for delivering a sigil like this to him. I'm not even sure he would want to hear from me. He got what he always wanted. He is a high priest. And—" Aral broke off with a heavy sigh. "I don't know what to think. Are they loyal? Do they commune with the gods, as they claim to? Can I trust him? I want to, but—"

"Tomorrow I will go to the temple to pray. I do so every week." Arlanz smiled kindly. "I will bring this letter with me. I am willing to risk letting you talk to him through me. He knows I keep in touch with you, so this will not be enough to condemn me if he has been corrupted. After that conversation, then you shall decide if he can or cannot be trusted. Will this be fine?"

She relaxed and nodded her head. "Thank you. I can't tell you how I appreciate your help."

"For such a pretty lady, it is the least I can do."

Aral blushed, laughed. "Such shameless flattery! I need to end this before you tell more lies. Go on, finish setting up for the day. I'll see you again tomorrow." She disappeared, but she did so with a genuine smile.

Yes. This spring would indeed bring renewed hope. Arlanz patted his pocket and headed into the kitchen to tell Bretav the good news.

Aral sat back, satisfied with the first test of the projection spell. It was a lot simpler and less taxing than she had thought it would be, especially with some the herbs Raev had on hand which produced some interesting results when used as ink for different spells. He had been such a help to her over the last few months...

"It worked, then?" Raev asked, touching her shoulder.

Aral jumped and flinched away in surprise. "It worked beautifully. Thank you." She smiled, trying to soften the blow of her first reaction. "At first, he thought I was actually there, and then he thought I was a ghost when he couldn't touch me. It's exactly what I had hoped."

Raev nodded and took a seat beside her. "I am sorry. I forgot that you do not like to be touched."

"No, I don't like to be surprised."

"Aral..." Raev leaned forward, toward her, and put a hand her arm.

Her muscles tensed, and the smile was gone from her face, but she didn't flinch. It took willpower, however. "See? I'm fine. "

"You are not fine!" He let out an exasperated breath. "You have not been fine since you arrived here. Something happened before you came here that made you afraid. Byrek looks at you with concern when you cringe at even trivial contact with another, but he will not say a word. I see these things that you do not want me to know. I grew up in a family of merchants, it is our gift to watch people, and to see the truth. Watching you for this long, it has been hard not to notice."

"It's none of your business," she muttered. As soon as the words left her lips she regretted it. Raev had been so patient and kind. He had been the perfect host and protector. "I'm sorry. I didn't mean it." Her fingers covered her mouth loosely, as if that would recapture words that had already escaped.

"I think that you did mean it," Raev stood and walked toward the door. "I think you do not wish it to be my business. I think that you wish nothing about you would be my business, and I am sorry that I hoped things could be otherwise."

Aral was silent until Raev reached the door, and finally she forced herself to speak. "Wait."

Raev was very slow in turning around. His deep brown eyes were soft and warm and spoke of a pain that Aral hadn't thought to look for until that moment. She realized he'd been trying to reach out and offer comfort for a very long time, and all she had been able to do was to push him away.

Aral found herself walking to him about two steps after she had started. She reached out, touched the tip of his beard and realized she had not done this even once since she had arrived.

The day they'd arrived she'd reached out to him. She'd felt a pull within her soul. He was a kindred spirit. She could trust him.

But later that first night, alone in the dark, Aral had realized it was foolish, dangerous, to trust a man she did not know. To trust any man that far, again.

In the darkness, all she could see was Porrellid. His smirk. His sneer. His rage.

He had been a large man, as was Raev. Not as tall as Raev, but he'd seemed taller, dragging her by the hair. Even now, standing beside Raev, Aral relived her helplessness at Porrellid's hands.

With her eyes closed, she still felt the same terror of that morning after.

"You scare me," she admitted slowly, pulling away again. "It's not your fault. Something very bad happened to me once, just before we met, and the nightmares hadn't started yet at the time. So, no, I don't want anyone touching me, because it reminds me of that, but especially when it is you."

"I see," Raev said softly. "Is there anything that I can do?"

"I don't know." Aral closed her eyes and leaned against him, reminding herself over and over that she was safe now. She felt his arms come around her and after a moment she managed to relax. "It was just a very bad night. One bad night. It shouldn't bother me."

Raev tucked a finger under her chin, forcing her to look up at him. "You have lost your parents. Your brother's life was put in peril shortly afterward, and now yours is as well. If this priest did what it is I suspect that he did, there is no reason for you not to be upset."

Aral's blood ran cold and her eyes flew wide open. "You...suspect? What do you suspect happened?"

"I have heard terrible things about priests and what they sometimes do to adorable young ladies such as yourself," Raev said with a scowl. "Such things that are best left unspoken."

Rage battled mortification as she knew what he must think of her. "What occurred was of my own free will, no matter how distasteful I found it. I am not some victim for you to feel sorry for." Her hands clenched in fists, fingernails digging painfully into her palms. She held them before her, resting them on his chest. A threat? A need to seem more powerful? "Unfortunate things have happened, but I am not some frail flower that will die without your nurturing. I am a mage of great power, I have studied at the greatest university of magic in the world, and I did what I thought needed to be done to save my brother's life. I was betrayed, but I was not raped! So, if that is the word you find too distasteful to utter—"

She was choking on tears and anger, too consumed by emotion to go on.

Raev put gentle hands upon her wrists, looking into her eyes with nothing but compassion. Aral relaxed her hands and leaned into him. He hugged her and stroked her hair. He didn't hold her like a lover, but like a father comforting a child. It melted something inside her. Something that had been holding her together for the longest time.

It was the first time Aral found herself wanting to be touched in so long it made her heart ache to realize just how cold and distant she had become. She stood within the comfort of his arms and cried, just cried, until the desire to fill the silence grew unbearable.

"He made me feel stupid for believing his lies," she said, voice small and fragile. "That was the first great nightmare I faced when I realized—when the shock began to fade. It doesn't matter that he wasn't kind or gentle. I wasn't there for my own pleasure.

"He was furious that I didn't react to him, that my body didn't respond. Then he entered my mind and found my secrets, and I stopped him...and I assumed that was the end of it. I thought I'd won." Aral's voice pitched upward, throat tight. She took a breath, fighting for control. "The sex was over. The spell weakened me, and I had fallen asleep when he was—after he finished.

"The next thing I knew he was dragging me out of bed by my hair. I was naked, half-asleep, and couldn't think. I felt like I was watching everything happening to someone else, even though it was my body he threw into the streets, my body he spit on, my body that all the people had—" Aral stopped, looking up but at a point across the room.

"That's the thing that gave me nightmares. Still gives me nightmares. I knew to expect what happened that night, but the crowds are what finally made me feel helpless. I was losing everything, and the world went away, and the magic took me. The next thing I knew I was at Master Arsat's door. And I was so relieved it was over."

Raev kissed the top of her head, gently. She looked up at him and reached up around his neck and pulled him down for a proper kiss.

She didn't know what came over her. His kindness after reliving that cruelty? Her loneliness? The need to erase all of the horrible things she'd been through and replace them with something better?

Aral undressed him, hesitating now and then. He didn't make a move except to cooperate. Raev let her do what she wanted. No sudden movements, no words, until his pants lay at his feet.

"The couch?" The question was accompanied by a slight gesture.

It was big enough. Close enough. If they went to either bedroom, Aral thought she'd stop it all and shut down, let fear rule her again. And so she nodded, undressing herself as they walked over to it. She was clumsy and hesitant from so little experience, but Raev was patient. He guided her, taught her, pleasured her in ways that her previous experience had not prepared her for.

When it was over, both of them spent, Aral sprawled over Raev and listened to him breathe. Listened to his heart beat. Raev was nothing like Porrellid. Nothing at all.

That was all she'd wanted. To erase that memory. To feel in

control of her own life again.
 But what did this mean for them?

Chapter Ten –

SMOLDERING EMBERS

"The goddess will hear your request, my child."

The phrase had no meaning.

Krecek said it every day, nearly all day. They were words to placate the masses.

Nothing more.

He placed his hand on top of the human girl's head, briefly, as if he were bestowing a blessing. In honesty, it was a signal that she could leave.

"Thank you, High Priest," she said. She seemed to think it meant something, because as she left she was beaming, giggling with her friends.

He forgot what she'd asked for already.

"Just bed one of them already," Mirasen murmured beside him, bending close to his ear. She was one of the high priestesses, and she'd been goading him to enjoy his position to the fullest.

"Why?" Krecek stared at her. "They're all so...human." He paused. It wasn't their humanity he found beneath his notice. It was the fact that he'd touched greatness. He'd been embraced by a goddess. "Well, mortal. What could they have to offer that she doesn't?"

"Just something to pass the time," Mirasen laughed. "A diversion. A way to warm up, if you will."

Krecek stared at her in silence until she walked away. She was laughing at him, but that didn't matter.

Maybe he should. Maybe it would make him seem more normal for his position. It might help keep their eyes off of him, keep them from questioning his motives all the damn time.

He didn't want some random supplicant, though.

He wanted to find Aral. To keep her safe.
To tell her what he'd done for her.
To erase everything Porrellid had done to her.
These thoughts were useless. Worse than useless, they were dangerous. His mind always returned to Aral on the days Arlanz came in. The café owner would probably arrive at any moment. He'd been coming regularly, every week, since his wife had last miscarried.

They'd spoken a few times, prayed together several times, but Krecek would stop the conversation short of asking anything about the others.

"Are they alive? Are they well?"

"I promise you, if ever they are not, I will let you know as soon as I can."

"That's all I need to know."

It was as good as a pact. If he was busy on a day Arlanz came in, Krecek would still take the time to catch his eye, holding his breath until Arlanz nodded. They were safe. It's all he needed to know.

Arlanz strode through the temple doors at a pace that spoke of purpose and importance.

He didn't bow his head reverently or wend his patient way through as he always had before. People made way before him, muttering resentments he seemed not to hear.

Krecek's mouth went dry. Sounds around them became muted.

Something was wrong. It had to be.

Had one of his friends died?

Was it Aral?

"I beg an audience," Arlanz said, stopping just an arm's length away to give a perfunctory bow. "In private."

"Of course," Krecek managed in a normal tone. He couldn't risk looking distressed, or in any way like this was an unusual event.

There were eyes everywhere. A fact he was intimately aware of, since many of them reported to him, as well.

Every step they took toward Krecek's office his dread increased. He kept thinking of the last time he saw Aral, and how gloriously beautiful she had been. Despite the tears on her face, despite position she had been in, she was stunning.

He hoped that would not be the last time he saw her.

They turned a corner and he started thinking of the others. Something could have happened to Davri or Naran. Naran was still a small child, wasn't he? It would be such a tragedy for the boy to meet his end so soon, after all they'd done to keep him alive.

And Davri, of course, was...

Well, he was Davri.

Krecek was just as drawn to Davri as he was to Aral, but he hadn't worried about Davri. The young man was strong, both physically and magically. There were rumors now and then that the Beran family had divine blood in their veins. It wasn't impossible. In fact, it would explain much of the magic they possessed.

His attraction to Davri had been put from his mind for some time now. There was no cause to worry about Davri, because he was so naturally adept with magic. But now, with the thought that something was wrong, it was impossible not to think of him. He'd never told Davri, never told Aral, how he felt about them. What if he never had the chance?

Krecek closed his office door, heart in his throat. "What happened?"

"I bring good news," Arlanz said. "It is urgent, but not dire. There is a spell that Aral has found to communicate with covertly, and she did not wish to wait to see you again."

Krecek was so relieved he slumped against the door, closing

his eyes briefly to clear his mind. "I didn't expect good news." He chuckled, shaking his head. "Death or capture, but...thank you. For a moment I really thought someone had died."

It was Aral's voice that answered him. "Still very much alive," she said. "Happily so, some days."

Krecek opened his eyes in an instant. He wanted to smile but all he could do was gape. "You almost look like I could — touch you." There were currents of magic floating in the air around her, creating this perfect image of her. Channeled through...something Arlanz held? Yes. It flowed from a sigil he never would have noticed if it hadn't been active. "What an amazing spell."

"My father did most of the research," Aral said demurely. "I just had to put a few things together and find the right inks and herbs. Raev helped with that." She waved that aside and leaned forward. "Krecek...it's so good to see you again. I've missed you so much."

"I've missed you as well," he said softly, absently raising a hand toward her, though he could feel within the currents of the spell that it would come to naught. A flash of irritation swept over his face as he forced his hands to his sides. "So much has happened. I don't know where to begin."

"I'll start, then. Congratulations on your new position. I know you worked hard all this time, and it's what you've wanted for years."

This brought out a bitter laugh from Krecek.

Aral and Arlanz exchanged confused looks.

They didn't understand. They couldn't. No one would have told them...

"I wasn't chosen for it," he said, the weight of what he was confessing pulling on his shoulders, bending his back. "I took it. I murdered Porrellid. I demanded his position."

Arlanz gasped.

"What?" Aral looked...stunned? Disgusted?

"It's more common than you'd think," Krecek said. A terrible hollowness had carved a spot in his chest. Saying these things aloud to two people who knew him, who lived outside these walls, forced him to think about what he'd done and what he'd seen from the others. Living it was somehow easier than admitting it. "The high priests are corrupt, and the gods are at best amused by their corruption. I had no idea, until I set my faith aside and became one of them. Not a day goes by when I don't think that something should be done, but what? Who could do a thing?"

"We will." Arlanz's voice was a deep and soothing rumble, full of assurance.

"That's right," Aral said. "If my life is forfeit anyway, I'm going to go out with purpose. We're gathering like-minded people to join us, to make changes. Byrek, Davri, Raev, Arlanz, and Bretav have already agreed to help me. We're all making lists of people we trust, that we think would help us. You've been at the top of those lists."

Krecek stared. "How do you plan to do all this?" Some part of him was afraid of her answer. He was a priest. He had power. And the things he shared with Nalia that no other could understand or — "Wait! No. Tell me nothing. Arlanz, you need to leave. Aral, you should never talk to me again. I need to think. I need to do...something. I'm not sure what to do. She'll find out—"

"It's okay," Aral started.

"It's not!"

"We've got—" Arlanz tried to interject, but Krecek cut him off as well.

"You don't understand!"

How could they understand?

"I'm trying to protect you both!"

He wanted to explain, to tell them, but how could he?

Living this life was easy. He could tell himself he was doing what was necessary to survive.

Admitting to what he'd done, to people he loved and respected, was something else.

Admitting it to Aral was impossible.

"Nalia fucks her high priests."

It was a new voice that said it.

The blunt shock of the word, the crudity, made Krecek cringe. He clutched his arms around his stomach as if he was going to be sick.

He knew that voice.

"Literally and figuratively," this new person went on, laying the crux of Krecek's dilemma exposed before them all. "She's a pragmatist like that. It keeps them loyal and keeps her amused and informed." He paused. Smirked. "Oh. I'm sorry. Did my little word shock and offend?"

"Krecek, this is—"

"I know who Agruet is," Krecek said, though speaking was difficult when his mouth felt like it had been filled with ashes. "God of secrets and deceptions. I'm the one who taught you his name, remember?"

"We've been working together," Aral continued as if she had actually made the introduction. "Without his help, I never would have figured out this spell. Especially the part that keeps other gods from spying on me while I'm using it."

Krecek looked around at the three of them. His heart was pounding, and he really did feel sick. "Aral, the spell Porrellid used against you. You know—"

She nodded and reached for him, but it was useless. Her touch was nothing but a wisp of magic through the spell.

"You'll have my help," Agruet said.

"Why should I trust you?" Krecek shook his head, confused

that the others weren't questioning this as well. "Why are we trusting you? Why you, of all the gods?"

Agruet stepped close and looked into Krecek's eyes with a somber, serious expression. The trickster god was, for now, not playing around. "Krecek Alavraneth, you know the stories. The myths, legends, tales...my past. Our past. You're a priest and an elf. You are your father's son. You know them all." Agruet waited until Krecek nodded. "Now, think back to when my brother and I were coming into power. We were destined for something, but we didn't know what. So, we slipped away to explore the darkness. Lost, afraid, and searching—"

"—they looked to the void from whence creation had come, and the void unmade them, then created them anew. Baedrogan found peace in the unmaking and brought that gift and knowledge to all creations of the gods. Granting that they would know an end and yet be remade. No mortal knows or can comprehend what Agruet saw, except that it was the secret of all."

"That was beautiful," Agruet said. "Quoting Ashavan?"

"My father said his was the most accurate account of this particular tale."

"True. Ashavan died long ago, staring into my eyes and begging for more of my secrets." Agruet paused a moment, perhaps indulging in the memory. "That line of scripture should have been that I had learned all secrets, but some things are lost in translation when the writer is going mad. Can you imagine? Mere glimpses of what I saw drives mortals insane. I chose to become the god of secrets, deception, lies, half-truths, and not telling anyone else a damned thing because I know too much. It can't be healthy for me."

Krecek shifted his weight from one foot to another. Was Agruet saying that he was insane?

This line of conversation wasn't inspiring any trust.

Agruet laughed. He was suddenly standing directly in front of Krecek, and he leaned in close. "I know things that will give you nightmares. I know things that will give all of the gods nightmares, and they don't know because they don't want to know.

"When my mother touches your flesh and takes your secrets and sees this conversation, she'll look at it and forget every word because she is afraid of the things I know. I have seen our end. Our demise. My brother's hand upon us all. And I know that you will lead us to that fall."

His voice was soft, but the words burrowed into their minds like maggots to meat.

"I should hate you for it." Agruet stood tall. Shrugged. "If you think I'm betraying my brother-gods, it's nothing next to what you, Krecek, are about to bring. You want to end the suffering of your friends? I promise you they will suffer eternally if you do not follow this path.

"You're out of choices. The day you said hello to Davri, spawn of my half-mortal daughter, was the day you became the instrument of our deaths. You are the greatest betrayer of us all, Krecek. Every god but me curses your name without knowing they curse it.

"I bless you. I love you above all others. I praise you. I would worship you if I could. Krecek Ceolwyn, Wizard and murderer of gods."

Krecek had gone perfectly pale, feeling the blood drain from his head in shock, knees trembling under the weight of those prophetic words. "No," he whispered. "I'd never."

"You will," Agruet said. "Aral already agreed to this. Davri was born just for this purpose. You… Well, you and I still have a choice, I suppose. But knowing where it leads, neither of us would take it."

"Why?" Krecek had to ask. "Where does it lead?"

The Arcane War

"It leads you to my mother's bed, my mother's side, as a favored toy while everything you love, everything you've sacrificed for, rots."

He could see it. Krecek could see exactly that happening.

"…fuck…"

Agruet nodded, solemn as a funeral, and disappeared.

"Ceolwyn?" Arlanz asked. "Wizard?"

The words snapped Krecek back to the present. He stumbled to his chair and sat down heavily. He had to compose his words carefully, to explain without giving away too much.

Elf secrets.

Priest secrets.

It was amazing he was able to say a word to anyone.

Aral had the answer before Krecek could answer.

"Wizard is an ancient word for one who has as much magic and power as a god. It hasn't been used because the sheer hubris of making such a statement was deemed offensive by the priests generations ago. Mage has been used instead, for those who work with and understand the nature of magic. The title of wizard is said to be cursed."

"And Ceolwyn?"

Krecek shook his head, opening a drawer in his desk and pouring himself a glass of strong red wine before he answered. "Before the gods gave their creations permission to speak for them, and created the priesthood, it is said that the lands were divided into countries ruled by wizards. They were mostly the bastard children of gods. Elves comprised the majority of the wizards. They changed their surnames to match their titles. Their countries were called by the same name, to show that the wizards were one with the land they ruled. Wyn is an elvish suffix, only ever used for those names."

He picked up his glass.

Frowned.

The wine rippled, almost sloshing around the glass, his hands were trembling so hard.

He forced them to stop.

"So, you're going to be a wizard?" Arlanz asked. "What's that supposed to mean?"

"What if you're not actually a half-elf?" Aral wondered aloud. "What if you are half god?"

"I'm not a wizard," Krecek said with a wry grin, "and I'm not half-god. Trust me, I know my father. He's decent, for an elf, I suppose. But he is no god." He punctuated this by draining his glass and pouring another.

Gods, the way he felt at this moment, he should just drink direct from the bottle and drain the whole thing.

He'd heard the name Ceolwyn before, from his father and other elven relations, and he knew exactly where the kingdom had been. They were in the center of it, at the seat of it, and the temple of Nalia had been built upon the razed remains of the sacred cave the wizard had ruled from.

Part of the mountain had been blown apart to wrest the power from that wizard. He'd been the last who had remained, and they destroyed him in order for the priests and the gods to erase wizard rule.

Were they destined to repeat that cycle?

Elves said that events happened in circles, and all of history was made up of endless events that rotated around themselves. Humans had forgotten all about wizards over time, but elves spoke of them as if they had been around only yesterday. Would it be the same with mages and priests some day?

Would they rise again and tear down what he was about to build?

That thought was when he realized he would do what Agruet wanted of him. It was folly, but the god had been right. Krecek had no choice.

Not if he wanted to be able to live with himself.

"I need to tell Raev and, uh, Byrek about this," Aral said at last. "I'll transcribe and send you the spell I used, Krecek. We'll be able to keep in touch. I have so much to tell you. Later. In private."

"Thank you," Krecek said, but that was all he managed before her image vanished. "And thank you, Arlanz. I need to rest and think."

"I feel the same," Arlanz said, looking wistfully at the bottle of wine. "If you need me, for anything, my door is still always open to you."

Krecek offered the bottle, but Arlanz shook his head and placed his hand on the door. "I hate to leave Bretav alone right now. This pregnancy is also not going well. I pray to appear devout, but I am afraid the gods know better. They will not leave a child in our care." He took a deep breath and turned the knob. "Thank you for giving me a moment to speak of my troubles."

"My door is open as well," Krecek said gently.

"Perhaps next week."

Summer was coming to an end.

Aral took a deep breath of the salt air blowing off the bay, starting to get a sense of the weather the way the locals did. She was fairly sure the days to come would bring a change in the air, some summer storms to say farewell to the season in style.

The breeze carried something heavy, but crisper and sharper than the heat they'd been sweltering under. Underneath it all was a hint of the arcane, whispering to her that the changes to come were not just rain.

She took laundry down from the line, loosely folding it into the basket. Raev was busy with a customer or might insist that he do it instead. Aral had a mind for magic, of course, but household chores…well. She wasn't exactly inept, but Raev was better at the mundane details than she was.

In a household of mages, it only felt natural for the one who practiced least to handle the practical things.

Still, it was nice to help out and feel the sun on her face once in a while. Especially on such a beautiful day with the sun shining and the sounds of life carrying on the wind. The chant of the fishermen, the calls of the dockhands, the cries of the children at play, the horses clopping on the cobblestone lanes…

Aral was nearly finished when she heard a familiar voice. Magic whispered to her of the presence of someone she loved. Was it true? Were they really here? She savored the thrill of being on the brink of joy for just a moment.

This was what living was. Happy surprises among the mundane.

"Davri," she said, turning around to look. If that was Davri's voice, it meant the deeper and unfamiliar voice had to be, "Naran!"

The basket of clothes fell, forgotten, as the three of them hugged and laughed and talked at each other in the way people do when it's been years and they love each other. "You've grown!" and, "You've lost so much weight!" and, "You look so happy," and, "I missed you," of course, followed by, "Why didn't you come here sooner?"

"How'd they get you to do chores around here?" Naran teased. "Did the world run out of books?"

Aral laughed and picked up the basket again. "Come inside," she said, guiding them into the back door, away from Raev's shop front. "I wouldn't have recognized either of you just by looking, it's been too long. Come on, inside where it's not so hot, and I'll get the both of you something to drink."

"She's changed," Naran laughed.

"Almost domestic," Davri agreed. "Who has done such a thing

to a mage of such renown?"

"Infamy, you mean," Aral said, chuckling. "Have you heard? There's a price on my head now. They're claiming there's new evidence linking me to Porrellid's death. It's something I arranged with Krecek."

"Why?" Naran asked, alarmed. "That's not something you should want, is it?"

But, Davri was nodding. "I'd heard about that, actually. Just as people were starting to forget."

"What else is being said about me?" Aral looked at her brother, walking backward as she guided them downstairs. "You've heard at least some of the rumors, yes?"

"Yes." Naran said. "I've heard things, like you are some kind of tragic hero. A victim of the priests and gods. I mean…a lot of it is weird, like you cursed him and he died at your feet because he wronged you or something. Um. Davri…well, I mean, we helped a little bit." He added the last bit sheepishly.

"Thank you," Aral said. "I could kiss you for that. Bards are telling my story, and the bounty for my capture has kept everyone talking. It's making me a legend."

"That's why you planned it?"

Aral nodded. They reached the bottom of the stairs and she swung the basket to her other hip to open the door. "Exactly. It's a strategic move to increase the divide and polarize the people."

They all walked down the narrow staircase single file. Aral followed to close the door behind them. She grinned to herself, knowing the reaction to expect.

The first time she had walked these steps, she had expected a simple root cellar or sparse basement. The door was innocuous, looking like any other cellar door in the town.

Instead, at the foot of the stairs, a sharp left opened into a vast hub-like room. Doors and hallways hinted at a labyrinthine complex extending from it. Aral had immediately called it the war room, rather tongue in cheek. The name had stuck, and the function had followed.

"It's not like being with the dwarves," Naran said with a chuckle. "Wouldn't Deeg hate it here? It's so…quiet."

"True," Davri said, "but I think he'd appreciate it for what it is. It's not a home. It's a refuge."

Aral nodded. "This room we keep fairly stark. We have a library, though. Byrek is probably in there…"

"I'm sure he is," Davri murmured. He took a deep breath and nodded to himself before smiling once again at Aral. "How have you kept in touch with Krecek? Wouldn't that be exceedingly dangerous for you both?"

It was the question Aral had been waiting for. "Last year, I finished a spell that's let me keep in touch with him across distances. I've got copies for each of you, too, but the components are too expensive to have risked missing you." She walked over to a cabinet and handed each of them a blank page. "I've been disguising them as simple letters, seeming to be normal correspondence if anyone found them. It's not easy to cast, and you two kept moving around, so I didn't want to risk you missing the letter with the spell." She took a breath, then released it slowly. "I really have missed you both. So much."

"Me too," Naran said, and suddenly Aral had an armful of little brother, who wasn't so little anymore. "There's been so much. But, we're here now…"

"You're here and you smell like you've been on the road for ten years," Aral laughed, clinging to him for a moment before holding him at arm's length. "Go, bathe. I'll talk Raev into closing up the shop so that we can prepare the two of you a proper meal to welcome you here. Baths are down that hall, to the left." She pointed, and then picked up the laundry basket one last time. "I'll be upstairs if you need anything." She rushed out the door and up the stairs.

There she paused.
It was overwhelming, seeing them again.
Naran had grown so much.
Deep breath. Shoulders squared. Ignore the tears in her eyes until she could wipe them away, unseen.

Chapter Eleven –

Fanning the Flames

Davri chuckled to himself as he toweled off his wet hair. He was looking around the dining room, at the heavily laden table. The quick meal Aral had promised seemed like a feast. The last time he'd seen such a variety of food had been at the university, where a varied spread was necessary for such a diverse set of students and tastes.

"Aral! You didn't have to go through so much trouble," Davri called out.

"It wasn't my idea," Aral said. She walked in with a large bowl of bread rolls. "Raev insisted you and Naran should have choices, since traveling gives you none."

"It is true," the large man himself said, walking in behind her and wiping his hands on an apron. "I am Raev Madri, and my home is yours. Eat your fill."

"You're certainly a Madri," Davri chuckled. "The family features are unmistakable. Is Naran still bathing?" Davri looked around, wondering where the young man could be.

"He ate first," Aral said, shaking her head. "He changed into fresh clothes and insisted that a bath could wait, silly child." She sighed. "He won't be a child much longer, will he? He'll be taller than I am, soon."

"It has been some amount of time," Davri said, sitting.

Aral sat down as well, and she grimaced. "I wanted to talk to you without Naran around anyway. I want to ask you about something."

"I'll try to answer around bites of food," he said, filling a plate with a little bit of everything.

Aral laughed and sat across from him with a glass of wine and a few grapes. Davri figured she wasn't actually hungry, had probably helped "sample" everything as it was set. Raev had already slipped out of the room without Davri noticing.

So, she was going to ask something personal. Something he might not answer honestly in front of others. Davri bit into some chicken, waiting, and wondering just how honest he was prepared to be.

"The first time I managed to talk with Krecek since leaving Anogrin, something odd happened." Aral's words were careful, deliberate. Rehearsed. "We were using the communication spell I mentioned earlier. Agruet appeared, and he intervened. He said a few things that have been running through my mind since."

Ah.

Agruet.

The great thorn in his side, and dark mark in the family tree.

"My great-grandmother was his daughter, if that's what you wanted to know. It's the reason for my visions. His blood runs through me, though rather diluted at this point."

Aral nodded, absently popping another grape into her mouth. "He mentioned something about that. But, that's not what I wanted to ask you about." Chew. Swallow. Drink of water. "Actually…what do you know about wizards?"

Oh.

That was…tricky.

How could he answer that, keep her respect, but not destroy that vision of the future by speaking of it?

Damn Agruet for playing with fire like this! Shouldn't gods know better? Particularly him?

No. Davri just might not be thinking of the right perspective from which to come at this question. He could leap into a literal history lesson. It didn't have to be about the future, and a possible outcome of this war.

Except, she knew all of that. She'd see through that as an effort to obfuscate and misdirect.

"Go on," she prompted. "You were about to say something and thought better of it. Just say it."

Compromise. Start somewhere between.

"I don't need to tell you the basics," Davri said. "Or where the word comes from. Krecek would have explained that to you. You're not asking what I know about wizards, but what I know about what wizards will be. Am I right?"

"Essentially," Aral said. She picked up an apple and began idly playing with it while Davri ate a few more bites. "Agruet called Krecek by the name Ceolwyn. There shall be wizards again, and you've just confirmed it."

Damn it.

"What else?" She continued. "I watched the emotions play across your face enough to know there are things you don't want to tell me."

"It's complicated," he said, then swallowed the bite he'd been in the middle of. "Nothing is set in stone. That great vision Agruet had? It's possibilities. All of them. And he's dedicated his life to unraveling them and finding the best path away from...well. Something terrible. Another god is working against him, and right now he can't tell who. But right now, we're at a cusp of two futures. The one he wants, and the one I've tried to help him attain, is...it's terrible. But it's better than the alternative." He took a drink of wine, then rested his elbows on the table and leaned toward her. "In that future, there will be wizards again. The priests will fall and be hunted as fugitives. The gods all die, and a few mortals take their places. Krecek being Ceolwyn is news to me, but good for him. I've had dreams where I'm Verwyn, with a sprawling country estate and everything I could wish for. In others, I'm just dead."

"And me?"

"I don't know," he said. "There's so much still up in the air, even if we succeed. Or partially succeed, which looks more and more likely these days. I've tried to ask Agruet, but he said it's even harder for him to pick a possibility out of the mess everything's become. I'm mostly mortal, so I only saw what's pertinent to me. He saw everything."

"You said...you said that all the gods die. How?"

"We kill them."

Glass shattered in the kitchen and they could hear Raev cursing from the other room. Coincidence? Probably not.

"I know that. They told me that." She hesitated, glanced toward the kitchen, then plowed on. "How? How do we kill the gods?"

"You have all of your father's notes?"

"Most of them. I've been trying to make sense of them, organize them, the last couple of years. Byrek has been helping me. Why?"

"Years ago, he was supposed to be the one," Davri said slowly, gazing intently into her eyes. "He was going to stumble on the spell and, when pushed too far by grieving for his son, he would use that spell to kill them all."

"But that didn't happen," Aral whispered.

"No," Davri said. "And I think it's my fault. I was a child, and I told my mother a dream I'd had. We were in public. I will never forget how pale she was when she slammed her hand over my mouth, or how her lips looked like a purse drawn tight. I never had a dream of Master Tennival again, and my mother was furious with me. She said that some visions should never be spoken of aloud. She then told me that many people were going to die who should have lived, and it would be my fault."

"You said yourself," Aral's eyes flashed in anger as she spoke, "you were a child. She can't blame you for that."

Davri nodded, but he didn't agree. He'd known better. With such a curse passed down in his family, of course he knew better.

But he'd wanted to save the little boy. Even then, he'd wanted to save Naran. And he'd known that if he destroyed the dream he'd had, the boy would live.

"The point is," Davri finally continued, "the foundations of the spell should be in your father's notes. Even if Agruet and I never intervened, you'd have come across it and completed his research. It's inevitable. We kill the gods, or they destroy us and Agruet tries again in a century or so. Thankfully, the god of death is on our side. He swore to me that if we fail, he'll make sure that our souls are utterly erased. As a kindness."

"Kindness?" Aral's eyebrows arched in confusion and alarm.

"So that the other gods can never find our souls and torment us for eternity for the attempt."

Davri ate again while she mulled that over.

"So…I have to sort through decades of books, notes, journal entries, and random scribbles, so that I can find a spell that will…what? What happens to this world when the gods are dead? Chaos and anarchy, to start with. But…"

"We have to take their power," Davri said around a mouthful of food. "We're taking their places, sort of."

"So, use my father's notes to come up with a spell to kill the gods, another one to take their power, and then we take over the world. All just to save Naran."

"And to help my decrepit old great-great-grandfather, who doesn't deserve our help."

"But…Naran…" Aral slumped into her chair. "Promise me you won't tell him. Ever. If he knew we're doing all of this, just to save his life, I don't know if he could handle it."

Davri sighed, nodded. "I know. I promise."

"Thank you," she said. "It's just too much for me to take sometimes, so I can't imagine how he'd feel. When this is over and we're safe again, I'll do everything in my power to keep him safe. Anything, just to make sure he's never hurt again. I want him to have a normal life. As normal as I can make it."

That, of course, was one potential future. "I'm sure you'll do your best." He smiled, right to her face. He'd said too much. It would affect the future. But...

He cast the spell. The one he hated above all because it was such a violation of trust and self. It was cheating at the worst level.

It was an admission of failure.

"You'll forget this conversation," he said, planting the suggestion. "You'll remember that we talked, but you won't think about the specifics."

Aral stared at him blankly.

Davri wasn't hungry anymore.

"I should go unpack. Settle in." He pushed his plate aside and stood. Still smiling.

Her face lit up with a mischievous grin. "Finally go see Byrek?"

"Maybe."

Aral stood and took Davri's plate. "His face lights up whenever he gets a letter from you. Go on, silly. He wants to see you as much as you want to see him."

"Are you sure about that?"

"Go see for yourself." Aral grinned. "He's down in the library. Downstairs, second corridor to the right, third door. He knows you're here." With that, she left.

Davri's heart was pounding.

As he walked, he replayed every thought, every letter, every vision he'd had featuring Byrek.

Shoved aside his failure with Aral. Distracted himself from the thought he'd just erased knowledge from someone's mind and hijacked their free will.

Damn it, no. Think of Byrek.

He remembered the certainty he'd felt when they met. The unshakable feeling that they were meant for each other. Every vision he'd had since they met had reinforced that.

But nothing was guaranteed.

"Byrek?"

His feet had brought him to the library before he knew what else to say. Davri stood in the doorway, waiting.

There was a sound of a book being snapped shut from behind a book shelf. The elf immediately poked his head around, eyes wide at first.

Byrek's expression softened, and mirth sparkled behind his eyes. "Shouldn't that be 'Master Arsat', Davri?"

"I'm not your student anymore," Davri said. He walked over as calmly as he could force himself. He wanted to run and kneel before Byrek and kiss his feet and beg for affection.

He didn't.

"No, you aren't," Byrek murmured, head cocked to the side. Assessing. Weighing. Judging.

It scared Davri. Despite the few letters they'd managed to exchange, despite the words they'd written each other, what if Byrek found Davri lacking?

What if he could tell what Davri had just done?

"I'll never be your equal," Davri said. "I'll never live that long. I'm going to die impulsive, impatient, and human. But when I do, I want it to be at your side."

Byrek walked over and reached for Davri's hand. "I've missed you," he said. "I didn't know that I would. I've lived thousands of years without you in the world, you know. I never missed you, then. It caught me by surprise. Your smile. Your teasing. Your confidence. Your kindness. You always looked at me and saw me, not some source of history and information."

"You'll really give this a chance?" What would he do if Byrek said no?

"Love between humans and elves never ends well." The words hung between them a few moments. Then, Byrek bowed his head. "Despite that, yes. I'll give this a chance."

"Thera, damn it all."

Thera jerked her head up, blinking away the stupor she had drifted in.

There was no vitriol behind Master Dershan's words, just weariness. A year or two ago the words would have been shouted across the room, and she'd have cringed at the thought of disappointing her professor. Now?

"Come here, girl. You're overworked, and you've just added a second spoon of sulfur."

Oh. Damn it.

Volatile potions and lack of sleep were not a good combination. "I could try to scoop it out. It's still sitting at the top."

"No," he said. "I have a use for it in that state, but you need sleep more than I need another bomb tonight."

"I'm sorry, sir."

They were behind schedule. It was an arbitrary schedule, since they had no idea when their handiwork would be needed, but in this case, it was better to be prepared too soon than too late.

"Come here," he repeated, patting the workbench beside him. "I've done the same thing five times in the last week."

Thera only hesitated a moment, but she walked over and sat down beside him. It always surprised her just how small he seemed when she got close to him. Hobgoblins were short, shorter than the northern elves, and as ugly as elves were beautiful. But Master Dershan somehow managed to carry himself as if he were taller, filling a lecture hall on sheer personality and impatience.

"Perhaps we should take an evening off," he said. He looked

as tired as she felt. "We've done enough for half the library and the laboratories, at least. The rest of the library should burn readily enough."

"The books are packed in so tightly that most will just smolder around the edges a while." Thera recited the words she'd been telling herself for the last month. "The priests might be able to salvage them. They can't be trusted with any of it. Not a single page."

Master Dershan nodded, but he pulled out two tiny vials and a flask. "They're not ready to move against us yet." He poured, and she could smell the strong spirits from the glass he handed her. "As for the library, well, the books are not as tightly packed as they once were."

They tapped their glasses together and drank. Sweet fire burned its way down Thera's throat, and she only coughed a little bit.

The wrinkles seemed to smooth a bit from Master Dershan's face after a moment, and he relaxed visibly.

"Daichen and Garm have managed to smuggle a few books, then?" Thera asked when she could speak again.

"More than just a few," he said, actually smiling. "I think they've recruited Mistress Esandir. We've saved considerably more books than I'd expected to by this point."

"We're not supposed to talk about or speculate on who else might be recruited," Thera frowned a little. More of a pout, really.

"Child," Master Dershan chuckled, "I'll be surprised if the entire university hasn't been recruited by now. Oh, there are a handful who aspire to be priests of magic still, but I've kept an eye on them. No one is happy with the most recent edicts coming from the temples."

"Yes, but, one of my contacts said that one of their recruits had been arrested. I'm worried we'll be compromised."

"And it's kept you up nights?" Master Dershan poured more

spirits for them both.

Thera nodded and drank, hoping that the heat of the spirits would melt her worries as the warmth spread through her body.

"You're not the only one," he said. "Thera, these are hard times. Harder than I've ever seen. I'd bet only elves remember a time where we were so close to rebellion against the gods. It's terrifying, and you're right to worry. But don't let it rob you of sleep. Accept that people will die, people will betray us, and even innocents will suffer for no reason.

"My people are generally hostile to outsiders, and to us an outsider could just mean another hobgoblin you've never met before. We're always at war. I grew up with war, with losing people I love, and watching people suffer who didn't deserve it. It's why I left. I wanted my life to leave behind something lasting, to have had a greater meaning, even if it meant living among humans instead of my own kind. My only advice to you is take a night to say goodbye to everything. Visualize the city in rubble. Picture burying each of your friends. Move on before they're gone and be thankful for every moment that isn't a disaster."

"That's a cheerful thought," Thera slouched, handing him the small cup. He put it away and Thera frowned. She would have liked more. He probably knew best, however.

"It's practical advice for the times to come." Master Dershan patted her on the knee in a paternal gesture she'd never have expected before they'd started working together.

"I'll try," she said.

"Go, say your goodbyes in your mind, and get a night's rest. We can start again after classes tomorrow."

How was the rest of the growing rebellion preparing? Thera wondered as she walked down the dark halls to the dormitories. What were they doing to help the city, to fight the priests? How many people were there, really?

It was impossible to know. They didn't gather. They worked

in small cells, the smaller the better. They all had something to do.

And Thera was about to say goodbye, in her heart, to them all.

Chapter Twelve –

The Fall of Anogrin

"My back is killing me," Thera grumbled as she opened the door to the café. "Those 'extra credit' potions for Master Dershan are going to be the death of me."

"Better that than the library," Daichen replied. He headed to the nearest empty table and flopped into a chair. He waved to Arlanz, then leaned forward and slumped onto the table. "When I'm not going cross-eyed from transcribing, I'm about to collapse from moving stacks of books to the next wagon. We had another go out last night."

"My fingers stink," Thera said, shoving them into Daichen's face. "Why can't explosives smell like roses?"

"Gross," Daichen turned his head away from her hand. "Fine. Books smell better." He sat back up as Arlanz brought over their usual drinks with a plate of berries. "Are they still in the cellar?"

Arlanz shook his head. "They'll return in a few moments," he said. "Relax. We're among friends."

Friends? Thera sat up straighter and looked around. Raev walked over to a pair in the corner. They wore their religion around their necks. Damn it. At least they weren't priests, even if they were almost as bad. Supplicants were out doing the dirty work, while the priests gave commands.

No wonder the others weren't here right now.

"It's not like they'd recognize Davri," Daichen said under his breath, barely loud enough for Thera to hear. "It's been years since…you know."

Thera nodded. "It doesn't hurt to be careful," she said at the same volume. Then louder, "Washing flasks for extra credit is the worst, though."

The Arcane War

"Stop falling behind and you won't need it," Daichen teased, pushing his glasses further up his nose.

They bantered back and forth along those lines until the two "friends" in the corner stood to leave.

"If they wouldn't give us this much work—" Thera was saying, thrusting her arms wide to show him just how much. She was interrupted by an outraged gasp from the dour young woman who wore the emblem of the sun on her necklace. "Sorry, sorry," she apologized with a laugh.

"How dare you raise a hand to me?" the supplicant demanded.

"Um, you were behind me? You almost walked into me." Thera rolled her eyes. "If I wanted to hit you, you'd have been hit."

"Disrespectful cow," the woman spat.

Arlanz was shaking his head, looking alarmed. This was neither the time nor the place.

But, Thera hadn't done anything wrong!

"I apologize for my friend," Daichen said before Thera could react further. "Let me pay for your drinks. It's the least I can do. She's been studying too long and has forgotten how to be polite."

"It's true," Thera said, doing her best to fake being contrite. "Been awake for three days. I'm a beast to everyone, not just the devout."

The woman with the sun pendant narrowed her eyes, but her companion convinced her to back down. They left without paying, making a point to tell Arlanz that "the girl" should be responsible for their order.

Thera didn't relax until they were out of sight entirely. "She called me a cow. Bitch is lucky I didn't turn her into one. If we'd been anywhere else…"

"You wouldn't have turned her into a cow," Daichen said, laughing. "Cows are big and can do some real damage. Turn her into a slug."

"Are you calling me big?" Thera demanded. "Careful, or I might do some damage!"

Arlanz laughed at them both. "Wait until you meet Raev. He will make you feel like a tiny little doll. Drink up, and do not worry about payment. I am just glad to those two gone."

The front door opened again. Finally. Davri and Master Arsat joined them, sitting down. Bretav came from the back door, nodding that all was clear.

"I'm surprised everything has gone so well, so far," Davri said, grinning.

"If you consider this going well," Master Arsat said. "Anogrin's streets have never been so quiet or tense. People scurry away and avert their eyes, or they strut like they are looking for an excuse. They're saying the word execution openly now, instead of sacrifice."

"Exactly as planned," Daichen muttered, then took a long drink of his tea.

It had been simple enough to do, Thera thought. The mistrust had already been there. People were begging for a rallying point, for a leader to channel their frustration and anger. It didn't take much to turn Aral Tennival into a mythic figure. Too many people had witnessed her teleporting away, like a god. The legend almost created itself.

Emotionally, though, it was the hardest thing any of them had done.

"Anything could start a war at this point," Thera mused. "I don't like it. But it's what we needed."

Master Arsat patted her on the arm. "The world will be better for it, or so I've been told."

"If you say so," she said, skeptical.

Anything he would have said was cut off when the door flew open.

A high priest stood in the doorway.

His wild white hair flew in the breeze that had followed him into the room. He was the half-elf, Thera realized, recognizing him by reputation. Bloodthirsty and depraved, cruel.

Everyone in Anogrin knew who Krecek was. He was once quoted as saying, "Let me investigate this rebellion. I'm bored and executing the riffraff will give me something to look forward to, mid-week."

The café fell silent.

"The high priests are shutting down the university," he said. He stared at Arlanz, eyes intense. "They're to confiscate the books, use them as evidence of heresy. Now." Krecek looked around the room. "Warn the other students." His eyes met Thera's. Held them a moment. "Go. Run!"

Thera nodded. Grabbed Daichen's wrist. Ran out the door.

They knew what this meant.

They'd planned for this moment.

It was sooner than they'd hoped, but it's what the bombs and emptying the library had been for. The time had finally come.

"If we survive, I'll find you," Daichen said.

In a moment of bravery, she kissed him.

"For luck," she said.

She then ran straight to Master Dershan's laboratory.

It was time.

Krecek collapsed at one of the vacated tables, elbows braced on his knees, hands covering his face.

Bretav had the presence of mind to make him a strong cup of coffee and bring it over. The others were too stunned by what they had heard, and the sheer shock of him being there, to figure out how to respond.

"Here you go," Bretav said softly, setting the cup before him.

"Take your time. The students know what to do from here. Thanks be to Agruet, they've been expecting this day."

"They have?" Krecek looked up, faint hope in his eyes. "The books...?"

Arlanz cleared his throat. "The library is set to explode. It is a trap. We could not let you know."

"It's why we're here," Davri said, gesturing to Byrek in inclusion. "We came to oversee the removal of the last of the most important volumes. They're being sent to Plath, most of them. But we knew we would have to sacrifice some, to bait the trap."

Bait the trap.

Krecek frowned. "You might catch some priests off guard, but not likely. They know they're going into a stronghold of mages."

Damn it all. Some of them were counting on it.

"And we know," Byrek said, "that our enemies are priests and faithful of all levels, of all gods. To our credit, we have not been caught unaware."

"There's more," Krecek said. "The other priests know that I've come here, to warn you. They all but sent me, to prove that what I've been doing won't make a difference."

Silence.

Byrek seemed to digest that thought the fastest. "They're mages." There was resolve in his voice. "This is war. The fact that both sides are aware changes nothing."

Davri shook his head, though. "What did the priests have planned?"

"This is just the beginning," Krecek said. "Without the mages to keep them in check, they'll lock down Anogrin with absolute rule. Any mage must first be a priest, and all magic must be done only with their permission. From there they mean to impose this human idea of priestly rule upon all races."

Byrek straightened, tense, eyes narrowed.

"I told them the elves would never stand for it," Krecek

continued. "They said humans breed faster and will overtake them in sheer numbers if elves do not submit to the will of the gods."

"This won't end well," Byrek muttered darkly.

"It was never meant to," Davri said, placing his hand on Byrek's arm. "They've raised the stakes, that's all. We're still going to win."

"I'm done with them," Krecek said. "I'm not going back to the temple, not after that. I'm fully on your side, if you'll have me."

"Of course," Davri nodded. "We're lucky to have you on our side, and your value isn't limited by your position."

"You've been invaluable to us," Byrek agreed. "We'll find another place for you, you've done what was needed."

"Look," Arlanz interrupted them, pointing out the window.

Thick, black smoke billowed into the sky, tinged orange in spots from what must have been an intense fire.

"It's begun," Byrek said, stepping toward the door. "That was much faster than I thought it would be."

"That's not the direction of the university," Bretav said, picking up her skirts and rushing outside.

"Those are homes," Arlanz said as they all filed out, following. "They might start a fire brigade, but not if everyone has gone to save the university."

"Look," Bretav grimly pointed toward the source of another pillar of darkness that rushed toward the clouds. "That's the direction of the library. It's smaller, but it's there."

As they all stepped outside they could smell the smoke. They could hear cries for help and calls for water and shouts of people trying to organize what was surely to become the worst disaster in history.

"We need to do something," Byrek said urgently. "We need to help!"

Davri shook his head. "Where? This won't be all of it. Over

there, there's more!" He pointed behind the cafe, and this was clearly closer to them.

"I am going to help evacuate people," Arlanz said. "I will make sure they can leave their homes safely. They will follow me because I am so tall, they will see me easily."

"I'm going with you," Bretav said in a tone that brooked no argument.

Davri and Byrek exchanged a look. "We're going to the university," Davri told Krecek. "Are you coming with us?"

Krecek shook his head. "They'll panic if they see me," he said. "Go on. I'm going to the temple to tie up a few loose ends."

He knew that those who had set the fires would not burn down their own homes. The temples would be safe, unscathed. For now.

The bells clamored their alarm, filling the streets with their tintinnabulation through every district within Anogrin.

Bretav exchanged a look with her husband. It had certainly taken long enough for them to start ringing. The streets had been clogged with people in a panic for what seemed like hours already.

"Thank you," the old man said, eyes watering in gratitude as he looked up at Arlanz.

"It was nothing," he replied.

They'd just helped the old man down some stairs. A small gesture. One anyone would do.

One that not many others had thought of in their panic, however.

"You should hurry," Bretav said, looking around. The bells had whipped people into a new frenzy. "To the square, at least. Or, to the gates if you can. There are many fires burning now."

He nodded, moving at what must have been a rushed pace at his advanced age. It seemed painfully slow to Bretav.

"We seem to have this block roused," Arlanz said. He looked around, seeing over the tops of the heads of those around them.

Bretav pointed. "The fires are coming closer. We should—"

An anguished scream cut through the noise.

A woman was standing in front of one of the homes that were burning, pointing to the second story and calling out for help. She had her arm wrapped in a makeshift sling and two others held her back from running into the house. "Kestra! Someone save Kestra! She's still up there!"

The girl in question stood in front of the window. Her hands were pressed flat against the glass, and then she slapped ineffectively against it. She couldn't have been more than four, not nearly old enough to break it.

Smoke was filling the room. The roof was aflame.

Any rescue attempt short of magic would be futile.

"Gods, that poor girl." Bretav started to cry, just seeing her up there.

Before she could react any further than that Arlanz left her side. He rushed into the house.

"It's not safe!"

One of the men who held back the mother shouted a warning. He reached a hand in Arlanz's direction, but the mother nearly escaped him, and he was forced to hold her back yet again.

Bretav knew the warning was useless. Arlanz wasn't the type of man to leave a child in danger.

Timbers groaned and the smoke grew thicker.

A heartbeat later flame poured through every opening of the house.

Windows shattered.

A blast of heat washed over the spectators.

The Arcane War

The house began to crumble and Bretav let out a scream.

The library had turned into a riot between mages and priests.

Spells were flung with near disregard for who they might hit. Aim toward an enemy and hope.

Byrek paused. These were his students, his friends, his colleagues. Even a good number of the priests had been among the people he'd tutored or counseled. Krecek hadn't been his only student to join the priesthood.

"We won't make any difference here."

Gods curse it all, Davri was right. "But..."

"I know," Davri said. "Come on. We'll check below."

Below. To the laboratories.

Every space where experimental magic was tested, a safe zone needed to be established. Somewhere that minimal harm would befall when things went wrong. In a school these needed to be especially reinforced, so they were nestled deep in the stone of the mountain.

They rushed down the numerous stairs and down a long corridor lit by a dim glow of magic. The door Byrek sought was ajar, and papers were scattered even into the hallway.

Were they too late?

"Keevan! Are you—"

"I'm here," the hobgoblin snapped.

"We've got to go," Thera was with him, holding a folio of hastily gathered pages. "If we dally, the priests might find their way down here."

"Wouldn't that be worth seeing the surprise on their faces?" Keevan's lips twisted into a wicked grin. "Might be worth it to wait here to see it."

Thera laughed. "It might."

"Don't worry, girl," he said to her. "I'm almost finished here. Get to a safe distance. Half way down the mountain might be good."

"I'll see you at Hodarian's Bay."

"Be safe, Thera," Keevan said. "It's been an honor working with you."

"The honor's been mine," she said, dashing out of the room.

Keevan watched her go, unmoving. There was a grim set to his eyes as he pulled a device from a drawer. "The two of you should leave, too. I've received the help I needed. I just need to burn what's left in here."

He waved a vial of liquid fire under Byrek's nose.

Davri took a step back, and Byrek nearly did the same. That much?

"Are you planning on burning down the whole university?"

Keevan nodded. "Every inch of it."

Byrek and Davri exchanged a look of alarm, then understanding.

"That's been the plan all along?" Byrek stared at Keevan.

"Indeed. The students are only delaying and distracting. This," he hefted the device in his arms, "just might destroy the entire city. It's my present to the priests." He grinned and strapped the device to his back, then clasped Byrek's hand. "It wasn't the same here, without you. Thank you, for…" He broke off with a nod.

"It was an honor to work with you, my friend," Byrek said solemnly. "Goodbye."

Davri left then, to sound alarms and spread the word for evacuation. He knew Keevan Dershan did not expect to survive the night.

Many people would not.

The Arcane War

Arlanz knew he was dead as soon as he crossed the threshold of the burning home.

Baedrogan stood before him, shrouded from outside view by the thick smoke. The god of death had his arms crossed before him, glowering. "You're wasting your life. The child has no chance to live. Your wife stands outside, mourning already."

"Bretav is strong," Arlanz said, pushing past. He ignored the heat and dashed toward the stairs. "This child is not."

"What of your child?" Baedrogan followed. He stood easily when Arlanz wavered on his feet.

"All of my children have been taken by you," Arlanz coughed. "I shall finally meet them." His eyes burned from the smoke, and his throat itched.

He kept going.

The stairs were intact. He hurried to them, meaning to take them two or more at a time.

Arlanz stumbled forward upon them, on the first step. The air shimmered around him from the heat. His head...he was so dizzy now. He had to be quick.

"It will be a long time before you meet your last," Baedrogan said, leaning down close to Arlanz's ear. "Bretav carries a girl for you, even now."

It was hard, but Arlanz did not hesitate. Falling had given him a few moments more, bringing his head under the layer of smoke. On all fours, he dashed up. He reached the top of the stairs and crawled forward to the girl's door. "Then my daughter shall live knowing that her father died to do what is right. To do what I must."

It was the only thing he had to say to the god of death.

Arlanz pushed open the door and released the awaiting inferno. The pain was excruciating as the flames engulfed him, devouring his flesh. He could not stop the gasp that pulled the fire into his lungs.

Even still, he was reaching for the girl.
She was whole. Untouched.
Unharmed.
This girl must live. Arlanz reached toward her as he was consumed. His soul cried out. *I give my life for hers.*

Clack, clack, clack, clack.

The sound of Krecek's boots striking the marble floor echoed in the empty hall.

The Temple Magica was a bastion of peace, the eye of a great storm.

It was odd to see the halls so empty in the light of day. It was so still, so empty, that the shifting of his clothes seemed as startling as a shouted profanity. Krecek was tempted to hold his breath, just to be silent. He already felt like an outsider, an intruder, in these sacred halls.

His chamber doors hung open.

They'd been locked this morning. It was a habit Krecek had formed after he'd found a young supplicant naked in his bed. Thief, peace offering, or bribe, perhaps. The intent didn't matter. The invasion of privacy had not been welcome.

The key sat heavy in his pocket as he entered. The air was heavy, thick with a familiar scent.

"You don't think you're going to sneak out of the city that easily, do you?"

Nalia was lounging upon his bed, naked as the supplicant he'd been reminded of.

"I had no plans of sneaking." Krecek turned his back on her and gathered his belongings. "I thought I'd simply walk away."

"Walk away?" She laughed. "After all I've done for you?"

"After all you've done **to** me, yes." He slammed shut a drawer and whirled on her. "I can't do this anymore. I can't live like this. I'm nothing but a pampered pet! I need more."

Nalia stood, a gown of darkness and glittering jewels forming upon her body as she walked toward him. "I'm a goddess, Krecek. Do you think you can be my equal?"

"Of course not."

But, wasn't that exactly what Agruet had hinted? Wizards were as powerful as gods.

Their equals.

Their betters.

Wizards knew what it was to be mortal.

To have empathy.

To have morals.

"Leave then," she said, voice suddenly light, flippant. "Burn the whole town if that's what you want." Nalia placed a hand on his chest, over his heart. "It's the most impressive tantrum I've ever seen from one of my own."

"I'm not yours anymore." A whisper. A plea.

She ignored him.

"There's beauty in so much destruction," she continued. "I appreciate beauty when I see it. When you're finished, when you tire of it, you'll return. Your little rebellion is cute, but futile." Nalia's hand slipped downward. She grabbed his cock with a smirk. "You'll never be free of me. You're mine, Krecekarmalin Alavraneth." The goddess spoke his full elvin name as if it was a leash made of words that would bind him to her.

The name only his parents should have known.

The one only his mother had ever used.

He was enraged by the violation.

"Not anymore!" This time he shoved her away.

"Always."

Nalia vanished as if she'd never been there.

Krecek stood shaking in rage and fear.

A tantrum?

She'd called this a tantrum?

Fine. He grabbed his small pack of belongings and tore through the temple. He dispelled the enchantments that held it together, one at a time, and reveled in the destruction as everything crumbled.

He'd spent the majority of his life maintaining those spells. He'd poured his soul into their longevity in honor of the goddess of magic, and to honor those priests who had come before him.

No more.

"Fotar will never forgive me for this," Baedrogan muttered as he came to a decision. He stood between Arlanz and the little girl, Kestra.

She was weeping, confused but unscathed. Probably terrified.

The girl could wait a moment more. It wouldn't kill her.

Baedrogan knelt beside Arlanz. Sighed. "You may die."

Arlanz's suffering ended at the sound of that command.

"You've done the right thing," Baedrogan said to the smoldering corpse before him. "You deserve your rest. Better you die now than to see what is to come." He then turned to Kestra. "You're going to be a great mage, when you grow up. Come, child. You get to live."

The god of death held out his hand and Kestra took it. He guided her out to the street safely and looked her in the eyes. "Remember what you've seen tonight."

Kestra's mother ran to them, snatching her away. "My baby!" she wailed. "My baby!"

Baedrogan turned to the mother, eyes cold. "Five other children her age are dying at this very moment. There are ten infants in the city burning to death in their cribs. Your father is trapped under a fallen beam on the other side of town, and you can't save him. This girl is the only one I'll spare. See to it her life is worth sparing. Get off your knees and run!"

The woman stared, white as a sheet.

Baedrogan raised his eyebrows.

She grabbed Kestra into her arms and ran.

The others ran, too, but Bretav held her ground.

Baedrogan glared at her for her defiance.

"Please. Did he suffer?"

This. This made Baedrogan pause. "Yes." He eyed her, impassive.

"Did he...did he, even once, wish he hadn't...?"

"No." He touched Arlanz's widow with a frigid hand. "I gave him every chance, every motive, to turn back and let the girl die. He would not."

She nodded, biting the heel of her hand to keep from screaming her anguish, even as the tears ran down her face.

A small sound escaped her, but she inhaled sharply to keep it in.

So brave. So compassionate.

Mortals were so oddly self-sacrificing and needlessly noble at all the most inconvenient times.

Baedrogan looked around them, only to ensure any other gods would not witness this moment of weakness. He opened his arms to Bretav.

She clung to him, almost collapsing as the emotions took her over. Now she wailed. Now she screamed. It would be good for her.

He stroked her hair and gave what comfort he could. "I would take you now," he said, offering the greatest comfort he could give, "but I promised Arlanz that his child would see this world."

Bretav looked up at him, the question clear in her tear-filled eyes.

He nodded.

"Go now. Save yourself and the innocent life within you."

Baedrogan watched her run for safety. His eyes followed her a long while.

Lives were ending all around and he gave them barely a thought.

He gave them peace, gave their souls sanctuary, but the afterlife was his domain. His own creation. How would the dead enter, once he came to an end?

If Bretav and Arlanz were to be reunited, he would have to take her too soon.

And their poor child...

"What the frilly feathered fuck, Baedrogan?"

The voice was like nails on a chalkboard to the god of death.

Fotar, god of fire.

"Uncle," Baedrogan said, bowing his head so Fotar wouldn't see him sneer, or roll his eyes.

"Since when do you save lives, or give out hugs?"

"Since when has it been your business what I do, or don't do?"

Fotar waved a hand dismissively. "I could have taken them both, cleansed them both before their deaths. Why did you save the girl?"

"I liked how she wasn't afraid," Baedrogan said.

The older god looked at the god of death, nonplussed. "Why would you like that?"

Why indeed? Mortals were supposed to be afraid of death. It's all that kept them alive.

Kestra was afraid of dying, as she should be. What had touched him was...she wasn't afraid of him, the god of death. Even while she watched him take a life.

Baedrogan turned and walked away without answering. He had a busy night ahead of him.

Just for spite, he made the girl immortal.

That should irritate all the right people.

He'd always wanted to do that to someone who hadn't begged for it. This would be his last chance to do so. The other gods were too distracted to stop him.

A great mage and an immortal. That was sure to annoy someone down the road.

"Aren't you supposed to be off terrorizing students and ending innocent lives?"

The question rang out, echoing through the expanse of the great hall, as Krecek entered it. The gruff voice was familiar, but not one he'd expected.

"Keevan Dershan?" What was the old professor doing here? Now?

"In the wrinkly old flesh," the hobgoblin replied. He looked Krecek over, eyes narrowed in obvious suspicion.

"I've decided to take the night off," Krecek said to grandiose effect. "Permanently."

To make his point, he waved a hand and the wrought iron candle rack flew into the pews, splintering the wood and setting them on fire.

Keevan's eyebrows raised.

"That's just the beginning." Krecek lifted his arms upward, pulling the final spell that kept the sacred tree of magic afloat above the temple. It would hover for a few more minutes, but it was doomed.

No turning back.

"Would you like some help?" Keevan shrugged and turned, showing off a strange device strapped to his back.

It was magic, whatever it was.

"What is it?"

"Pure destruction."

"How much?"

Keevan grinned. "I'm not entirely sure. It's the most powerful explosive I've had the chance to put together."

"Well then." Krecek found himself impressed. "Let's find out."

Chapter Thirteen –

Refugees

Krecek awoke to a living nightmare.

Before the explosion, he'd placed himself and Keevan in a protective bubble. They'd been thrown a great distance by the blast, and he vaguely remembered being tossed around inside the bubble. Then they'd hit something. Crashed through it, perhaps. Krecek couldn't remember beyond the point of impact.

He hadn't bothered with a powerful, more permanent spell. Hadn't thought they'd need it. The spell ended the moment Krecek wasn't pouring power into it. In this case, when his head crashed into his own barrier on impact with a wall.

There were screams.

There was white-hot pain.

Everything was burning around them.

Everything was confusion and madness.

Krecek knew his arm was broken. It certainly felt broken, useless. What could he do about it? He made a sling for himself with a handkerchief from his pack, tightening the knot with his teeth. Slipped it over his head, lifted his broken arm into it, and cursed from the pain the entire time. Not much good, but it would keep him from trying to use it.

The damn thing was uncomfortable as hell.

His arm wasn't just broken, it was burned. The fabric holding his arm in place was excruciating.

Not that complaining about it would help.

Worse, so much worse, was Keevan.

He'd torn out a chunk of flesh from his back, and what wasn't burned seemed to be bruised.

"You look like shit," Keevan said, coughing weakly.

"And you look ready to take on the world." Krecek had meant to be sarcastic, but he couldn't put that sort of an edge to his voice.

"Feel like it, too," was all Keevan said.

They both gritted their teeth, knowing that to stay in the city was to invite doom.

People were already looting whatever could be salvaged while they were hidden by the dark of night. Maybe they were only grabbing what they could to help injured loved ones. The reasoning behind it didn't matter in the end. Desperation would drive them to other acts soon enough. Survival always brought out the best, and the worst, in men.

There was rubble.

There were abandoned carts and wares scattered in the streets.

This made their journey from the city all the more painful and frustrating. They had to pick their way carefully. Luck was briefly on their side when Keevan found a sturdy stick he could use as a cane.

One stroke of luck.

They'd need so many more. As they rounded a corner and came to sight of the city gates, Krecek feared that luck had run out.

"A mountain city has so many advantages," Krecek said, standing, watching. "They're very defensible against outside attack, for one. Having limited ways into or out of the city safely is a great strategic move in most cases."

Throngs of people pressed through the gates. Only so many could get through at a time, and all were tired of waiting their turn. Fights had broken out, or had continued from elsewhere, blocking the way further.

The carriage doors were wide open, for all that was worth. A wagon lay in splintered ruins, it and its cargo blocking most of the gate.

"It's a gods-be-damned nuisance," Keevan growled. "We can't fight our way through that. Look, priests are in that knot of fighting. And over in that area are some of my own students, losing their damn fool minds."

"One way or the other, one of us will be recognized if we try to walk the main thoroughfares." Krecek was amazed at the calmness he found in his own voice. Was it a carryover from living a double life for so very long, or had he just reached his emotional limits? "We'd be killed."

Keevan nodded. "If we're not killed by design, we'd be killed by accident. We've both seen better days, and neither of us are what one would call tall."

"Both of us, formidable mages, and if we try to magic our way through this mob we'll be worn down to oblivion." Krecek sighed. "But we can't remain here."

"No, we can't. They're going to run out of supplies, soon. The true criminals are going to start running the rubble so they can pick the city's corpse clean." Keevan spat, clearly disgusted.

They watched in silence for a while. They could face these people, or…

"We don't have much of a choice, do we?"

Keevan stared at Krecek with hard, narrowed eyes.

"You want to take an enchanted path in our condition?"

Krecek poked at his broken arm carefully, feeling a giddy queasiness when it just didn't feel put together right. Some of his skin was crispy, and all of it felt like it was on fire just by having air upon it. "I want to see my father. Elves can heal things that humans can't seem to conceive of. Byrek is, hopefully, long gone from here."

"Hobgoblins aren't much good at healing, either. We blow shit up like masters, though."

"Yes, you did," Krecek smiled. The pain was driving him mad, but he still smiled. "We should go. The roads to Naeriloran won't have too many shadows. We'll take our time."

"We'll be sitting prey," Keevan said. "But, die here, or die there...at least it will smell better in that half-realm."

Krecek nodded. What did they have to lose?

Aral looked across the table at Bretav. The young widow had arrived the day before and still looked exhausted. "It seems unreal to me," Aral said with a shake of her head.

Davri had contacted her by spell to let her know what had happened.

She'd been cleaning up after Naran's birthday party. Fourteen.

Such an innocent activity while Anogrin was in the process of being razed.

"I was there, and I feel the same way." Bretav picked up her cup of tea, looked at it blankly, sat it back down. "I just want to go home, and there's no home to go to. No café. No Arlanz. I haven't heard a word about my parents, or my sister. Thousands died, and I don't even know who survived."

Aral reached a hand across the table, resting it on Bretav's arm.

It's the only comfort she had to give.

The refugees who made it as far as Hodarian's Bay were all in good health. If they hadn't been, they wouldn't have made it so far.

Thera, Daichen, and a few of their compatriots were the first to arrive and take shelter with Aral and Raev.

The smell of smoke and carnage had followed them on the wind for days.

People had overwhelmed the roads leading down the mountain. Many who had been otherwise safe had been pushed off ledges or trampled to death.

"The girl Arlanz saved," Bretav continued. "I don't even know if she made it out of the city. What if he saved her, but she fell when everyone ran? What if her mom brought her right to where the explosion was while they were trying to get safe? What if he died for nothing at all?"

It was heartbreaking.

But...

"What if she's fine? What if she'll be fine?" Aral squeezed her hand against Bretav's arm like a miniature hug. "You can't tear yourself apart with possibilities. It'll just eat you up inside until you do find out one way or the other. It's out of your hands for now."

"You're right," Bretav said. Her voice was small, soft, and the corners of her eyes pinched. "It's not even my biggest worry right now."

Of course not. It must be so small next to losing her home, her family, her husband...

"I'm with child again."

Oh. Given her history and inability to carry long enough, that would be bigger. Yes.

"You're sure? I mean, you don't look..."

"I suspected a few weeks before," she said. "I didn't even want to tell Arlanz, never had the chance, because I couldn't handle disappointing him again. But...I was told...just after he died..."

Damn.

"If there's anything I can do for you, I will. I'm sure I speak for everyone here."

Aral was startled by the sound of someone gently coughing from the doorway behind her. She turned to see Raev, slouching, with a grimace on his face.

"You are not wrong," he said. "Aral...I need to bring up something...that is..." Raev took a deep breath, then joined them at the table. "Bretav, according to the customs of my people, it is my duty to care for you and treat you as my wife. We are traditionally nomadic, dealing with harsh conditions, and marriage is treated with pragmatism rather than romance."

Wait. What?

It took a moment for Aral to understand what he'd said.

She frowned and pulled her hand slowly away from Bretav.

Then, she laughed. "That's a little fast. The two of you just met."

"Pragmatism," he repeated. "As the closest unwed man of the family…"

"What of intimacy?" Bretav asked softly.

"That is entirely up to you," Raev said, hands held out before him as if to ward away any impropriety. "I will treat your child as my own. I will give all that I have to your care. I ask nothing for myself."

He was serious.

Aral stared at them, back and forth.

They were both serious.

"Since when do you care for old traditions?"

Aral didn't mean to sound sharp, accusing, but there it was, assaulting her own ears.

"Always," Raev said. "I have always upheld the traditions of my people." He looked at Aral sadly. "Were I wed, this would not have even been broached."

What could she say to that?

She'd had the chance.

He'd asked, many times.

No. This wasn't happening.

"Is this what you want?" Aral turned on Bretav. "I know enough of their traditions to know that you can always refuse."

"His traditions are my traditions," Bretav said quietly. "It's what I promised Arlanz when we were married. His family is my family; his ways are my ways. But if the two of you—"

"No." It was probably the firmest no that had ever passed her lips. She stood up. "I have... There are things... Outside."

Aral knew she didn't make any sense. The important word had been the "no."

The answer between Aral and Raev had always been no.

She wasn't a wife. She was a mage with duties.

But it still hurt to walk away from a warm bed and a man who loved her.

Somehow, she managed not to slam the door on her way out.

Too stunned to be angry enough. For now.

There was a spot under a pier that she loved to visit at low tide. It was a good spot to think a while. Her feet took her there without conscious thought.

The anger hit her as she reached the shade of the pier.

How dare he?

Raev could have mentioned it to her ahead of time. Could have warned her last night, even.

Instead he'd...he'd...well, he'd been quiet. Pensive. Troubled.

Aral had assumed it was the stories the refugees had told.

She'd assumed he only grieved for his cousin.

Would it have been better to know ahead of time?

She had no claim on Raev. Had never wanted one. But it stung to be so abruptly and easily replaced.

Well, not replaced.

Displaced?

She had a room in their underground base, but she hadn't used it much.

The base was filling up as more refugees arrived. She'd thought about abandoning the room to make room for others, but now...

The water lapped at the rocks and sand.

She usually brought a bag of food to feed the turtles and the birds, but this time she came empty-handed. She apologized, and after a while the birds flew away.

She sat on her favorite rock to perch from, and she stared out to sea.

Someone was swimming in the water. She wore a dress of seaweed and discarded sails, awkwardly covering most of the expected areas. A bit of the seaweed drifted aside to reveal a nipple, but it was a valiant attempt at normal clothes. The strange girl's hair trailed to the water, seeming to be made of it. She rose to just above the waist and beckoned Aral closer.

"I am Shista," she said once Aral was within earshot. "I represent the merfolk of the sea."

Merfolk?

They were hardly ever seen this close to a human town.

"It is an honor."

"You are the human Aral of the Tennival family?"

"Yes."

"You lead rebellion against the gods."

Aral's breath caught in her throat. It sounded like an accusation.

The mermaid wasn't attacking, though.

In fact, all of her words had come out flat, monotone. So, maybe just a statement, not a prelude to an attack.

Defensive spells sprang to mind, but Aral stilled herself. She nodded, unmoving.

"Your rebellion and your plight are known to the free people of the sea. If you have need of us, we will be there." Shista then turned and slid back into the water, discarding the makeshift dress as soon as she was clothed by the water again.

Aral continued to stare.

That had been abrupt.

Unexpected.

Merfolk never came to the land. Never. They tricked sailors sometimes, or aided others, but they never concerned themselves with humans who did not travel on the sea.

What was she doing to do with an army of merfolk?

Aral heard the crunch of sand behind her. Someone new approaching. She closed her eyes, hopeful and afraid that it was Raev.

"Sorry!" Not Raev's voice, at least. "Hope I didn't startle you!"

As Aral turned, she realized Shista must have a magic of her own. Aral started to shiver. She turned and rushed as fast as she could out of the frigid water, toward the stranger. "What's going on here?"

The newcomer was short and stout, covered from head to toe in thick clothing. He carried a thick canvas parasol and wore a floppy, wide-brimmed hat, despite the sun being firmly hidden behind a thick layer of clouds. Bits of beard stuck out of the fabric here and there, and tinted goggles poked through as well. "We've been gathering."

"We?" She was still shivering, surprised it hadn't made her stutter.

"I met your brother and your friend Davri a few years back," said the little man. "They told us what happened. My uncle took them in for a time. We dwarves have been gathering information on the priests and their movements ever since. We try to keep track of the gods as well, but there's not much of a point to it."

Aral nodded and returned to the rock she'd been sitting at before. "Do I have you to thank for bringing the merfolk?" There was a bit of driftwood laying around, but it was waterlogged. Damn it. That wouldn't burn well, and it would smoke horribly if she forced it. She'd have to use a pure magic flame, which would take more energy. But, she had to warm up and dry out.

"You have yourself to thank," he said, sitting next to her. He stared at the sudden flame warily, then looked at her legs and realized what it was for. He relaxed. "I did come across her on my way here, but she was already searching you out. You've earned quite a reputation. Disappearing from Anogrin was one thing. Surviving this long…amazing. But you brought Anogrin down, you destroyed the temples, without setting foot in the city."

Aral felt she had to demur. "I didn't do that last myself. I was throwing a party when it happened."

"A party?"

"Celebrate when you can, right? It was my brother's birthday. I just happened to have all the right people in the right place when the priests initiated the attack."

"That's what a leader does."

"Anyone could have done it. If I hadn't, someone else would have."

"Would they, though?" The dwarf shook his head. Well, he seemed to. The fabric shifted, and the bits of beard that poked out moved back and forth. "In all this time the gods have remained the same. And in all this time, no one has struck such a blow against them."

That was something Aral couldn't refute. The idea made her uneasy, and that must have shown on her face.

"Every good leader feels like they're in over their head, but that doesn't make them stop being leaders." He nodded at his own sage words. Again, it seemed like a nod from how the fabric moved. "I've heard many times that without you the whole rebellion would never have happened. That without you making decisions, the rebellion wouldn't have a chance. You've done extraordinarily well at knowing who to trust with what. Even over a distance, you've coordinated the escalation of hostilities like a master. You even managed to get Byrek and Davri to the right place at the right time, and I think I'd go sober a month to learn how you managed that."

"How do you know all of that?"

"We dwarves are resourceful, and my uncle is Deeg, master of spies. I am Breev, one of the greatest spies we have. Perhaps you have heard of me?"

"I'm sorry," Aral said, shaking her head. Great, she was about to insult a dwarf on their first meeting. That always went well. "No, I haven't."

Better to insult him than lie. Right?

"OF COURSE NOT!" Breev shouted. He then howled with laughter, either at his own joke, or the expression on her face. "Some spy I'd be, if anyone knew my name!"

"Then why are you telling me?"

"Because you're a leader, and you have a need to know." Breev sobered quickly. "I'll be honest. It seems that Davri sees himself as a leader, but not the leader. You've others beneath you that seem similar. Thera, who only made local decisions for Anogrin. Sirale, out in Fenrenborough. How did you get him on your side, anyway?"

"He was a friend of my father's," Aral said. "We ran into each other the last time I went to my parents' grave. He said a certain god sent him. I've learned to trust that, if they know his name."

"You've got a god on your side while you fight the gods?" Breev jumped up and took a step back, nearly tripping over a dangling piece of fabric.

So. Agruet hadn't had a hand in sending Breev or Shista. It had been unusual a year ago, but more and more people were coming to her without divine intervention.

"Do you honestly think we could win without some help?" No sense revealing another was involved if he was distrustful of mention of one of them.

"You trust him?"

Trust. That was a hard question to answer.

"I don't know," Aral said at last. "I need to trust him to some degree, but I know he's doing this for his own purposes. He's helped us a lot, but in the end, well, he's a god. If that makes him our enemy..." She spread her hands before her.

"Then what are your plans?" Breev looked momentarily frustrated. "I thought it was just to get their attention and get them to change, and why would you have help from other gods if that was all you were doing?"

"War. Rebellion." Aral stood and began walking back to Raev's shop. "We're not looking for attention. Our aim is to bring real change. You said yourself, you're a spy. For now, only people I trust know the larger plan. Earn that first or leave."

She managed only a few steps before she heard laughter behind her.

"She's either brilliant or she's mad," Breev cried out to the sea.

"Let us hope she is both," Shista's distant voice replied.

Thera looked around the empty room with a small sigh. Hodarian's Bay was crowded with refugees. They'd been doubling people up, at least two to a room, in the underground base.

This room was the only room left vacant.

"What if he doesn't show up?" Thera looked over at Aral, fussing over the empty bed. "He might not. No one's seen him since Anogrin's fall."

"I know," Aral said. "But he's a good friend. He took care of me. He taught me more about magic than anyone else except my father. He was there for me when I was at my lowest. He tried to warn me about the priest that betrayed me."

Her shoulders slumped as she said that bit.

Thera stilled, looking at her friend. Aral probably regretted not listening to that, more than anything. It had to be hard, knowing she'd brushed off a friend when she could have used it the most. Even now, years later.

"I'm not giving up on him," Aral's voice was quiet. Nearly

inaudible. "He never gave up on me."

Thera picked up the pillow and threw it at Aral. Time to break the tension. "You sound like you're pining after a lover. Something you're not telling me?"

Aral stared for a minute.

Thera made a silly face, and Aral finally laughed. "No! Believe me, no way. There are too many reasons not to, ever. Starting with Porrellid. When things...were intimate...with that...with him...I could feel the eyes of that goddess, watching us, the entire time with...him. Krecek has the same look in his eyes, now. I can feel it it even through the communication spell. I have it on good authority that his goddess has sexual relations with her high priests, and I just can't. He's a friend, and I miss him, but no."

"They...he did that? They DO that?" Thera found herself unable to put all her thoughts into words at once, as warnings and lessons and memories all scrambled for attention at once. "You trusted him, even knowing that? I mean—" She huffed a little, nose wrinkling. "You're the one who told me that sex could reveal our secrets, and you go off and befriend someone who has slept with one of our most powerful enemies? How...I mean...he betrayed us, just by being...what he is. Or was. Or whatever."

"No," Aral said with a firm shake of her head. "I don't trust him. He trusted me."

Did that really make a difference? Thera grimaced, not even trying to hide how skeptical she was.

"He knew what would happen. He warned me from the start not to trust him with any of our secrets. And, there are certain spells that can keep gods from knowing certain things."

"Wait, what?"

Aral held out a hand, stopping Thera. "We couldn't even rely on that. So, he was only given as much information as he needed to be able to help us. Meanwhile, he told me everything."

"Wow." That was, well, it explained a few things. "So, what's this spell? I've never even heard of anything like it."

Aral sat down beside her. "It's time I trust you. Completely." She was wearing her "leader" face. Serious. Sincere. Profoundly removed from emotion and attachment. "You showed great initiative and a level head in Anogrin. I've been told that you helped save many lives that night. You guided people to safety. You organized them as they fled. I want you to be one of my closest advisors."

"Wow. Um. Sure! I mean, I'd be honored," Thera said. "So, the spell?"

"It's not a simple spell that keeps our secrets. It's, well, the god of secrets is on our side. He's been guiding us and helping us from the start. I know it's dangerous. He's a god. He might betray us just because he's bored. But if he does, we still fight. His help has been invaluable so far. We use his name, and his complicity. Without it, we'll all fail."

"Wait. So. We're rebelling against the gods. because another god told us to?" That was the last thing she thought Aral would confide. Thera chewed the inside of her lip, thinking. "You think we'll actually be able to...change things?"

"We already are." Her voice was firm. Resolved. "I don't think we'll end up with everything we want. I wouldn't even make a bet on any of us surviving. I'm willing to risk it." Aral paused. Nodded. "I know. I have nothing to lose. If we don't win, I'm dead anyway. How can I ask that from anyone else? So, I'll be up front and honest with you. That's where we stand. Figure out now if you'll stay, and advise me, knowing the truth. Or, go home, subject yourself to the whim of gods and priests, and live a safe life. I won't hold it against you. I mean, I might, if I had the choice."

Thera stood up and started pacing the room. "I'm fighting because, well, there's so much to gain from forcing the gods to listen to us and take us seriously. Things can't keep going the way they are. I want my death to mean something for everyone that's stuck here, still alive." She stopped, looked Aral in the eye. "Sure, I've got a lot to lose. But I'm in. I couldn't live with myself if I just walked away."

Aral shook her head, and the words that followed were flat, emotionless. "The gods aren't going to take us seriously. Let go of that idea right now. I'm not going to convince the gods of anything. No one will. We're toys. We're playthings. The only way anything is going to change is if we change it."

"What?"

"Total honesty," Aral said, "and all cards on the table. Right now, the only mortals who know the real, ultimate plan are me, Davri, and Byrek."

"What do you mean? What's the real, ultimate plan?"

"We're going to kill the gods."

The words hung in the air. The impossibility of it. The audacity.

The appeal.

"How?"

"Well, it's going to take a lot of magic," Aral said. "We'll need the most powerful mages in the world. I've been getting to know them, corresponding with them, and gathering them for years. You're one of them, Thera. I've had you in mind from the start."

Flattering. Undeniably flattering.

But it didn't keep Thera from realizing that it wasn't actually an answer.

"Do you know how to kill a god?"

Aral grinned, looking sheepish, like she'd been caught doing something naughty. "Not yet."

"Until we do, we're still just puppets and playthings."

"That's nothing new."

Well, that was a sobering thought.

It wasn't new at all.

That's all they'd been since the gods created them.

The thought that they could be more was thrilling. Sure, the forbidden always was, but...

They might do more than just stand up for themselves and protest.

They might change the world. Forever.

What would the world be like without gods?

"Whatever you need," Thera said, "ask me. I'll do it. This is going to be the best, ever."

Weeks later, the site of Nalia's temple was still a smoking pit.

Agruet schooled his face, as always. Appearing triumphant at the destruction would raise a few eyebrows. And some unwanted questions.

He was the god of secrets. Answering petty, nagging questions over inconsistencies in behavior was completely beneath him. Total waste of time.

"It's plain to me what this is," Brinn said in his deep, rumbling voice. He sounded like the echo of cannons on the horizon.

"The humans have declared war," Thar agreed, almost laughing in glee. Her voice was a sharp staccato, like clashing blades.

Agruet almost rolled his eyes at the pair. God and goddess of war. The war had been declared long ago, and not by mere mortals.

"This was mine," Nalia said, pacing. "I'm not only talking about the building they destroyed. The city was mine. The university. The mortals responsible for it were mine as well."

The assembled gods were nodding, murmuring.

"So, we raise an army," Thar said sharply. "The two with the bomb were not the only ones responsible for this."

Fotar stood. "We should make all the mortals pay for their complicity! Make them suffer!"

"They'll only rebel harder against hardship," Hastriva murmured sadly, next to Agruet. She was a younger goddess, the lady of peace, and Agruet thought he would have liked her more under different circumstances. Her kindness was refreshingly different from all the rest.

And Baedrogan, the sucker, put a hand on her shoulder. "Yes, but they won't listen to that," he told her quietly.

This time Agruet rolled his eyes.

Kindness wouldn't serve necessity. Not at this stage.

Kindness was a tool to be exploited for greater ends.

He saw a shadow slipping through the assembled gods.

Yda. She knew.

Yda had orchestrated all of this.

She had to be dealt with. But not yet.

The outcry to assemble armies grew, bringing glee to faces that usually looked bored. It could all be resolved with magic, of course.

If they did that, no one would get their chance to show off and play around for a while.

After all, what was the purpose of mortals if not to play with, right?

"No!" Nalia interrupted. Her voice echoed through the ruins of the city. "I didn't bring you here to raise armies. I can handle this. They targeted me. They tricked one of my own high priests into betraying me. They made it personal. I want revenge."

This gave a few of the assembled pause.

This was Agruet's cue.

"Mother," Agruet said. He stood slowly and drew out the word. "Perhaps you didn't notice. This pile of rubble, right here? Off to the side, as always. This, here, where I stand, was my temple. There were temples to, well, most of us. They called it the temple district because there were so damn many crammed into the area. Yes, yours was special because it was so very pretty, but did you know that all of my high priests in this temple died that night?"

And, of course, Baedrogan nodded to confirm the deaths.

All two of them, because he'd warned the others away.

Details...

"We'll be gathering armies," Thar and Brinn said in unison. "We lost priests, too!"

Nalia opened her mouth and was shouted down by the rest of the gods.

They all had stakes.

They all wanted revenge.

Not petty, personal revenge against two mortals. They wanted to take down this entire ridiculous rebellion. A lesson had to be taught, or the mortals might do this again.

Agruet leaned in close to Baedrogan. "Entropy wins. As we knew it would."

"Yes," Baedrogan said, expression blank. "As we knew it would."

Nalia would still work against the rest to further her personal vendetta. It didn't matter.

War was inevitable.

They'd all be gathered at the right place, together.

And then they would die.

Chapter Fourteen –

GATHERING OF THE ARMIES

The autumn turned to winter, which was always hellish off Hodarian's Bay. In the middle of a great ice storm, Krecek stepped off of an enchanted path, alone. He wore simple mage robes with a sack slung over his shoulder.

Davri met him there, offering his own heavy winter cloak, and ushered Krecek inside.

"What went wrong?"

"Too many things." Krecek slumped his shoulders and shook his head. He didn't want to recount it.

Not yet. There'd been too much.

"It's fine," Davri said. He showed Krecek around, introduced him to people. They ran into friends, but only Aral walked with them.

Krecek didn't have much left by way of belongings. When he was given a room of his own, he nearly laughed. What was the point of it? "You saved this for me?"

Davri slipped away, giving Krecek a grin behind Aral's back.

Aral nodded. "I had faith that you'd find your way here eventually. And, see? Here you are." She giggled, and it sounded shrill and forced. She was fluttering her hands around, making half gestures toward one empty part of the room, then another, then toward the small bed.

Krecek looked around. There was a lot of empty space. "Just for me?"

"Well," she said with another fluttering gesture that might have meant to indicate the whole room, "I thought that since you were used to such large and ornate rooms at the temple, you'd want your space. It's not much, and we don't have any fancy furniture or anything, but I saved it for you."

"Thank you," Krecek said. "I appreciate the gesture."

He wanted to tell her it wasn't necessary.

He didn't want to be alone.

Awkward silence filled the space between them.

"I need to...I was in the middle of...I'll see you later." Aral wavered back and forth, then almost dashed from the room.

There went his chance.

He didn't have the energy to talk to her anyway. Not now. Not today.

Krecek emptied the pathetically small sack. Everything he'd had of any value had been either destroyed or given in compensation for safe haven and healing spells. All he had now was a change of clothing and a broken hairbrush.

He'd changed into his freshest and most intact robes before stepping from the enchanted path, but he couldn't afford the luxury of throwing either away.

The reminder of ornate rooms and the temple stung.

He could have stayed.

He could have relaxed and enjoyed himself more.

He could have turned a blind eye to suffering and injustice.

There were many times he could have put an end to it all by convincing Aral to visit him. He could have betrayed her and watched her die while Nalia consoled him. He could have—

Except he couldn't.

"I've done the right thing," he whispered, just as he had every day since Anogrin's fall.

He'd drive himself insane like this. Krecek had been left alone among the elves; not quite shunned, but close to it. Months alone with his thoughts. Alone with his temptations.

It was toxic, being alone with his thoughts so much.

He quietly slipped from his room and sought out Byrek. There were things he had to tell the old elf, messages to convey. It wasn't a conversation Krecek looked forward to.

Still, it would be conversation. Sweet, beautiful words that didn't come from within his own head.

He found Byrek in the storage room.

"We have a bath." Byrek didn't even turn from what he was doing.

Krecek rolled his eyes. "I've missed you as well."

"Being missed doesn't excuse body odor. I went through the trouble of insisting our bath was to elfin standards. The least you could do is use it."

"I need just a few minutes. I don't want to be alone."

Byrek stopped, set down his paper and pen, and grabbed the tip of Krecek's ear. "You're still just a child, by elf reckoning. I'd put you over my knee if you were my son. Bathe."

It was still a better welcome than he'd received from his aunt.

"Elfin standards, you said?"

Byrek nodded, already pulling Krecek along by the ear. "I insisted."

That meant communal bathing.

"You don't have to pull me around like a child," Krecek insisted, wincing. "I'll go. I just didn't realize."

Byrek let go, but he didn't stop walking.

Krecek realized that if he'd been listening, he'd have saved himself the embarrassment of being treated like a child. Humans had odd notions of privacy and modesty, but elfin baths were a place to talk and relax with others.

All he'd had to say was, "Join me? We need to talk."

"Sorry for being an idiot," Krecek said, head bowed. "I'm exhausted and not thinking straight."

Byrek nodded curtly, then opened the door to the baths.

It was spacious. Beautiful. Krecek washed himself at the basin, where he was delighted to find running water. "How?"

"I cast the spells myself. With so much ocean water nearby, it's simple. A little filtering, and we have all the clean water we could need."

It was impressive for a team of mages to accomplish. Astounding that Byrek did it all himself.

Finally, once he was completely scrubbed off, Krecek relaxed in the hot bath next to Byrek.

It felt wonderful.

Byrek looked over at Krecek, raised an eyebrow. "You wasted no time in finding me. Davri had just told me of your arrival."

"I needed to talk to someone who would understand." Krecek relaxed into the water, staring vacantly across the room.

"You've been in the northern forests," Byrek sighed. "I can tell you've been among elves, even if they're not my kin."

Krecek nodded.

"Did you convince them?"

"I convinced my father."

Byrek sat up. "Just your father?"

"He managed to persuade a few others. We might get half of some of the younger warriors and mages. Ones who have never seen battle."

"No veterans?"

"Very few. A pervert asking them to join his mutt child? You know how some can be."

Byrek sighed. He sunk back into the water and nodded.

"Of those, many of them are taking the enchanted paths to try to convince the southern elves. You know better than I how well that will probably go."

Byrek nodded and slid down so that the water was to his neck. "Our people are difficult to goad to action. Even so few is more impressive a force than I expected."

"Keevan helped. I'm not sure how, since he's still a crotchety bastard, but he knew just what to say."

"You saw him? He's alive?" Byrek's eyes went wide, and a

smile graced his lips at last.

"He's alive," Krecek said. "He walked in with his explosive as I was trying to destroy the temple by hand." He grinned ruefully and shook his head. "If I'd known, I'd have helped him ahead of time. But, I couldn't be trusted."

Byrek started to make some conciliatory motion. "That's not—"

"It's not self-pity. It's fact." Krecek met Byrek's eyes, holding his gaze until Byrek nodded. "I told Aral not to trust me. I'm glad she took me at my word. Keeping the few secrets I had was nearly impossible. It's why I'm so relieved that that's over."

His voice had gotten louder as he talked, and the last echoed uncomfortably around the room for a minute. He winced, especially when he saw that Byrek had cringed at the volume.

"I'm sorry," Krecek went on, quiet again. "I've spent my life around humans, convinced of my superiority and maturity. Three months back among the elves, and I feel like an immature freak. They didn't even have to look at me for me get defensive. I began to walk around apologizing for existing."

"You don't have to defend yourself to me," Byrek said gently. "I understand more than you know."

"Thank you," Krecek said. They shared silence for a while.

"Why isn't Keevan with you?"

"He's gathering the hobgoblins. He'll come."

There was a longer silence after that.

Finally, "Aral didn't want to be around me," Krecek finally blurted out. "She was happy to see me, but—"

"You know why," Byrek said. "It's the same reason a room was saved for you. Alone."

Bitterness stabbed through Krecek's heart.

"She doesn't trust me, still. No one does."

"The goddess you served still dances behind your eyes." Byrek sighed and put a hand on Krecek's shoulder. "Aral will never see past that. Not after what happened to her at Porrellid's hands."

"I killed him. For her." Even to his own ears, he sounded like a child, petulant that the world wasn't fair.

"I'm sure she appreciates that." Byrek looked offensively patient. "She's intelligent. She knows what she owes you. But one can never owe their heart to another. Love is not a transaction. She's talked about it. More than once. How she feels about you. She's afraid of you. So long as the goddess is part of you, Aral won't touch you. Not willingly. Not the way you want."

Krecek took a deep breath. Nodded. "It's still all worth it," he said, voice small.

There was a mix of pity and understanding in Byrek's eyes.

Krecek couldn't face it.

"I'm finished here." He stood, nearly slipping on the tile as he numbly left the tub.

He dried himself and dressed himself, thoughts so loud that the rest of the world receded from his mind.

"It's still all worth it," he said again as he closed himself in his room. "It's all been worth it."

It had to be.

Within days of Krecek's arrival, Northern and Southern elves began to arrive. There were nearly a thousand of each.

There were grumbles and complaints among the humans at first. More mouths meant less food.

Well, it should have.

Elves wove magic into everything, making plenty out of scarcity.

Once the elves had laid their magical groundwork the sprites, dwarves, merfolk, and many others began to gather there as well.

Aral found herself overwhelmed. Every moment of every day

was taken by something needing her attention.

She was the one everyone turned to.

Others advised, but her decisions were always final.

Her word was the word that everyone looked to.

It wasn't a mantle that Aral felt sure she deserved. It wasn't a decision she had made for herself. Then again, she didn't shrink from it, either.

People followed her. When she asked for solutions, people gave them. Then, she made a decision. So far that's all leadership was to her.

Simple, if not easy.

Half of her had expected Krecek to take control, but he had all but disappeared as soon as he had arrived.

She found him in his room, alone, curled up around a book.

"I wanted to talk to you."

Krecek looked at her, wary.

Deep breath. This was important.

"Of the two of us, you have more leadership experience."

She blurted the words out.

Spewing them forth like word vomit.

"Now that you're with us, fully, well, you've more than earned your position here. If you would like to take over leadership of —"

"Me?" Krecek stopped her with his laughter. "Lead?"

It wasn't a kind, polite laugh. It was sharp as a sword, with barbs that caught on their way back out.

"Well, you're older. And, like I said, you're experienced."

He sobered quickly. "This isn't something you can just pass along to whoever you wish. The people will follow who they will. They've chosen you. Perhaps they showed up out of curiosity for what they'd heard, but they're staying through a harsh winter for your sake."

"But what if I mess up? What if I do something wrong?"

He scooted to the foot of his bed and offered her a spot to sit.

It embarrassed Aral how long she hesitated before she did so, but she did.

She also made a mental note to have a chair moved in here later.

Krecek's lips stretched into a thin smile. "You've tried to pass this to Byrek already? And Davri?"

She bowed her head, ashamed that he was right.

"Don't be so eager to throw this at someone else. If you make a mistake, you learn from it and move on. You'll never be perfect."

He was right, of course.

"I might be tempted, but I could never accept." Krecek leaned toward her.

Aral flinched away.

"That's why I can't lead these people."

It would have been nice to pretend she didn't know what he was talking about. To pretend there was nothing wrong. That he was still her old friend.

"It's like she's looking at me, too."

"I know."

"I mean, it's not...every other high priest I'd ever met, I felt, well, intimidated. Overwhelmed. But that was normal. But, since Porrellid—"

"I know," Krecek said again, more forcefully this time. "Aral, I understand. I think I understand it better than you do. It seemed like such a gift, once."

"A gift?"

"Before I met you, yes. Not as much, now." He stood, gestured to the door. "You should go. You have responsibilities to see to."

She could hear the unspoken words beneath it.

Please don't torture me with what I can't have.

Aral stood, but she hesitated.

"Be my advisor. You're wise, you're learned, you—"

"No," he said. "You already have more from others."

"Please?"

He paused.

Breathed.

"I'll think about it."

Days went by.

Aral refused to leave Krecek alone with his thoughts. She sent others to ask his opinions on one matter or another. When given the slightest excuse she called for him to give advice.

A week later he relented, spending time at her side. A show of trust and confidence neither of them really felt.

It didn't take much time for Aral to take comfort in his presence.

So long as she didn't look at his eyes.

False spring came upon them.

Refugees were eager to start planting or to move on. Many of them wanted to get away from Hodarian's Bay before battles found their way here.

Aral had lived here long enough to know better. "Anything planted now will die. Anyone who tries to travel from here will find the passes choked with snow again within a week."

One more crisis to handle on top of all the rest.

She was always busy, always answering some question or another, always listening to or reading some report or spell or taking something into consideration. It was remarkable she got any sleep at night.

She realized one night as she walked to her room that she hadn't had time to eat all day. She was so exhausted that she wavered in the hall, torn between two conflicting needs, when Davri came up behind her and steadied her.

"Something wrong?" he asked. "You look dead on your feet."

"I haven't eaten," Aral said, but she was still looking at her bedroom with longing.

"Come," Davri said. He wrapped an arm around her and led her to his room instead of hers. He ushered Byrek and Naran out, telling them to go sleep in Krecek's room just this night. "He's lonely, and he's the only one with a room to himself. Now go. Aral needs to rest without some idiot pounding on the door in three hours."

She slumped against him in relief as they left. "Thank you." She collapsed onto the bed he steered her toward. She left her feet hanging off the edge with a silent promise that she'd take her shoes off in a minute.

Davri took off her shoes and started massaging her feet.

She moaned in thanks. "That feels so good."

He smiled at her. "Roll into your back. No, feet still...there. This is as warm as I could make it, without lighting a fire," he said.

Aral was confused, then he set her feet gently into a basin of warm water.

It felt heavenly.

"You're going to spoil me," she said.

"Someone needs to. It can't all be hard work and business, day in and day out. You'll forget to live."

"I had that long enough," she said, thinking of Raev upstairs in the house, waiting on Bretav the way he used to wait on Aral.

"You didn't have so much weighing you down, then."

Aral said nothing. She stared at the ceiling. Davri continued working the tension out of her feet and her legs. He dried her feet off and washed his hands.

"You'll have to sit up for this part," he said.

Aral protested with a disappointed groan, but he sat down next to her and pulled her up against him.

"Here, I'll sit behind you, like a chair. You can lean against me and eat comfortably." He put a leg on each side of her, supporting her so she could relax while she ate.

The Arcane War

He offered her bread, water, and an apple. It wasn't much, but it didn't entail going all the way to the kitchen.

"This is just what I needed," Aral said, twisting around to kiss him on the cheek before she ate. She managed to finish the apple and ate half the small loaf before she completely drifted off to sleep, safe in Davri's arms.

She woke up just a few hours later. It felt so good to held while she slept. It was such a familiar feeling, and in a sleepy haze she didn't stop to think whose arms surrounded her. Something was strange, though. She thought at first it was just from being overdressed. She undid the laces of her dress and wriggled out of it.

That's when she realized.

The man beside her was too thin to be Raev.

Darkness hid her blush, but couldn't spare her the feeling of mortification. Her thin shift was hardly enough for sharing a bed with a man. But, Davri was fast asleep. If they were both under the blankets it might still pass for modesty.

And, honestly, wasn't she past that? An entire city had seen her naked.

She settled back into bed and waited for sleep.

And waited.

Her mind raced, though, clearing away even the gentle tug at her eyelids.

She was in a strange bed with a strange man she had always been attracted to.

With a thrill of apprehension mixed with anticipation she reached to his sleeping form and explored the strange curves and planes of him. She felt the compact strength of his muscles as she ran her fingers over his arms and across the flatness of his belly. His chin was covered in rough stubble instead of the full beard she had known the last few years.

Aral realized she liked the feel of it. She imagined the friction it would cause if they kissed.

He stirred a little.

She stopped. Left her hand still upon his cheek.

Even her own breath seemed too loud to her ears. She knew the pounding of her heart wouldn't wake him, but she held her breath until he relaxed again.

Davri shifted a bit, but his breath was still slow and even.

Still asleep.

She pulled her hand away, but only for a moment.

He was shirtless, and a sudden spark of mischief spurred her to discover just what other articles of clothing might be missing.

Or, more realistically, to find out where his pants began.

She grinned as she found the waistband, low upon his hips.

"Aral?"

He grabbed her wrist, sounding sleepy as he said her name.

Oh. Shit. Caught.

"I'm sorry." She pulled her hand away, rolling over onto her other side. "I got curious. And carried away. I didn't mean to wake you."

Shit, shit, shit. As soon as she'd realized it wasn't Raev, she should have clamped her eyes shut and kept her hands to herself. Instead, she'd gone too far, rubbing her hands all over while he slept.

"I don't mind," Davri said.

That surprised her.

"I liked it."

"You did?"

"Very much." He moved closer to her and placed a gentle hand on her waist. "I wasn't sure you were aware what you were doing. If you were sleep-groping."

Aral started to relax. "Your body is so different. My curiosity got the better of me."

"I see," he murmured in her ear. "Is your curiosity satisfied?"

Did he want this, too?

One way to find out.

"No," she said. "I want to know...what it's like to kiss you. And more."

Davri pressed his body against hers and kissed her on the neck. "How much more?"

"Everything more."

He nibbled her neck playfully, and his hand slid downward to pull up her shift.

She gasped and turned around to face him. His stubble was rough when he kissed her. It left a bit of a friction burn behind, but she didn't mind in the least. It was more of a thrill to feel that burn in places more intimate. Aral thought to herself that this wasn't at all like being with Raev. Davri was rough, playful, and passionate. It was awkward between them at times, but it was also fun.

By morning, they were both in a better frame of mind.

The change in Aral and Davri's demeanor did not escape the notice of both Byrek and Krecek the next morning. The two of them exchanged looks, understanding each other for the briefest of moments.

Davri kissed Byrek on the cheek. He must not have known how strong elvin hearing was, because his whispers were like spoken words to Krecek.

"We were both mostly asleep. She asked and I couldn't tell her no."

Byrek whispered something in return, too soft for Krecek to hear.

"No. You know I love only you."

Another whisper from Byrek.

"Yes, it was just for fun. And, it was fun. To make it up to you, what if the three of us..."

Krecek left the room before he could overhear any more.

Instead of having someone to sympathize with over the jealousy burning within him, Krecek stood on the outside, watching the three of them grow closer.

Days went by.

It was impossible not to notice.

He even overheard Thera and Bretav giggling over it, until they noticed him and went silent.

Everyone went silent around him.

Even meetings and battle reports were given with hesitation if he was in the room, despite Aral's assurances.

The three people he'd hoped would be able to accept him, despite the choices he'd made of necessity, choices that had aided them all this time...those three people were too wrapped up in exploring whatever triad they had formed to give him a second glance.

The three people who were his only three friends.

Was solitude to be his reward for the sacrifices he had made?

No.

He reminded himself that he hadn't done any of this for any sort of a reward. He was trying just to help others.

He was trying just to make things right. That was what he wanted to do. That was what he wanted to accomplish. Success would be its own reward.

Oh, but it was bitter and hard to watch Davri and Byrek enjoy the girl he wanted. The girl he had wanted for so very long.

Even if he knew he could never have her.

Days went by.

It was undeniable now. Krecek was Nalia's creature through and through.

She'd never been the hero of myths.

The Arcane War

Nalia was the original trickster. The one who made things happen, even when no one wanted those things to happen. She'd pitted the other gods against each other when they created the high magic races. Had brought them all together again when they had created humans. When she had birthed the twin gods Agruet and Baedrogan, she'd given them the strength to look into the void and not descend into oblivion or madness. With that, she'd gifted the world with death and secrecy, gods seen as a bane, but ultimately a boon. She'd always done what was necessary.

Even when others hated her for it.

Even when she received no reward.

Krecek left. He strode out to the edge of the town, refusing to glance at anyone as they passed and tried to greet him.

He glared at the ground, he glowered at the blue sky, and he grimaced at the everything that was between.

The air was crisp. Chilly. The very cusp of winter and spring.

Oh, how he loathed it.

His skin crawled with the force of his anger and frustration, and it wasn't until he was a good hour's walk into the woods that he finally released it in a soul-deep scream that he felt even in his toes.

"Something troubling you?" Nalia's voice came from everywhere around him. "The girl you want is willing to fuck anyone but you? And you think that's just so horrible?" Mirthless laughter filled the air around him. "You think that's so horrible, Krecek?"

Damn it all!

He wanted to be alone! To work all of this out on his own, get it out of his system, get on with his life.

"You chose me," Nalia taunted. "You killed to get my attention. It was so flattering. So beautiful. But when I granted you what you wanted, when I took you to my side, you know what your heart was already filled with? Her."

Flashes of thought pierced through his mind. Nalia's jealousy and surprise that any mortal could be placed above her. The insult of finding a priest already in love, unable to let go.

"She complains because I watch her through your eyes. What about me? That girl was everything to you, even after you dedicated yourself to worship me. And now you cry out to me that you can't have her?"

"It HURTS!" he screamed, staring upward as if he would find the goddess there. "I can live with it, but it doesn't mean I can stop hating how it feels!"

"Do you know what else hurts, Krecek?" Nalia took form before him, taking on the appearance of an elf, just to taunt him. "Death."

The word echoed around them, filling the air.

Oh no. Oh shit. Oh fuck. Oh, DAMN it all!

How did she find out?

"Your new friends want to kill me. And my brothers. And my sisters. My daughters and my sons." She stared into his eyes, trapping his gaze. "I plucked that bit of knowledge straight from your head. I saw it sitting there, glittering like a jewel. It taunted me and told me I should not know, but I found out."

"No," Krecek mouthed the word.

"You want me dead! I thought you loved me! You were my most entertaining high priest, and you want to betray me! How do you mean to do it? What imbecile gave you the idea that gods could die?"

"No one!" Terror made the lie difficult, but he forced it out. "No one," he said again, gently. At the same time his mind was a chant demanding that Agruet protect him and his secrets. "It's just wishful thinking. Mortals do foolish things when we're afraid. You made us this way."

"You're hiding things from me," Nalia frowned, eyes narrowed. "I can feel it, like worms crawling on my skin. You're trying to deceive me." She stepped in close and caressed Krecek's cheek in an almost loving gesture. "Agruet is MY son, you know. I gave birth to him. He can only protect your secrets for so long."

"I don't want to upset you." Krecek leaned into her touch. "My thoughts are just jumbled and unworthy of you." Krecek took her hand, and he kissed the palm of it. He had been so lonely. Her touch was like a balm. It was dangerous, touching her. But maybe he could talk to her. Change the course of events by turning her to their side. "You created mortals to be an entertaining distraction. We became more than that. You, Nalia, you gave us that. Despite what the other gods meant for us. You said yourself that if we were just puppets and playthings, we would grow boring. Treat us better, and all this can end."

Her eyes softened.

Nalia's fingers lingered, pressed gently against his skin.

Was it possible?

Was she as lonely as he was?

Did this goddess crave a deeper connection that she hadn't yet found?

She snatched her hand away.

"I can destroy you. I can unmake you so utterly that it will have been as if you were never born. All of you!"

"Please," Krecek turned away as if embarrassed for her. "Threats are beneath you. You are the most powerful of all gods. I've seen that in you, I know the truth. I've known you as intimately as you have known me. If you meant to do those things, they would be done."

She slapped him then, and it sent him to the muddy ground, clutching his cheek and tasting blood.

"You DARE?" Nalia straddled his hips, hitting him with bone-jarring force.

At least she remembered that he was only flesh and bone. She managed not to kill him.

But she wanted to hurt him, to teach him a lesson.

And she knew exactly how far she could go.

He saw all that in her eyes as she shattered his body upon the rocks and the trunks of trees, throwing him around like a limp rag, and he did not fight back.

He did not even attempt magic to heal himself or lessen the blows.

"You dare to tell a goddess what I can and cannot do? You are MY creation! You are MY high priest! You are MY lover! You are MINE!"

She looked into his eyes. They both knew further harm would be his death.

He saw her temptation.

Her hesitation.

Her sadistic glee when she thought of the one thing she could do that would hurt worse than physical pain.

That would hurt him worse than death.

She tore the magic from him and devoured it while he watched.

"Beg me for its return," she said, kneeling next to him.

Something whistled as he took a breath.

"No," he whispered, defying her wish with his last conscious act.

If that was how he died, so be it.

He had no reason left to live.

"Death walks among us."

Aral was in the library, and those words stole her attention from her work.

Death? Had someone died?

Or, was Baedrogan here?

The Arcane War

Garm burst into the door. "Aral. You need to see this."
Probably Baedrogan, then.
"What is it?"
"It's Krecek. Something...I don't know. He looks half dead. The god of death walked in with him, scared the pants off of half the base."
As soon as the words "half dead" had left Garm's mouth, Aral was out of her chair and rushing down the hall. He was at her heels, still talking.
"I don't know what's going on," he continued, "but how's this fit in with all our plans? Can we tell him our grievances? Can we get him on our side?"
"He already is," she said curtly. "It doesn't change anything." She stopped. "Where am I going?"
"Krecek's room. Thera and Raev guided him there. What do you mean, the god of death is already on our side?"
"This first. Answers later. Tell no one."
Aral ran.
She burst through the door moments later.
There were so many people in the room. Gawking. Staring.
There was Baedrogan, a head above everyone in the room but Raev. He seemed to hover over them all, like a vulture.
His head snapped up and he met her eyes.
The others in the room noticed her then.
Moved aside.
Moved so she could see the broken form upon the bed.
She was hit with shock. Horror. Disbelief.
Gods, how had he survived?
The urge to cry was overwhelming.
Instead, she forced a smile. "Thank you for bringing him to us," she said to Baedrogan. "For sparing him."
"I have more to ask of him," Baedrogan said quietly. "Him. You. Everyone here. Heal him?" The god looked like a child,

asking a parent to fix a broken toy. "I hate to withhold death from anyone suffering this much, but I have to." He sat down in the chair by Krecek's bed. "I can keep him alive." There was a vulnerable quaver in his voice. "But, I can't..."

"We will," Aral said. Her voice was firm, no-nonsense.

In full leadership mode.

If she didn't fall back to her role, to the emotionless state of making decisions and barking orders, she would break.

Aral scanned the room, eyes meeting Thera's. "Do we have a list of mages with healing aptitude?"

"Yes."

"Ask for volunteers. Strongest ability first, but I'll take anyone who is willing. Set up a rotation of shifts, so no one burns themselves out."

Thera nodded. "Good idea," she said over her shoulder, already in motion to follow orders.

The room emptied, leaving Aral alone with Krecek and the god of death.

Baedrogan shook his head. "This is a message. A warning. From my mother. She means to end this war herself. Without the aid of armies. Without the other gods."

Not good, not good... "Does she know what we mean to do?"

"She does."

Chapter Fifteen –

The Beating of the Drums

Aral cursed under her breath, profanities passing through clenched teeth with a well-practiced cadence. She paused. Oh, right. Baedrogan was a god.

"Not you, of course," she said, embarrassed.

"I've said worse. Today, in fact." He gave a pained smile. "Agruet and I are being pushed to our limits right now. She knows my brother and I are behind this. She pulled it from Krecek as she drew him away from here."

"I can't sit back and let her do this," Aral said. It was hard to think when all she wanted to do was help her friend. But, leaders lead, even when things are falling apart. "We'll call for attacks in Eglian and Beronasvan by the end of the week. I'll send out word to step up our efforts. If we attack the other great temples, the other gods won't be able to let her take it all on herself."

"Agruet and I are doing all we can," he said. "Your aid is appreciated." Baedrogan stood and put a hand on her shoulder. "I don't want to, but we need to speed everything up. We can't risk Nalia destroying everything for something as petty as revenge."

"Will you fight at our side, when the time comes?"

Baedrogan fell silent, staring into her eyes. He looked sad.

What could make a god look so sad?

What could make death look frightened on top of it?

She put her hand over his, about to say something comforting, but he shook his head.

"I must be the last," he said.

"The last?"

"The last god to die. If I'm not the last, or if I don't die, it won't work."

A shiver went down Aral's spine. She didn't like the thought of killing their ally.

Or, was it allies?

"What about Agruet?"

"My brother promised to join me," Badrogan whispered. "When this is over, we won't be alive to aid you further. The world will be yours."

Aral the leader dried up and disappeared at those words, set aside so that she could be a protective big sister to someone in pain. She hugged Baedrogan, beyond words.

She'd had no idea. The plan had been to kill the gods. A nebulous idea that had always been the ultimate plan somewhere down the line. None of them who knew the plan had thought of what to expect if they won. The compassionate side of her wanted to tell him they'd stop; they'd find another way. It was impossible, though. If there'd been another way, these two gods would have found it and jumped on it by now. He and Agruet had come to them, their mortal creations, to work toward this very end.

She couldn't back out.

Byrek walked in.

It was like a splash of cold water. Baedrogan took a step back, squared his shoulders. He wore composure like it was his everyday disguise.

"Did I interrupt?" Byrek asked.

"No," Baedrogan shook his head. "We were finished." He shot a look of gratitude at Aral for her compassion.

"I volunteered to heal Krecek first, but I'm glad you're still here. It's been some time since I've seen your brother. Is he doing well?"

Elves were usually guarded with their emotions, especially ones as old as Byrek. Aral was surprised to see such strong concern and agitation written across his face.

"Agruet is well. Busy, and trying to keep you safe on top of it, but fine." Baedrogan smiled. "You'll see him again." The smile disappeared. "We're accelerating the plan. Mother's gone off again, and we need to end this soon."

"Oh, joy." Byrek's voice was heavy with sarcasm. "Alternate plan?"

Baedrogan turned to Aral. "It's time to gather all the mages you can trust. Byrek, teach them the spell. We can't wait for a human to discover it." His eyes flickered toward Aral when he said "human".

Aral furrowed her brow. "Me?"

Silence.

"I was supposed to figure out how to kill gods?"

There was something familiar about the idea.

Baedrogan sighed. "Your father was. Events unfolded in less than optimal fashion."

As he said it the feeling of somehow knowing that struck Aral, but when she pressed further for how she'd known, or who she'd been talking to, the idea retreated.

"Oh."

"You were our second choice, but your studies were derailed when you took command. Now that time is of the essence, we can't wait for the spell to be discovered naturally."

"I'm sorry," Aral said. What was she sorry for? Sorry for being too busy to think of ways to kill gods? Sorry for not being her father? Sorry for not taking on the responsibility for the end of the gods?

Sorry for not remembering something she couldn't remember being told?

"Everything must end," the god said. "Everything."

Byrek nodded, face placid once again. It took Aral a bit longer to compose herself, but she knew Baedrogan was right. All things needed an end. It was the reason there was a god of death in the first place.

She nodded.

"I'm sorry to ask this of you both. Your hearts are kind, and this will leave an indelible scar on your souls and your psyches." Baedrogan bowed his head. It was surreal for Aral to see a god apologetic and humbled before them. "It's an unfortunate necessity. I tried to keep the burden from you both. There has been an unseen hand fighting us at every turn. Remember this, when you need it."

With those words, Baedrogan disappeared.

Aral and Byrek looked at each other, reading the expression on each other's faces.

"No time to figure out what he meant by that," Byrek said, looking Krecek over. "We have work to do."

Krecek mended slowly.

Most people had at least some innate magic.

Nalia had taken it all from him.

The horror, the depth, of what it meant to be utterly bereft of magic hadn't dawned on anyone until they tried to heal him.

Without magic, Krecek had no internal reserve to fix himself, of course. That had been obvious and expected. The true problem was that other mages couldn't tap into his magic, couldn't synergize with it. Couldn't use his power to aid their attempts.

When he realized why it was taking so long, why it was tiring them out so quickly, he tried to regain it. He felt around within his mind for some way to unlock it or sneak it back.

She knew. Every time he reached for it, he heard Nalia's voice mocking him, telling him to beg.

It was tempting.

A hunger strike, with a goddess of food dangling a gourmet meal in front of his mouth.

All he had to do was beg.

Krecek wasn't sure how he managed not to give in.

Perhaps it was because Aral spent so much of her time by his side.

She smiled and held his hand. She worked her healing magic upon him whenever she had a chance.

People were constantly coming and going, needing to talk to Aral, but she stayed. When she wasn't healing she was doing her paperwork by his side.

"Why are you still here?" It was the first thing he'd managed to say, coherently, in days.

"You're one of my best friends," she said. "I'm not letting you go, and I refuse to let you suffer."

Krecek tried to smile. The attempt ended with a wince. It was too painful.

"You're not just keeping an eye on me? To make sure I don't leave again?"

Aral laughed, setting down her paperwork. "Yes, if I took my eyes off you for an hour, you might reach the door."

If smiling was painful, trying not to laugh was torture. It ended in gasps for breath and tears streaming from his eyes.

Still, it felt good.

"I'm sorry," Aral said, placing a hand on his forehead in a comforting manner. "I didn't think that through. No more jokes, I promise."

He nodded, but he attempted a smile again.

"I hate to see you like this," she said. "God or no, I'll see to it she pays for doing this to you."

"How?" Krecek croaked, his voice giving up after talking, laughing, coughing. His vocal cords had been just as abused as the rest of his body, mostly by screaming in pain while it had

The Arcane War

gone on.

"I'll kill her myself." She set her jaw and determination glowed within her eyes. "I know how."

Krecek shook his head, squeezing her hand as hard as he could manage. "Not you," he whispered hoarsely. "She's jealous of you. She'll fight harder."

"All the more reason for it to be me," Aral said. "She won't be thinking straight."

Krecek knew in his aching, shattered bones that it was a mistake, but he wasn't in any position to stop her.

Davri had finished searching the woods, examining the scene of the conflict between Krecek and Nalia, without learning much that was new. It gave him insight into her frame of mind, by the strength of the traces of magic she'd left behind, but that was all.

Days of going over the minute details, for what? To learn she was upset? Angry? Scared? Possessive and growing irrational? He could already guess that. The faint stirrings of a plan began to gather in his mind, but what good was that? They were running out of time. They had to gather the rest of the gods to the same point, not just bring her solitary wrath upon them.

He realized it wouldn't do any good to stay out there any longer. It was time to help the healing efforts.

As Davri neared Krecek's door, he heard Aral's raised voice. "I'll kill her myself. I know how."

Well, shit. That would do no one any good. He could hear a rasping protest, but the words were lost to him. Too quiet, too rough and gravely.

Aral's reply was crystal clear. "All the more reason for it to be me. She won't be thinking straight."

"Neither will you," Davri walked into the room, coming up

behind her, and he put a hand on her shoulder. "You shouldn't go after Nalia or Garatara."

Aral glared. "I don't get revenge?"

"It's a tricky spell. You'll need to keep a clear head, or it'll rebound and kill you." The nebulous thoughts he'd had in the woods coalesced into something he could use, and he grinned. "If you want revenge, though, I think I have an idea."

"I'm all ears," Aral said dryly, arching an eyebrow.

"The first thing we need to do is get Krecek's power returned to him," Davri said. "If Nalia is jealous, she—" He stopped himself. Scowled. Saying her name was growing increasingly dangerous as she fought Agruet directly. "I'd feel safer talking about this if Agruet was here. He could let us know if it is a viable idea, and he'd keep others from listening in better than I can."

"Work on it and get back to me with your idea when it's fleshed out," Aral said. She sighed. Stood. "I have a lot to finish up today, and I only brought half the reports from this morning." Gathering her papers, she gave a terse smile. "Some of the scouts have reported some odd things. Maybe we'll see some activity soon."

And then, they were alone.

Davri sat down at the edge of the bed, staring at the closed door. His thoughts were awhirl, creating a plan. He hated it, but it was the only thing he thought would work.

They were fighting an enemy that wouldn't play fair. It limited their effective options.

Well. They'd deal with the fallout as they needed, not before. He looked at Krecek. Talking with that much damage to his throat must be terribly uncomfortable. "She didn't get much healing done, did she." He placed a hand over Krecek's neck.

Davri hadn't had much practice healing others, only himself. He closed his eyes, visualized the damage, and rearranged everything to as it should be. Things that had already healed incorrectly had to be ripped apart, and the beginnings of scar tissue were erased. It took a few moments, but—

Krecek gasped and muttered a short curse. "Yes, but she's gentle about it. The pain takes a lot out of me, you know."

"You can sleep when we're done," Davri said. "We need to talk."

Krecek looked away. "You talk while I recover."

"I'll be blunt," Davri moved around the bed to meet Krecek's gaze. "Nalia is jealous because you are the first high priest she's had who loves someone else more than they've loved her. Right?"

Despite the healing, Krecek didn't say a word. He just stared with narrowed eyes, radiating suspicion and resentment.

Davri didn't have time for that. He needed Krecek to listen to him, damn it. Not hide from everything because his feelings were hurt. Taking a cue from how much healing Krecek's throat had hurt him, Davri grabbed Krecek by the shoulders and healed them just as quickly, just as forcefully. "I can do this to every inch of your body before anyone else would walk in. I have the sheer power for that, and you know it. I don't flaunt it, but you know what I am."

Krecek let out a whimper of pain and nodded.

Davri let out a slow breath, letting go of his anger. He'd gone too far. It was time to concentrate on soothing the raw nerve endings. Convince them to ignore the pain...

Krecek let out a relieved moan. "What do you want from me, Davri?"

"I know you're hurting, but I need you to listen to me. Aral..."

"I know," Krecek interrupted. "I've heard it from everyone, now. She doesn't feel for me what I feel for her. She never will. Between Porrellid and Nalia, I have no hope of winning her over, ever."

"That may be true," Davri said slowly, running his hands over more of Krecek's body, combining the soothing with the healing, now. He wouldn't go overboard, he didn't think Krecek could take it, but he owed the half elf this much. "It's not the point I want to make. I'm not here to mock your pain. I wanted to apologize for increasing it."

Krecek stared up at him, skeptical. "You have a hell of a way of showing it."

"I'm sorry," Davri said. He covered his face with his hands, closed his eyes. "You weren't listening to me. My temper got away from me." He opened his eyes, looked at Krecek intently. "That was stupid of me. I won't do it again."

It was frightening. Davri had caused that much pain. Negligently.

With healing magic.

Hurting the people closest to him, with magic, because he didn't get his way. First with Aral. Now with Krecek.

He was generations removed from godly blood. They had all been weak enough that the gods hadn't destroyed them for starting the wizard threat anew.

Too weak for the gods to notice.

Too powerful for most mortals to stand up to or fight against.

And this rag-tag group of mages and refugees were fighting to bring wizards back into the world?

Sure. There was no way for that to end badly. Not at all. Right?

It didn't bear thinking about for too long. They were dedicated to this course of action, for good or ill.

"Why you...with Aral?"

The question sidelined all of Davri's fears and self-recriminations.

"It just happened," he said as gently as he could. "I was half asleep and didn't think much beyond how nice it was at the moment. I assumed Byrek would be fine with it, because he has another lover. That assumption, well, it was a learning experience on my part."

"But," Krecek interjected, "it is fine now?"

"It is," Davri said. "I'm young. Stupid. Impulsive. And I didn't think much beyond the three of us. I didn't mean to add to your pain..."

Krecek trembled as he lifted his arm, placed a finger against Davri's lips to silence him. "I don't blame you," he said. "I want to. I could. But I also could have fallen in love with anyone else. And I'd still be alone right now."

Davri shook his head. "That's not—"

"It is. The problem isn't with anyone else. It's me." He dropped his hand, exhausted. "It's this fundamental feeling of being unworthy. I'm half elf and half human. I'm not pretty enough or delicate enough for other elves. I'm too short for human women to take me seriously. I am a priest, but I betrayed my goddess. I am a man, but I betrayed the girl I wanted. I'm nothing. I have nothing. I own two robes and a pair of shoes. One robe now, I suppose. I still frighten everyone who looks at me. I'm not even powerful anymore. The only thing left to me is my pride, and even that's rapidly eroding as Nalia dangles the promise of power over me. I've never felt so small."

"If I can return that power to you, will you recant the rest?"

"The robes are hard to recant. There's physical evidence."

Davri bit his lower lip to keep from laughing. "The rest of it," he said, chuckling despite himself. "Including new robes, because I've already replaced them for you and bought you more."

"You did?" Krecek narrowed his eyes slightly in suspicion. "Why would you do that?"

"Clearly," Davri drawled, "because you are a hideous, unlovable beast who gives me nightmares."

"If I'd known you have a soft spot for hideous, unlovable beasts, I'd have tried to be more of one sooner."

"You're unbelievable," Davri said, taking Krecek's hand in his. "After everything you've done for us...and you didn't ask for anything in return. You suffered in silence. You left to sacrifice yourself so you wouldn't bring a goddess's wrath upon our heads. If I weren't in love with Byrek, I'd have chosen you."

Krecek's eyes were half-lidded, drifting further closed in small increments with every blink. "You couldn't...have found...a better time...to tell me that?" His words were breathy, barely audible, but intent.

Davri bent down, kissing Krecek so very gently. "You should sleep more, now. I promise to be gentler next time I come in to heal you."

"It's okay," Krecek said as he closed his eyes. "I feel better now...than I have in years." An instant later he was asleep.

"I didn't tell you the best news that came in today. They're gathering armies, this soon into spring," Aral said triumphantly, eyes sparkling with joy.

Just seeing her smile raised Davri's spirits.

Seeing her sprawled naked across Byrek, also naked, was a happy bonus. A memory to treasure, to be sure.

"So, that's the source of your enthusiasm tonight?" Byrek teased, pinching her nipple.

She gasped and giggled. "Only part of it, I promise."

"I don't care where the enthusiasm comes from," Davri said, laying back in full satisfaction. "It's just nice take advantage of it."

"Don't ruin my good news," Aral said, nudging Davri with her foot in a half-hearted kick.

Davri caught her foot in one hand. He made a tickling motion with his other hand, inches from her skin, making her squeal and pull from his grasp.

"Go on," Byrek said, reaching to light a few more candles. "I'd like to hear the rest of the news."

"Mmhmm." Aral settled in and relaxed. "I feel like I shouldn't be excited to say there's an army within a few days from us, and they're clearly poised to attack. Priests and other devout. Several elves, sadly, but not as many as we have. No dwarves, unsurprisingly. Many faeries, though. That could make things tricky."

"They're delicate," Byrek pointed out. "Very susceptible to magic attacks, too."

"Natural healers," Davri murmured. "Also adept at spying. We should adjust our strategies to compensate."

"Already working on it," Aral said smugly. "Meran had a few insights into how to handle the faeries. You'll see."

"Mmhmm." Byrek kissed her on top of her head.

It was so sweet. Davri felt warm through and through, watching them. He was adrift in euphoric afterglow.

He wanted to take this moment and wrap it up like a Nightwatch gift to himself. He'd open it at down after the longest of nights and warm himself with how perfect life could be.

"Davri," Aral said gently, after a few moments of content silence, "I hate to bring the mood down, but I wanted to ask. What did you and Krecek talk about, after I left?"

Davri propped himself up with some pillows, frowning as he composed his thoughts. "I apologized to him. For what the three of us have here." He didn't mention the threats and frustration he'd felt, ashamed of his abuse of power. "He was depressed. Feeling sorry for himself. I told him that if I hadn't already been in love, I'd have fallen for him." He couldn't look either of them in the eye, just letting the words come out. "It sounds horrible, like I'm rejecting him too, but I think he understood. I think it helped." Deep breath. "Krecek mentioned that she-who-is-a-total-bitch is dangling his magic over him, tempting him with it. I don't think we have much time. He's strong, but..."

Silence settled upon them.

The Arcane War

The last was bad news. About what they'd expected, but still bad.

Aral sat up, pulling her legs up to her chest. "I'm sorry. I could go to him. I could try. But he'd know I was there out of pity. I'd just make everything worse." She closed her eyes, forehead resting on her knees. "I don't think I can handle love, and he doesn't deserve anything less."

"Don't be too hard on yourself." Davri reached over, put his hand on her shoulder. "He'll find someone, eventually. So...don't ruin that for him by offering more than you can give."

Aral nodded, but it still didn't sit well with any of them.

"What about in the interim?" Byrek propped himself up on his elbows. "Is there anything I can do to help him?"

Davri grinned. Byrek wasn't asking for wisdom. He was asking for foreknowledge. Anything that Davri might have gleaned from visions.

"He looks up to you." Davri said. "You were the only other elf he knew in Anogrin, and you made adapting seem so effortless."

All gleaned through magic, none of it something Krecek would say aloud.

"Effortless?" Byrek shook his head. "It wasn't, believe me. I struggled constantly. I hated being away from home and family. He was raised among humans. He helped me adapt more than I could have helped him."

"That's not how he sees it." Davri shrugged. "When he met you, he'd just met his father. He'd just failed at living with the northern elves. He needed to see it was difficult both ways."

Byrek nodded slowly, thoughtful.

"We're drifting off the topic," Davri said. "My point is, I admire him. You admire him. He admires us. It could be the start of something. At the very least, a closer friendship. He needs that right now."

Aral looked back and forth at them, a small line between her eyebrows. "What about me? What can I do other than make him miserable every time he sees me?"

That was an easier answer. He didn't even need magic and visions to know what to tell her. "Keep doing what you've been doing. Be his friend. Don't lead him on. Trust him. Be yourself around him. Leave the healing to us."

Aral scowled, but she nodded. She clearly wasn't happy with the idea, but Davri wasn't about to suggest anything else. It was the only thing she could do that would help.

"Davri, that's going to make you sound like a hypocrite when you tell them your plan."

The bed had been a little crowded, but now it was full.

Davri jumped, shocked to hear that voice. Here of all places. Now of all times.

Aral shrieked and grabbed the closest blanket, pulling it up to her chest.

The newcomer had dressed to fit in, showing his entire godly glory.

Only Byrek seemed completely unruffled.

"You're later than I expected," the elf said mildly.

"I've been a busy god," Agruet laughed and settled in against Byrek. "I've missed you, too."

Byrek's response was to wrap an arm around Agruet and nuzzle his cheek.

Aral stared, tugging the blanket tighter around herself.

Davri just stared. This was the secret Byrek had been keeping? This had been his other lover, all along?

That was completely unexpected.

Although, it explained a few things.

Agruet looked at Aral, then Davri, amusement dancing on his lips. "Should I have waited? Thrown some pants on? Joined the three of you mid-coitus, perhaps?" His eyes sparkled as he looked Aral over. "Relax, adorable. I've seen your body before, remember?"

Aral pulled the sheet over her head. "I remember, thank you."

"Let's get to the point before we get to the fun," Agruet said, tugging at the blanket playfully, just enough to make Aral squirm. "Tell them your idea, Davri. I swear that Nalia won't hear a word."

No point in stalling.

Davri took a deep breath. He outlined his idea as quickly as he could. "It really does make my advice sound hypocritical, I know. But, I've figured out a way to set a trap. All we need is bait."

Aral poked her head out from under the blanket. "I'm bait?"

"You'd certainly reel in something interesting," Agruet said, giving the blanket a sharp tug and revealing all.

"You'd only be the initial bait," Davri said, trying hard not to let the conversation be completely derailed. "I want Nalia herself to be the bait for the other gods. If she screams loud enough, they'll all come. Then, I kill her."

"You?" Aral interrupted with a glare. She seemed to have given up on the blanket. "Is that why you won't let me have my revenge? So that you can take it?"

"No." Davri reached over and placed his hand on her thigh, assuring her. "I need to kill her so that I can release Krecek's power. I know how to do it, and you don't."

"Teach me," she said.

"It's not that easy," Davri said. "I need you to distract her first. As soon as I attack her, you'll need to lead the others. Warn them that the other gods will be arriving. All of the armies, all of the mages. This area is going to become very dangerous for everyone."

"It's a good plan," Agruet said before they could argue further. He'd grown somber, perhaps melancholy.

Aral noticed, and she reached over to touch Agruet's arm in a show of compassion.

"The rest of the details can wait a while," Davri said, watching that little byplay curiously.

Had Aral found out how this all would end? Or, just part of it? Had she remembered? Or had she been told?

Told, he decided, or she wouldn't trust him enough to be here right now. Probably Baedrogan, the other day...

How she knew didn't matter. What she knew must have been enough that her heart was softened toward Agruet.

She wasn't shying away in false modesty anymore.

"You've got a week," Agruet said. "Maybe less." He covered Aral's hand and squeezed gently, then turned his attention to Davri. "Longer than that and Nalia has a chance of fighting her way through my spells. She's relentless, but secrets are still my domain."

Davri closed his eyes. Images flashed across his mind in rapid succession. "Three days, maybe less." He blinked.

That soon?

He wasn't ready for this.

"I can't narrow it down further, and I can't tell how it's going to start. There's too much in motion. I'm sorry."

"It's enough," Agruet said. He sat up, gave Davri a hug. "I understand," he whispered.

Warmth spread through Davri's heart. He would understand, better than anyone.

Agruet then sat back on his heels. "I seem to have ruined the mood."

Byrek shook his head. "We were on the way to doing that ourselves. It's nothing that can't be fixed." At that, he grabbed Agruet's butt and gave a squeeze.

"Is that an invitation?"

Aral's face was turning red, but she smiled. "You never did seduce me, the way you said you might someday."

"Consider yourself seduced," Agruet winked at her playfully.

She hit him with a pillow. "Not until you've finished the job. That left Davri.

Oh, hell, why not? There's no such thing as incest when it's among gods, right?

And who would it harm?

"Did we want to invite anyone else while we're at it?" Davri asked in mock exasperation.

Aral smiled, though her face was red again. "We could see if Thera's busy. Too many men in here, not enough women." She giggled.

"I like the way you think," Agruet said. "She's not busy. Go ask if she wants to join in."

Aral grabbed the blanket back and wrapped it around herself. She was out the door in an instant.

Silence fell upon the room.

Davri cleared his throat.

"So. The two of you?"

Byrek nodded. "Off and on."

"For a few centuries." Agruet shrugged.

"Over a thousand years."

"Really?"

Davri watched them banter. It felt good. It felt right.

Three days.

In just three days, Agruet would be dead. Or they would.

Or, they all would.

Impending mortality grabbed Davri's heart. Squeezed.

"None of that," Agruet said. He kissed Davri. Gentle, cautious at first.

Davri didn't want gentle.

There wasn't time for caution.

Only passion.

By the time Aral returned, Thera in tow, the party had already begun.

Byrek raised the book to his nose, inhaling the scent and calming as he did so.

It had been two days since Agruet's unexpected visit.

He knew a time like that would never come again. Still. Any moment of peace needed to be appreciated. Savored. Even in the midst of chaos, he was glad to stand in the eye of the storm and breathe it in.

Like now.

He caressed the leather cover of the book.

Sex and books were the purest pleasures, and he was lucky to have time to indulge before events came to a head.

The others were in a strategy meeting, and he just wanted to feast his eyes upon new knowledge for an hour or two.

With a self-indulgent smile, Byrek carried the book from the library and headed toward his room. He was nearly run over by a girl he vaguely recognized.

"He's gone," the girl said, nearly in a panic. "What do I do? I can't interrupt their meeting. Can you tell her, Master Arsat?"

Byrek set the book aside and held the girl by the shoulders, bending slightly to look into her eyes. "Who is gone? Who do you want me to tell?"

"It's her brother," she was nearly in tears. "Naran. He was sitting outside. I saw him. They took him, just now. Please, tell Mistress Tennival. She—"

He didn't wait to hear the rest of what the girl had to say. He didn't pause even to think. "Go in there. Interrupt the damn meeting. Tell Aral I'm going to go save him, and she needs to stay here."

It had to be Nalia.

They'd been warned that she was trying to put an end to this.

That she wanted revenge.

Holding Naran hostage for Aral's surrender would probably do it.

And maybe, if he were thinking like a god, so would taking the sacrifice so long overdue.

Byrek didn't bother with preparations.

He'd been trained by gods to hunt gods.

To spy for them.

To spy on them.

To end them, if need be.

He, alone, could stop this plot.

Aral, and the rebellion, could not afford the distraction.

Aral was furious when Mirren burst through the doors. She had just been a first-year student at the university when it had been destroyed. What business did she have, interrupting this meeting?

"What's the meaning of this?" Aral roared.

They'd taken so many steps to keep faerie spies out that Aral's first thought was they'd been compromised. The fear she felt twisted into anger immediately. She'd given orders that they not be interrupted except under dire circumstance.

"Mi-Mistress Tennival." The girl prostrated herself on the floor at Aral's feet. "Master Arsat told me to interrupt. He's gone."

"Byrek is gone?"

"Your brother." Mirren flinched. "Master Arsat went to save him. To save your brother. He was taken. Master Arsat said you must stay here."

What?

He expected her to stay here, when Naran had been snatched? After so many years of not being able to help? Of not even seeing him? Of wondering if he was still alive?

She was a heartbeat from running out the door to catch up with them, but reason prevailed.

There was nothing she could do to save Naran that Byrek couldn't do better.

Aral clenched her fists. Swallowed.

Bowed her head.

Stayed.

"Tell me everything." Aral knelt beside Mirren, lifting her shoulders. "Every detail you know."

Any mage candidate needed to possess a powerful memory to be accepted into the University Magica. Mirren lived up to that, and more. From scents to clothes to the faint hum in the air just minutes before.

"The man who grabbed Naran had an unsettling aura about him," she said at one point. "I looked into his eyes and had the feeling of being watched by someone unseen."

"A high priest," Aral said. "Go on."

She took in every detail Mirren said, steadying herself, when a sound like thunder tore through the room.

Davri was the first to react. "That was close," he said.

Mirren was shaking her head. "There's been no hint of a storm all day," she was saying as another boom echoed around them, rattling the door in its frame.

Aral could feel magic in the air, and it was building once again.

"Sound the alarms!" Deeg was wrapping himself in layers of clothes to protect himself from the sun as he shouted orders. "Get out into the fields and scatter! Spells ready! We do this now!"

At the same time Raev barreled into the room. "We need to draw them away. Bretav is in labor. This cannot be the epicenter."

Mirren looked pale, but she turned to him. "I can help. I can get her to safety."

"How?" he demanded.

"An amulet my mother gave me," she said. "It should hide us and protect us long enough to get us out of town, at least."

"Go then," he said to her. "Thank you."

"It's too soon. Isn't it?" Aral felt torn in three directions. Bretav's baby wasn't due for another month. Maybe more. They would need magic to help the baby live.

But, she needed to find Naran.

But, they'd been attacked.

Raev was nodding, looking near panic.

"Aral," Davri's voice was firm. "We don't have time for these distractions. That's all they are. You know what you need to do."

That's all it took for her to regain her sense of perspective. She turned to Thera. "We need to evacuate the town of any non-combatants who stayed after our warning yesterday. If they don't leave now, they fight. The priests are here, but the gods are not yet."

Thera nodded and rushed out the door, giving her own orders as she went.

"We'll fight them back," Aral said to all who were left. "We're ready for this."

"We just have to follow the plan," Davri agreed. "We let them fight. We save our strength for the real battle."

Aral nodded.

They just had to survive the day.

Chapter Sixteen –

Vengeance

In the burning shades of twilight it didn't look as bad.

Krecek balled his hands into fists.

A significant number of houses in Hodarian's bay were still standing. As the shadows grew, one could almost miss the rubble in the streets. One could almost ignore a slumping roof here or there where a wall had been partially knocked down.

It was almost dark enough that the scorch marks here and there simply blended into the night.

One thing could not be ignored.

The gaping crater where Raev's home and shop had been.

The collapse of the entire underground complex they'd hidden in.

Krecek trembled, seeing it again.

Remembering.

He'd barely escaped.

Davri had healed Krecek within an inch of his life just after the bombing had started. They'd scrambled toward the stairs, Krecek barely able to stand yet. He'd told Davri to just go on, he'd catch up.

The next thing he knew they were both huddled on the stairs.

The door above them was closed.

Krecek was struck dumb, wondering why the world was bright as day.

Davri had shouted something.

But for a frighteningly long time, neither could hear.

The burning twilight couldn't erase that memory.

"Your tent is ready for you."

It was jarring, being snapped out of the memory. "Thank you," he told the young man.

It was only fair. He and Keevan had blown up the temples.

The gods had simply done the same to the home of their enemies.

He was reduced to one tattered, blood stained robe, once again.

And nowhere to call home.

Again.

He followed the young man to his tent, slipped inside, belatedly realized he didn't even know the person who had showed him where to go, told him it was ready.

It didn't matter now.

A basin had been set up in one corner of the tent so he could wash. Someone had managed to find him new clothes. Plain clothes, not mage robes, but it would do.

As soon as Krecek and Davri had emerged from the rubble, they'd been surrounded by battle. Krecek was all but useless, weak as a newborn, and with no magic. Davri had stayed by his side, protecting him as well as fighting.

The rebellion had pushed back the priests over the course of the day. It was hard earned, considering the sneak attack, but they'd managed it.

The illusions and trickery from both sides had been spectacularly devastating in some cases. The battle in Anogrin had been more of a riot by disorganized rabble.

This...this was all out war. Everyone was a combatant.

Everyone but Krecek.

The dwarves had been digging pitfalls and tunnels into the landscape for weeks. The advantage quickly turned to those who knew the terrain and had trained there.

Right now, there were pits of broken bodies, filled with those who, as Krecek once had, believed in and followed the gods.

He couldn't help but think he'd escaped that fate by sheer luck.

All Krecek wanted was to sleep now. He'd survived. Davri had kept him alive.

Couldn't that be all that mattered this day?

The crackle of the campfire outside his tent was soothing.

He just wanted to forget all he'd seen that day.

Instead…

"Are you finished in there?"

It was Aral.

Despite himself, his heart skipped a beat.

"Come in," he said, opening the tent flap for her.

"It's a chilly night," she said as she walked in, rubbing her arms for effect. "I washed as quickly as I could. That water was so cold."

She wore a dress. The fit was loose, hanging on her like a child playing dress up. The skirt was short, coming to mid-calf, and the sleeves ended just past her elbow. Neither in a way that looked like deliberate fashion choices.

They'd given her clothes from a short, fat woman. But they were clean.

And, despite the poor fit, she was regal. Commanding.

Beautiful.

"They managed to make up a soft bed," he said with a gesture. "I could keep you warm."

Stilted. Awkward. Stupid.

With a line like that to woo girls, it was a wonder he didn't have to beat them off with a stick.

Aral stood still. The tent was dark now, and he couldn't see her expression.

His imagination filled in a few possibilities, of course. None of them flattering.

Finally, finally, she nodded. She took his hand, and they sat beside each other.

It wasn't much of a bed, to be honest. A bit of padding. Thick blankets that barely smelled of smoke.

His hands stalled a moment as he reached for her.

This was impossible.

Within his mind played every instance of rejection she'd dealt him, large or small. He couldn't force himself to move.

She circled her arms around him and leaned in close. "Forgive me," Aral whispered in his ear.

Krecek closed his eyes. He took a deep breath and held her close against him, breathing in the scent of her.

She felt exactly how he had always thought she would. Soft and strong and warm. She melted against him, laying down and pulling him down with her. Beside her at first, bodies barely touching along the length of them. She rolled so that she was on top of him, a breath away from the kiss he'd longed for all these years. It was a dream come true for him, even if the situation was nightmarish.

"It will all be over soon," he whispered in return.

"Don't think like that." She propped herself up and looked him in the eyes. He felt that unnerving sensation of her being doubled, or of being watched, that he'd felt before. "Think of how you love me. How you want me. How I mean more to you than anyone else. It's true, isn't it?"

"It is," he said as he ran his fingers through her silken hair. He kissed her neck, let his hands wander over her body.

She kissed him, and it was...painful.

No, he shoved that thought aside, thinking only of how much he'd wanted this moment.

The curves of her body beneath her dress. Small breasts, flat stomach. Flared hips. Aral was beautiful. He thought only of that. Only of his desire. Of the love he'd had for her that survived the years. His love hadn't just survived the eclipse of Nalia's attentions, but in the end surpassed it.

She disengaged from the kiss and let out a breathy moan.

"Here," she said, grabbing his hand. She guided his fingers to the juncture of her legs.

So warm.

So soft.

It was enough to make him hope that this wouldn't work.

That he could just keep going, never stop—

Aral yelped in sudden pain.

"That is more than enough of that!" Nalia appeared, standing over them both. She yanked Aral away by the hair. "I've shared enough with you."

Aral tried to fight loose, but Nalia pulled tighter, lifting Aral to her toes.

Nalia then turned her attention to Krecek. "You're doing this just to hurt me! I can hear it in your thoughts! Why?"

Krecek got to his feet. "Why?" He stared at her, defiant, daring her to hurt him more. "After what you did to me, you can ask me why? You almost killed me!"

Nalia tossed Aral aside and stepped right up to Krecek. "I didn't kill you because I'm merciful. Don't test the limits of my mercy. I can hurt you even more once you're dead."

"I lived because Baedrogan spared me," Krecek said coldly.

Aral rose to her feet behind Nalia. "Baedrogan would stop you." She was glowing with power. "He'd never allow you to keep hurting any of us, or anyone, after death. I know your sons better than you do, and I've only known them a scant handful of years. Don't you know why he brought death? To make sure that everything, especially suffering, would have an end."

"I'm more powerful than my sons. I—" Nalia paused, leaning toward Aral to look at her closer. "Oh. I see what you've done. You slut. Did you sleep with them both?" She paused a moment, then sneered. "No, just the weak one, Agruet. Oh, I can't wait until I see him again. He will suffer for—"

"You're calling me a slut?" Aral gaped. Her expression was a mixture of surprise and indignation. "Should I start with a list from the annals of mythology? Or stick to more recent events?"

Nalia looked mildly amused. "You want to keep playing games with me? Exchange a few insults? See who can hurt who the most?"

An image of Naran, tied, chained, and gagged, appeared in the air before them.

He was crying.

Alone.

Unharmed, so far.

Krecek relaxed.

"We can play games," Nalia said. "For every insult you throw in my direction, your brother gets whipped. How many is that so far?"

"He's still alive," Aral breathed the words. "We can still save him."

"You'll never get him back," Nalia said. With a wave of her hand the image was gone.

There was a flash of light and a rush of sound an instant later.

Aral turned to Krecek. "I want to go get him."

"No," he said. "We have to trust Byrek. We'll be down by two of our best mages if you leave now."

"YOU'LL NEVER SEE HIM AGAIN!" Nalia shrieked. "I—" The goddess stopped. Confused.

"We're done with you." Aral said, expression emotionless.

Krecek shook his head, turned, and held open the tent flap. "What took you so long? She could have killed us at any point. You know that, right?"

"Relax," Davri said as he walked in. "Byrek sends love, kisses, and I just told him exactly where Naran is. I set up a trace. Why have a bargaining chip, if you're not going to bargain? I was just waiting for her to tip her hand."

Nalia struggled against unseen bonds. "What did you do?" She held her arms outstretched and pushed, to no avail. "What are you doing to me?"

"The same thing we're going to do to the rest of the gods, once they arrive to rescue you. If you can gather them all here, they might be able to save you." Aral grinned wickedly. "Or, they might fall into our trap and die like you will."

"Gods can't die!" She pounded her fists against empty air. Each thrust was slower, weaker than the last.

"According to Baedrogan, you can. I'll take his word over yours."

"I tried to warn you," Krecek walked over to Nalia.

The barrier only stopped her. Not anyone else.

He touched her cheek, looked into her eyes.

This was it. The last time he would see her.

"I tried to stop this," he said with the last of his goodwill toward her. "You wouldn't listen to a mere mortal like me. You were too convinced of your superiority to entertain the possibility that there could be forces beyond your ability to stop."

"Free me, Krecek." Nalia lowered herself to her knees before him, looking up at him with wide, frightened eyes. In her own twisted way, there was love for him there. Too late. "I'll return your power. I'll give you everything. I'll make that girl your slave." She bent lower and pressed her forehead to his feet. "I'll give her to you as a present, wrapped up in a bow. Just love me again. Free me. Don't let me die."

Krecek took a deep breath.

She could do it.

Would do it.

He knew she would.

He forced himself to take a step back.

"Without my power, I can't free you. With my power, I would kill you myself."

He walked out of the tent, covering his ears to block out

whatever else she might say.

Her words followed him across the length of the camp, but he never looked back.

He just sat and waited for the other gods to arrive.

For Nalia to finally die.

"It was fated, you know," Davri said once he was alone in the tent with Nalia. "Hello, grandmother. We finally meet."

"Mortal." Nalia sat back on her heels. Sneered. "How dare you address me as such?"

All hint of vulnerability had left as soon as Krecek was removed from her view. Now, she was a caged animal.

Davri tilted his head to the side, thinking as he watched her. Nalia was a pitiable figure. She still thought she would survive this. Would get her revenge.

"My great-great-grandmother was Agruet's child," he told her, voice calm and even. And, well, why wouldn't it be? She'd be long dead before she could win her way free. He was using her own power against her to fortify this trap. "The rest of my family may have lived in awe or terror, but I never have. I've seen the future, and you're not in it. The world will go on without you."

"I created this world." Nalia frowned. "I had a hand in creating all life upon it. I shape everything touched by magic. There is no world without me in it."

"It's not something to take pride in." Davri took a step closer. "You created suffering. You created greed and injustice. You created people who see those things and know they are evil and wrong. We will fight against that."

Nalia stopped moving. Stopped struggling. "You fight against yourselves. When I get free, I will destroy you for your hubris. You think we did this to mortals? Mortals did this to us. You will have a tighter leash when this is over."

"Threats and posturing!" Davri threw his head back and laughed. "Do you even know what monsters you are? You have instilled in us a knowledge of right and wrong. You have given us the ability to learn and to think and to grow. I have learned that what you do and what you encourage are wrong. I think the world would be better without you and your ilk ruling it. We have grown beyond the need of you, and we will grow greater without you."

She put a burst of energy into one last attempt at freedom.

Davri was ready, absorbed it all, and threw it back.

"The age of gods is at an end."

Nalia began to tremble in fear, for the first time in her existence.

She wouldn't win her freedom in time to stop death.

She, who had created death.

She looked at Davri helplessly.

She knew what he was going to do.

She knew she was powerless to stop it.

Davri looked into Nalia's eyes, and she looked into his.

"Scream for me," he whispered.

She did.

Naran rubbed at his wrists, staring at Byrek in shock. "I thought I was dead," he whispered.

"The night is young," Byrek said, slipping his knife into its sheath.

Frighteningly ominous. Just what he needed right now.

Naran's fingers were itching with returning circulation. He winced, rubbing them together, shaking them, and his feet joined in.

Byrek uttered a hasty spell, touched Naran on the forehead. "We need to get away from here as quickly as possible."

"Back to Raev's house," Naran nodded. The pins and needles feeling faded quickly, thanks to Byrek's spell.

Byrek was looking him over, brow furrowed. "We can't go back," he said finally. "Where are your shoes?"

He was dressed only in a rust-red robe that left his chest and back bared. He'd been tied by his wrists and ankles for hours. Threatened. Beaten, though not severely. The goddess of magic had stopped her minions, telling them Naran was hers, not theirs.

No.

Now was not time to have an emotional meltdown, no matter how badly Naran felt the need. "I don't know," he said. "They took everything. I couldn't move, so I don't know where they put any of it." He tried to keep the fear out of his voice. He really did. "What do you mean we can't go back?"

"It's not safe."

Naran waited for more, but Byrek didn't say a word. He was looking around the tent Naran had been left in.

There was nothing.

The elf scowled and sliced some canvas from the side of the tent with his knife. He tied the canvas to Naran's feet.

"They were going to kill me," Naran said.

"I know," Byrek whispered softly. "Hush now. We need to sneak out and find safety."

"I won't say a word," Naran whispered. "I've done this before."

Byrek paused. Smiled. "So you have."

He cast his spell and they left. Within minutes he had brought them to an enchanted path.

Naran hesitated, looking at Byrek in alarm. Davri had told him, so many times, what the paths were like. The mysterious pops and bangs in the distance that could kill. The lifeless, dusty smell of it all. The shadow monsters that lurked within the stark boxy buildings that turned the landscape into a lifeless maze. When he'd been curious, Davri had warned him never to seek out such places. The shadows there wouldn't just eat you alive. They'd devour your soul.

Byrek paused. Looked at Naran questioningly.

Sighed heavily.

"We have no choice," Byrek answered the unspoken concerns. "The enchanted path will be safer than the real world tonight."

That wasn't at all reassuring, but Naran had no choice. He followed Byrek.

Krecek could feel it when Nalia died.

The night had been filled again with the sounds of war. Fighting and screams of terror, gurgles and gasps, moans and curses saturated the chill air with their cacophony. The gods had descended upon them to free Nalia.

They had failed.

He felt freed, and bereft. He'd loved her as much as he hated her. There were tears on his face as his own magic was released and flowed through him again.

Giddiness replaced his grief. A net had been erected to hold the gods within. He extended his will to add his power to the magic, and it felt glorious.

Without his magic, he'd stayed at the edges. He'd felt vulnerable, small, and weak.

With his magic returned, he felt invincible.

He looked into the eyes of the gods fighting around him. He saw the shock and alarm as they tried to process what had happened.

"That's impossible!"

The words were music to Krecek's ears.

The Arcane War

"Find her!" Fotar, the god of fire. was looking around. He was frantic, not five paces from where Krecek stood.

A distance swiftly crossed.

Krecek grabbed the god and threw him to the ground. "She's dead. There's nothing left to find."

"We're gods!" Fotar protested, summoning flame around them.

It was a mere show of force and intimidation.

That wouldn't be enough.

Krecek didn't flinch.

Didn't hesitate.

Davri had taught him the spell already.

The words came to him as if he had practiced them for a century. He wove his magic into the spell as if it was what he'd been born to do.

The god's death was swift.

The spell was done in three parts.

The first, to trap the god in physical form.

The second, to kill that form.

All the power remained within Fotar's body. It would heal him over time if left at this point.

Not a true death.

Not yet.

The last step of the spell was the most imperative.

Krecek used further magic as a blade to slice open the body before him.

It brought him back to the night he had killed Porrellid. The warmth of his life slowly cooled. The thick blood slickened his fingers.

This was like that. The difference was the heat. It was intense and did not fade as Krecek plunged his hands into the open chest to pull out the heart.

Before he could think about what he was doing he began to

devour the heart.

Don't think about the taste.

Don't think about how it burned.

Don't think, just do.

As the power began to course through him he cracked open the skull.

The brain had to follow the heart.

He was a feral animal, doing what he must to survive.

Around him the fighting continued.

He paid it no mind.

The world changed around him.

No.

His awareness of the world changed in myriad, indescribable ways.

He was only the second. He could feel it.

Davri, then him, and around him he could feel the fighting going on as his awareness expanded.

He didn't—couldn't—follow everything. There was too much. But the things that mattered glowed like embers within his mind. If he focused, he knew what they were.

It was greater than any magic he had ever known before. He felt it when Aral succeeded in killing Bogradan, the god of wind.

It wasn't over yet.

It was a start, but not enough to win.

He had to fight.

He had to help.

He opened his eyes and caught sight of Raev.

No one had taught the spell to Raev. He was a merchant, not a mage, despite his talent with magic.

With a surge of his newfound power, Krecek was at Raev's side, and he talked Raev through the spell so that the larger man would be able to help them. It was a spur of the moment decision, but in a flash of knowledge he knew it had to be done.

The Arcane War

They were about to need all the help they could get.
Because, if a god could be killed, so could a wizard.

Davri sat within the tent, alone. Blood seeped through his clothes to stain his skin. Visions flooded his mind and magic coursed through the entirety of his being.

He was aware of the fight going on outside.

He was aware of the armies of angels, of demons, of priests and their allies stirring again to action.

He was aware of those rebels who followed orders and ran.

He was aware of those who stayed and chose to give their lives to give the mages more time.

There was a temptation to intervene.

To save them all and fight.

Instead, he sat within the tent, alone.

It was Aral who brought calm to the chaos. She looked around at everything that happened. She encouraged, she guided, and she used her newfound power to diminish the influence of the gods and their minions. It was subtle at first, but with every god that fell she felt her influence grow.

She had one thing in mind. One driving goal that had to be met.

Aral had to see Garatara die for what he had begun.

For what he had done to her and her family.

When she did come upon him, she didn't realize it at first. The humble man before her didn't seem at all godlike.

He knelt, bandaging the wounded. Like any other healer, he said prayers and gave blessings. It didn't matter which side someone fought for, he saw to the injured.

It was only when Aral saw Garatara's eyes that she knew him for what he was.

"You are hurt," he said, reaching out to her. "Let me help you."

Daichen hesitated.

He'd watched gods and mages fall around him in horror.

The gods were torn apart in the bloodbath necessary for the spell's conclusion.

The mages were cast aside like bits of trash.

Somehow, the corpses of the gods outnumbered those of the mages.

Mages that Daichen knew. Studied with.

Fought beside when Anogrin fell.

Three of them lay the foot of the same god.

Baedrogan.

The god of death was practically roaring at those who came near. "I shall be last!"

Daichen watched, wary.

Tried not to look at the faces of the fallen.

Failed.

Donab Gratu, the youngest of them at just nineteen.

Agrad Merok, who had been Daichen's roommate their first year.

Shaia Taden. Her sweet face now bereft of what had once been an ever-present smile.

Something within Daichen shifted. His friends were dead. He knew there was something, an important thing he'd been told, but it slipped away. It was as if some outside force pushed him in the direction of his revenge.

The only thought on his mind was that this god, this creature, must pay.

And Daichen knew how to do it.

His heart was pounding with anticipation and fear as he took a slow step forward.

He clenched his fists.

Stilled his mind to begin the spell.

That's when it struck him. There'd been a plan.

What was it?

"I thought you were on our side," Daichen shouted. Pleaded.

Something didn't make sense.

Hadn't that been the crux of the plan? That two gods were on their side?

Hadn't Baedrogan been one of those gods?

Obviously, he'd been mistaken.

Daichen's resolve solidified. He couldn't hesitate.

He couldn't become the fourth body at death's feet.

They stared into each other's eyes. Mortal enemies.

Only one could survive.

"I am on my own side," growled Baedrogan. "And I will be last."

Chapter Seventeen –

THE ARCANE WAR

Deeg stared at the gloves on his hands.
The moisture seeped in, staining his hands red.
There was no light. His hands were covered. But he was aware of the color of the blood on his skin as he'd never been before.
The gods had blood.
And he was drenched in it.
"What have we done?" he whispered in horror. "I'm not a mage."
"Yet now you are a wizard," Raev said beside the dwarf. He had to bend over to pat Deeg on the shoulder. "I could not let her kill you."
Deeg nodded.
Raev's intentions were commendable.
But he was wrong.
Ceraan had been the mother of memories. The keeper of history.
She wouldn't have killed Deeg, or anyone here.
"Do not think of who she was," Raev said sharply. "Only what she was. A god. The enemy. They all must die."
Kill or be killed.
It's what this had been reduced to.
It was grim work, but they'd been given no choice.

Sweat rolled down Davri's cheek despite the cold air.
He hadn't moved since Nalia's death.

A death he now felt as if it had been his own.

Nalia had almost won free of her wizardly prison, despite the spells.

Hadn't Agruet once said, she flinched away from what he had seen within the void?

Davri had but to think of it and it appeared around him.

The void embraced his mind and unfolded the visions no other wizard was prepared to face. Everything Agruet had known assaulted his senses.

This...this madness...was the only thing that might keep her in check.

The void was pure chaos. Davri watched it, and it watched back. It waited, acting, about to act, but it could not touch him.

Could not affect him.

Within the void, Davri was a sole constant, and that sent ripples through it.

Visions from the swirling chaos accosted him.

He saw centuries of death and destruction that would be his legacy.

A child with hair of dark curls like the blackest of night.

Wide brown eyes that hummed with power.

Sweet innocence that would end it all.

Would end the world.

It was Davri's doing.

Davri's failing.

Davri's fault.

Davri's soul was this boy's soul.

The chaos around him grew bolder and clutched at his feet.

"I don't know this boy," he said. "He is a figment of the future."

More visions assaulted him.

Death.

So much death.

Undead horrors that had never before been called forth on this world.

Skeletal children with their skeletal parents reaching up through the ground, seeking more company in their ranks, filling the world with their empty stares and empty graves.

"I won't have it. I will not let this come to pass."

The visions did not stop.

In them, magic grew stronger, but so did the ingenuity of mere men.

War was declared on the secrets of the elves, the dwarves, the merfolk.

Humans with their plethora of children demanded more and more land, even reaching their towers to the sky, until they choked the very world of all its resources, and it was the wizards who allowed this to happen.

Without sacrifices to the gods, nothing could contain this plague upon the world.

It would die.

Humanity would be its end.

"There are other ways," Davri said, determined to see it through. Somehow.

Every choice he made he saw the world ending in fire, starvation, plague, disease.

Every shift of his thoughts only changed the when or the how, but never the what.

"There's a way! I know that there is one!"

Chaos stood before him, and she grinned a sadistic grin.

She was the reason he would fail.

"You will fall. You will die. Nothing will stop me."

"Don't touch him!"

The air crackled around the god who had run to Garatara's

side. Lightning danced across his skin, and the very atmosphere around him was heavy and oppressive.

Garatara looked at the other god in surprise, shaking his head.

"I'll see you both dead," Aral growled, advancing.

"Kedaran, no," Garatara said. He reached out to Aral, palms open, empty. "She needs help. I've hurt her somehow. I must fix this. I must heal—"

"Shut up!"

Kedaran deflected the blast Aral sent their way.

Staggered.

Shook his head.

That had hurt. Had actually hurt!

This stranger, this unknown, had inflicted actual pain!

This Aral Tennival was supposed to be a mortal. Not this.

Kedaran frowned. Shielded Garatara with his own body and will.

"You will not hurt him." Kedaran advanced upon her, despite the risk.

Two more gods appeared beside them, flanking the god of healing.

Thar and Brinn, the gods of war.

Their presence permeated the entire battle field. They gained strength from the fight.

Kedaran grinned. These two would turn the tide.

"He started this all!" Aral screamed, pointing an accusing finger at Garatara. "Every bit of this is HIS fault, for demanding the life of my brother!"

Garatara looked up at her, shocked. "I did?"

Aral attacked.

Davri blinked and the chaos was gone.

Fire still glowed from the other side of the tent walls. That was the first thing he noticed. He heard the fighting going on. The acrid scent of blood assaulted him next, followed by the stomach-churning flavor of it coating his mouth. Underlying it all was the oppressive weight of magic in the air, gathering to a bursting point.

Nalia's mangled body lay in a useless heap before him. He stared at it, almost disbelieving that he'd done such a thing. He knelt beside her, covering her with the heavy blanket still resting on the bed.

Someday, this would be him. Impossibly powerful, but subject to death.

The weight of what he'd done pressed upon his shoulders, stilling his breath.

He, Davri, had done this. He had killed the goddess, the guardian, of magic.

The world would never be the same, and his hands had wrought this change.

He would pay for this. Would suffer for this. There was a gaping hole in the fabric of reality that he now had to fill.

"I had no idea." The words were a rough whisper.

Nothing can make up for what you have done.

Davri bowed his head, accepting harsh reality of those words.

"Davri?"

Krecek was panting, covered in gore and sweat, green eyes glowing with power, skin flushed from exertion. He stopped in the doorway staring a moment while Davri rose to his feet. As soon as Krecek caught his breath he took two steps closer.

"Why are you still here? What--?" Krecek broke off, question forgotten as they both felt something new building around them.

None of the other newly created wizards would understand.

Disaster was upon them.

"Thar and Brinn," Davri muttered, jumping to his feet.

The Arcane War

They knew it would be too late, but they both ran anyway.

Sharp pain lanced through Raev's soul. He knew why. He knew what was happening.

He didn't know how to stop it.

Gods could teleport. It had to be possible.

There had to be a way for him to appear at Bretav's side.

To take away her pain.

For a moment Raev tried to appear at Bretav's side through sheer force of will.

Nothing happened. Whatever secret it took to reappear somewhere else, he did not know it.

So be it.

Instead, he would run. With a singular focus he pushed his way through the battlefield, past god, wizard, and soldier alike. Nothing mattered but her.

Nothing.

Until he reached a dead zone in the killing field.

Five figures faced off in the center of it.

Everything around them had died.

He recognized Aral right away.

She stood alone, facing off four gods.

Aral ran at them, screaming in rage, attacking them both physically and magically.

Bretav would be safe with the midwife, he told himself. Bretav would live. Arlanz's child would live.

Babes came into the world every day.

Early wasn't safe, but with magic they could live.

There was no one to pray to, to make it so.

But, between the danger he could not reach, and the danger he could now avert, he knew which he had to address first.

Baedrogan held off the young mage.

This one would do.

But not yet.

Damn it all, but not yet!

"Why are you even here?" the young mage demanded. He was circling, readying another attack, and Baedrogan's will was divided. His attention was stretched thin, even for a god.

There were more souls. So many more souls.

Faster than ever before, he took them. Placed them. Assured they were where they belonged.

He'd known coming in that some would be missed.

This mortal mage, Daichen Ronar, inched closer, increasing his threat.

"I owe you nothing," Baedrogan growled.

The words did not deter Daichen. He circled, avoiding the bodies at Baedrogan's feet, spell upon his lips and etched into his will and intent.

Baedrogan felt, once again, a burning rage that they'd been forced to this plan.

This plan, that was falling apart around them even as he fought.

There weren't enough mages.

There wasn't enough time.

Damn you, Yda. You're going to doom us all.

Laughter.

Other mages were stepping up. Helping teach the spell to others. Saving friends in desperation.

It could have been enough.

Should have been.

But there was no one to take Thar and Brinn. No one to take

Garatara and Kedaran.
One more soul.
He had to guide people over.
No one came.
"Brother!"
One more soul.
Agruet?
No. Not yet.
Baedrogan took a step toward Agruet, eyes wide in alarm.
Watched his brother being trapped by Garm Cerine.
Turned mortal.
Killed.
His twin, dead before his eyes.
No.
"No."
His own power coalesced around him, pulled in like a magnetic force, drawn in to one spot of reality. His will tied him into a mortal form.

Baedrogan turned, tears in his eyes, and stared at his murderer.

Stared helpless as Daichen destroyed the plan.

Thar and Brinn looked upon Aral with contempt. "Do you think you can win? Against us?"

"I know how to kill a god," Aral said.

She couldn't use the spell, though. There was no one to take the power into themselves.

Everyone around them had been slain.

Aral slashed through the air with her hands, using magic and wind to slice at her opponents. It came so easy to her that she gave it no thought. This made the gods flinch in pain and back away.

That was enough. Eventually someone would come and Aral would help kill them all.

Kedaran deflected the attack, but he was weakening. The god of storms had seemed immune to the attack at first, but Aral had been relentless, and Kedaran wasn't just protecting himself.

Aral pressed the attack, hands held before her like a spear, and ran at them.

Kedaran grabbed Garatara and dove out of Aral's way, but the other two held firm.

"We are not just a god," Thar and Brinn said simultaneously. "We are gods. You are just one wizard."

"Not anymore," Raev joined the fray, rushing them, planting his feet solidly and drawing his strength from the ground to hit Brinn solidly in the ribs.

Brinn bent double.

Froze.

Straightened.

Laughed.

"Yes, come at me, and feed us, wizard. Hit us again!"

Aral and Raev froze in their tracks, exchanging a horrified look.

The gods of war did not hesitate.

Brinn straightened and knocked Raev to the ground with one blow. He skidded across the ground until he hit a corpse, two, three, before he slowed to a stop.

Thar turned to Aral and charged her. She caught Aral by the wrist and flipped her to the ground with one fluid motion

"We would love to stay," the gods of war again spoke as one, "but we are through with this party. We grow tired of your hospitality. And we have no intention of dying."

Thar and Brinn grabbed Garatara and Kedaran.

Light.

The Arcane War

Sound.
Fire.
Death.
On the field of battle, no mortal survived.
The containment spell was obliterated.

Byrek had been down the enchanted paths at night before, but never while trying to protect someone.

It was harrowing, but they didn't go too far. They holed up in a small room together on the second floor of one of the dark structures. It was a windowless room with only one entrance.

He flooded the room with light to keep the shadows at bay.

There were loud, echoing pops in the background, but Byrek had never worried about those. Agruet had once told Byrek what they were, when the paths were newer, and the world was so much younger. He'd called it gun fire, from a weapon that humans would create some day. The problem with folding time and space to make travel quicker was time bleed in all directions. Here, the future was now.

He avoided every aspect of the future, of the time bleed, that he could.

When Agruet had taught Byrek these things, he'd been so young.

Young and in love with a god who loved him in turn.

He'd felt invincible.

Indestructible.

Immortal.

Byrek closed his eyes, feeling a tight squeeze around his heart.

Immortality meant nothing now.

Outside their room the distant pops and bangs were only one of many noises in the night. Incoherent whispers drifted upon the air, walking past their door. There were occasional inhuman moans that seemed to come from everywhere at once. Skittering sounds that were best left ignored.

And then, silence.

Byrek went still, eyes wide. The urge to hold his breath was both superstitious and overwhelming. It would do no good, but...

He put a hand on Naran's shoulder.

Something was missing. Something vital.

Unshed tears made his eyes itch.

But what, who, was missing?

His thoughts again turned to Agruet.

They'd long since stopped being in that hazy infatuation of being in love, had long since found other lovers, but they kept circling back to each other as the centuries wore on. There was love there. There'd always been love there.

He closed his eyes, willing away the tears he could not explain to Naran. The hollow ache in Byrek's chest would still be there when the boy fell asleep.

After all, it might not be Agruet.

Still, someone he loved had died that night.

That's when his thoughts turned to Davri.

They played a dangerous game this night. It was heartbreakingly probable that his human love would die.

Such a short life, with so much talent, so much promise.

So much passion, compassion, and —

An anguished wail filled the halls with sound.

It felt for a moment as if it had echoed the pain within Byrek's own soul, so heartbroken was the sound.

A shiver ran down his spine. and he checked and doublechecked his own will and his own magic to make sure he had not caused it.

No.

Something else, someone else, mourned as he did.

Soon the voice was not alone. A great cacophony filled the air, echoing around them.

Screams of agony.

Cries of disbelief.

Mourning.

Insanity.

Damn it all. Byrek realized where these voices came from. Some of the gods had escaped.

"Fucking damn it all!"

Naran's head whipped around to stare at Byrek in silent shock.

"You can speak," Byrek said. "The gods and the shadows are too distracted to hunt us now."

"Gods?" Naran's voice was hoarse. "We've lost?"

"Only partly." Byrek frowned. "Something went wrong, but…"

How much had gone wrong? Had he fooled himself? Had he let his worries trick him into believing that Agruet was dead?

"Agruet? Please. If you are alive, come to me. Let me know."

Naran placed a hand on Byrek's arm. "He helped us, didn't he?"

Byrek nodded, holding his breath, afraid and hopeful.

"Agruet?"

The god didn't answer.

There was one way to know for sure. It wasn't safe while trying to hide.

But, like he'd told Naran, the gods and the shadows were distracted.

He hesitated. If he was wrong, and Agruet busy, the god wouldn't be pleased. It was an intrusive spell that would temporarily link their minds. An ultimate show of trust between elvin lovers, used so rarely that to some of their young it was a myth. He'd done it with Agruet once before —

Nothing.

There was nothing.

"He's dead," Byrek finally breathed the words. "That doesn't mean we lost, but it doesn't mean we won. Someone mourns out there, but there's no telling who."

"We'll go back in the morning," Naran said. "We'll find out. I don't want to run anymore."

The young man looked ready to face his own death.

Byrek understood that emotion too well.

"Have hope, Naran."

It was hard to do as the night wore on and the mourning of immortals raged around them, but dawn would tell. Dawn would answer all.

Chapter Eighteen –

ENDS AND BEGINNINGS

Aral laughed into the wind. Being a wizard was amazing! She and Thera had spent half the night giggling at stray thoughts they'd sent in each other's direction. The effortlessness of it was exhilarating. They'd spent an hour, giddy, dancing around a bonfire naked. The rest weren't doing much better. The absolute power was so heady! They were invincible!

They were alive.

They were going to rule the world.

"We can do anything we want to," Aral said, looking up at the dawn sky with a dreamy smile. There were all these colors she'd never seen before, and she could still see the stars. So many stars hiding above the all the air between her and the edge of the atmosphere. "Anything. We'll make the world a paradise."

Deeg cleared his throat. It had to be to get her attention, because why else would he make such a sound now that he had the power of a god? It made Aral giggle again.

"I hate to bring you back to reality," he said gruffly, "but time is marching on. Look around you."

"I am!" she said expansively, arms outspread to take in the beauty of the dawn.

Deeg's hands gestured lower.

To the carnage around them.

To say the sight was unpleasant was gross in its understatement. Aral sobered at the reminder the light had brought. They'd been in giddy celebration on a field of slaughter.

"We can do anything," Thera echoed Aral's sentiment from moments ago. "We can make this all go away. Wave our hands and fix it all, except the gods. We'll bring our friends back—"

"NO!" Deeg cut her off. "Make monstrosities of your own people if you'd like, but if you turn one dwarf into a puppet of your desire, I'll find out what it takes to kill a wizard as well as a god."

"We're not reanimating the dead," Aral said firmly. "Any dead. Even gods could never get that one right, and without Baedrogan in the world, well, that's a line we shouldn't cross."

"I couldn't agree more." Daichen joined them, pushing his glasses up on his nose. "We need to agree to some rules, or we'll become exactly what we were fighting against."

"First, we should honor the dead." Deeg seemed to be of one mind on that. "My...my son died yesterday in this fight. I was no mage. I came to fight the gods as a way to honorably die. Raev..." He was scowling, but he shook his head and his countenance gentled. "He saved my life. Without that, I'd be among the dead here. I want to see them treated with the honor I'd hope you'd have given me."

The gathered wizards nodded.

"Spread the word," Aral said. "We'll do this by hand. No magic, not yet. We should do this and remember why we were fighting to begin with." She then turned to Deeg, smiled gently, and put a hand on his shoulder. "But look. The sun shines on you, and Deyson is among the dead," she said. "You and your people can move freely again."

He nodded with tears in his eyes, holding his hands out to the light and basking in it. "I'd noticed." His voice was rough. "My son may never see the light of day, but his children will. It is enough."

"We won," she said. "We have countless reasons to mourn, but we won. Don't be defeated. Your son wouldn't have wanted that."

They worked side by side, they collected the dead, they

collected stones to create cairns suitable for them to honor all the fallen. It was not a simple task for a single day. But it brought peace to the survivors.

Raev nearly collapsed as he found where Mirren had spirited the trio away to. It was a seaside cave that faced the bay and overlooked what was left of the town.

The town that had been obliterated when the remaining gods had blasted their way to freedom.

Mirren lay at the mouth of the cave. Blood had flowed from her ears, her mouth, her nose, and her eyes, while she'd still been alive. Raev realized she must have been warding them against discovery or intrusion when the magical explosion had reached the cave. If she'd channeled the spell, the backlash would have liquified her brain.

Had liquified her brain, he decided as he knelt beside her. He closed her eyes and used a whisper of his new magic to keep them closed.

Bretav was dead as well, but he'd expected as much. He'd felt her slipping from the world in a cry of agony and regret. She was finally the mother of a child who lived, as she lay there dying.

Further back into the cave, around a bend, he heard a soft sigh. The midwife was asleep, sitting propped against the cave wall, with the infant in her arms. The woman had taken a beating from the magical explosion, but she was alive.

So was the child.

Raev knelt beside them and the woman opened her eyes, blinking a few times.

"Master Madri," she said, voice rough from sleep. She smiled at him, though it was a pain-filled smile. "You have a niece. Or…a daughter. However you prefer."

The Arcane War

Raev nodded, staring at the infant in wonder. Legally, she was his own. Bound by blood and by law.

"What is her name?"

The midwife shook her head. "You will have to tell me that, I'm afraid. It all happened so fast…"

"Can I name her Mirren? For the girl who protected you?"

The midwife nodded, tears springing to her eyes, lips clenched a moment. "That would be a wonderful name. I'm sure the girl would be honored." She wiped tears from her eyes as she settled little Mirren in Raev's arms.

Mirren was almost impossibly tiny, Raev thought. Hardly bigger than his own hand.

"I will protect you," he whispered softly as he stared at her sleeping face. "I will keep you from all harm. I will see you healthy and happy, so long as I live." Mirren seemed to glow as he said the words. A trick of dawn's light reaching into the cave, he thought.

Or was it?

He had stolen the power of a god. Why couldn't he do exactly what he said?

"And beyond my death, if it comes, if I can. Mirren Madri, the embodiment of my hope. You will live for a very long time."

"Did we win?"

It wasn't as simple as winning and losing, Davri thought. He looked at Naran. Looked around the tiny room that he and Byrek had hidden in. To his new, heightened senses it smelled like ashes and death. There were echoes of terror etched into the walls. The two of them had huddled in that emotional miasma all night.

Had they won?

"Yes," he said. "You're safe now."

Byrek didn't say a word. He stood and he gave Davri a tight hug.

What could Davri say? He held Byrek close, understanding all that the hug said.

The fear.

The grief.

The sheer relief of seeing each other again.

Davri felt it all as if it were his own. They had a lot to talk about, once they had delivered Naran to the others.

Once they were alone.

"We should go," Davri said reluctantly. "An enchanted path is no place for a reunion."

"Where's Aral?" Naran asked.

"Busy," Davri smiled. "She's fine. She's alive. I told you that we won, didn't I?"

He realized he was on the verge of talking down to the boy…the young man. Naran had been only nine when they had met and had escaped death together. Now he was a very mature fourteen, having grown up quickly, learning to face hardship and loss with resigned stoicism. It wasn't fair to give him simple answers when the truth was so complex.

But, Naran just nodded and gestured toward the door. "After you," he said. "I'm not stepping foot out that door alone."

Of course. The night would have been full of horrors.

Then again... Davri took in the robe Naran still wore. Designed for sacrifice, from the low chest and back, to the blood-red color. That must have been a much greater horror than anything that lurked here.

They left together, Byrek jumping at shadows and echoes of their own footsteps. Naran was little better, flinching every time they turned a corner, walking as if he expected an attack any moment.

"Relax," Davri said, trying to soothe them both. "You're safe with me."

"You don't understand," Byrek said. "The things we heard—"

"I know what you heard," Davri said sharply. It was his fault they'd heard all of it. His fault that some of their prey had escaped. "I know," he said again, forcing his voice into a calm and soothing tone. "But you're safe with me."

"Will we still be safe if we run?" Naran asked.

Davri grinned. "Run? I can keep you safe if you scream or laugh or sing! Running is nothing."

"I'd like to run," Naran was starting to smile. "I want to get home and let Aral know I'm safe."

"Okay then, let's run."

Acknowledgments

I hadn't planned on writing this book to begin with. Elemental was supposed to be a complete story, all self-contained and one volume, when I'd had the idea. No fuss, no muss, no long and drawn out series of novels to play around with. When I'd reached the events of Part Eleven in Elemental, where Krecek is telling Agrad about the events of the past, one image began haunting me and would not let me rest. The image of Aral, begging for Naran's life, and being betrayed by those she'd turned to.

I still wasn't going to put that into a book of its own. Perhaps a short story, but it didn't need to be an entire book.

So, first I need to thank National Novel Writing Month (www.nanowrimo.org) for the existence of this novel. 2011 was my ninth year participating. I knew my chances of completing a novel that year were slim, because we were moving that month. Instead of going for a win, I decided to just participate while creating some internal backstory for Elemental that would never see the light of day. This was supposed to be a mere writing exercise.

Surprise!

I didn't win that year, as expected, and I irritated the hell out of my family by making the attempt. Many thanks go to my son and my husband for not killing me for stealing moments here and there while they were packing and unpacking. Sure, I pulled my own, but no one likes to see someone poking away at a "hobby" when there's work to be done. (They're proud of me now, at least, and realize how seriously I take my fiction.)

If any one person in particular is to thank for this book, it's my dad. For the usual reasons, yes, but also for being the first person to tell me that this was a better story than Elemental. His insight turned this from a hidden writing exercise to a story I'm proud to share with the world.

To Catherine White, my best friend and proofreader, thank you for all of your help, and for being so damn picky about the words I chose and the typos I missed. For helping me make this story complete, coherent, and beautiful. And for your endless support in all ways.

To my beta readers, every word of feedback, good or bad, has been more valuable than gold.

Josh, Claire, Aria, and Jasper, for the amazing artwork. Yes, I am thanking your entire family. Josh, you sacrificed more time creating the perfect cover than I deserve, and your family sacrificed quality time with you so that you could meet my deadline. I love all of you, and I'm lucky you're part of my online family.

To the Honored Exiles of Moonrunner, I'm still grateful for everything. For being my guild, for being my friends, for being my emotional support even now that I haven't been able to play.

Finally, to my amazing patrons on Patreon. Em Joyce Ascano, Amy Lauritzen, and Rachael Kelly. Your faith in me, and support of me, keeps me going. I am humbled by your continued patronage. I could never thank you enough.

ABOUT THE AUTHOR

Tam Chronin is a figment of the imagination, which might be why she lives there often enough to find her main characters and convince them to share their stories.

Before becoming an author she slayed trolls for many years in the wilds of the internet. She was occasionally granted the legendary weapon, Ban Hammer, to aid in this quest. It was a relief to retire from such harrowing adventures, but for a coin and a stiff drink she might recount them over a campfire.

She lives in Phoenix, Arizona, with her family, two parakeets, three cats, a bunny, a varying number of both fish and chickens, and a vicious attack tortoise who guards the back yard.

ALSO BY TAM CHRONIN

The Godslayer Series

Available now:
Elemental
The Arcane War

Upcoming:
Abomination
The First Wizard War
The Madness of Verwyn

The Graceful Death Series

Upcoming:
Everyone Dies Alone (Oct. 2019)
Zombies Half Price

Made in the USA
Las Vegas, NV
08 September 2022

54878963R00163